# DESIRE OR DEFENSE

## D.C. EAGLES HOCKEY
### BOOK 1

## LEAH BRUNNER

LEAH BRUNNER

# TRIGGER WARNINGS

This work of fiction contains mild language and references to alcohol.

This book has themes of abandonment, parental substance abuse, and grieving after the death of loved ones.

*To Tom Wilson.*
*I came for the good looks.*
*I stayed for the hockey.*

# CHAPTER 1
# MITCH

FLYING across the ice for our pregame warm-up, my muscles burn in the best way. Better my muscles, my body, and my skin than that pesky organ inside my chest. I needed this game after not playing for five days.

I don't want to think, to dwell on the fact that I have no family to spend these so-called *vacations* with. To know everyone else on the team has that. That they're immersed in festive activities with their loved ones.

Not me. But I don't need that, I need *this*. The challenge to my mind and body. To use my muscles for what they've been expertly honed in for. Everything I've ever worked for. The only good thing in my life that ever lasted.

For eighteen years, I've dreaded any kind of *vacation*. School vacations, summer breaks, and now… NHL time off for holidays. All that time off only means one thing: too much time to think.

Glancing over at the plexiglass, I take in the sight of my teammates fawning all over their offspring and wives on the other side. The kids all wear tiny jerseys with their fathers' numbers on them, and without seeing the backs, I know they say *daddy* on them. I sniff out an annoyed breath. So freaking cliché.

The guys wave and blow kisses to their girlfriends, which looks ridiculous with their gloves on. The girls don't care, waving right back, like these big, sweaty hockey players are the greatest thing on earth.

This is the worst part of home games. And the exact reason I prefer away games.

With a groan, I hit one of the pucks toward our goalie, Bruce. He's distracted, watching the families with a big grin on his face. The puck hits his helmet, causing his head to whip in my direction. He narrows his eyes at me, but a smirk plays at the corner of his mouth. Bruce seems to be the only one on the team who's not offended by what the rest of them call my "surly countenance."

Bruce has dirty-blond hair and green eyes full of mischief, everything about him is cheery and bright. Like a burly Christmas elf. He seems more suited to working in Santa's workshop than being a goalie, but he's actually a badass netminder. Best in the league if you ask me, but I'm biased.

"Don't be a grump!" Bruce yells across the ice—like he was reading my mind—before hitting the puck back in my direction.

I roll my eyes. "I'm just ready for the game to start already," I lie. I mean, I am ready for the game to start, but I was definitely thinking about how annoying the guys are acting. Like they didn't just spend an entire five days with their families.

Hitting another puck into the net, I spot a kid off to the side behind the glass. She's probably not quite ten, watching us in awe. A disheveled D.C. Eagles beanie covers her hair, but brown pigtails trail down her shoulders. The rest of her clothes look just as worn. She isn't surrounded by adoring parents or siblings, not decked out in the latest Eagles attire, and she didn't come with one of those giant, ostentatious posters that say something like "#1 you're my hero!" or "#00 can I get a selfie?"

She's an underdog, and I can appreciate that. Skating over toward the girl, she makes eye contact with me. Her bright eyes widen in surprise. Not sure if that's because someone noticed her, or because it's *me*... and I'm not known for interacting with fans. But weirdly, I see myself in this little girl. My pathetic childhood self. Which is why I take my stick and raise it up high so it slides right over the plexiglass separating us, and into her shaky hands. Her jaw drops as she reaches for my stick.

I read her lips through that glass as she nervously mouths the words *thank you*. Nodding my head in response, I hear our coach's voice yelling over the crowd. When I look up, Coach Young is signaling for us to head back to the locker room, warmups are finally over.

As I'm about to enter the tunnel, I hear Bruce's voice behind me. "I saw that, by the way. Better be careful, Mitch. Fans might realize you have a heart."

I know he's joking, but he's right. I need to be more careful unless I want fans seeking me out.

No, thank you.

We get settled in the locker room in our designated spaces and wait for Remy, Remington Ford, our team captain, to dole out our pregame pep talk. He stands at the front of the room, next to Coach Young, waiting for us to settle down.

Weston Kershaw joins them up front. Already donning the A for assistant captain on his chest. He's been on the team a little over a year and already moved his way up. I can begrudgingly admit he's a good player... It's hard to argue that fact when he's the highest goal scorer in the NHL this season—okay, fine. Last season too—but he irritates me. Not sure if it's the fact that he enamors people so easily and works them over with his "charm." Or if it's because he's already more settled in Washington D.C. in a year than I am after being here for five. Or because he and his fiancee will likely be adding to the "daddy jersey" club in the next few years. He's just one of those people everyone instantly likes, he has a loving family, and everything comes easily to him. He's like the comfort show you turn on after a long day, the show everyone's in the mood for and can quote incessantly. West is the *FRIENDS* of the team. And I hate him for it.

Colby Knight, seated to my right, elbows me in the ribs. I look up to see Remy and West staring at me.

"Hey, Mitch! You hear me?" Remy's booming voice is heard easily all the way across the locker room.

I run a hand through my already sweaty hair. "Sorry, I was focusing on the new plays."

Bruce, whose locker is to the left of mine, sends me a look that tells me he knows I'm full of crap.

Remy smirks and crosses his arms, and West looks at me with a bemused expression. Probably relishing in the fact that I wasn't paying attention and got called out for it.

"I said, let's all stay out of the sin bin. We don't need to be racking up penalties and giving the Renegades the advantage."

Bringing my chin up in a slight nod, I run my tongue along the edge of my teeth, trying not to be annoyed by the blatant call-out. But I know I deserve it. Last season I had to sit out five games and pay thousands of dollars to the NHL for slashing another player. It's not my fault he started a fight afterward and ended up tearing his ACL. Don't start a fight you can't finish.

Coach Young takes over the pep talk and everyone's attention is turned toward him. He's saying something about kicking ass for our first game, but I'm looking at Remy, whose eyes are laser focused on me. Apparently, I'm not the only one who has noticed that I'm especially prone to penalties after a break—and even more so against the Carolina Renegades, our biggest competition in the Metropolitan Conference.

Thirty minutes later, we're getting into position on the ice, ready for the game to start. I take a quick glance at the stands, the girl from earlier isn't there anymore. But I see a bunch of women with signs asking Weston Kershaw and Colby Knight to marry them and look away, swearing under my breath. There isn't a single sign with my name on it, which is fine. I like flying under the radar. But it's also a reminder that I'm the troublemaker of the group… the unlovable one.

I can practically feel my bottled-up energy and aggression rolling off of me, like water eroding away at the rocks beneath it, that's my self-control dwindling away with pent-up energy. And that can't come out in my hits tonight.

Freaking finally, the puck drops and I rush toward it, remembering our plays from practice. Number thirty-seven from the Renegades skates up next to me, his white jersey flashing in my peripheral vision. I've been expecting this. Not only does the smack talk that comes out of his mouth cross all normal smack-talking boundaries, but the guy I tripped last season was apparently his bestie. Whoops.

I try not to make direct eye contact with Ilya Adrik, I might turn to stone from how evil he is.

"Anderson!" His accented voice comes out with a lisp since he has his mouth guard in.

I ignore him, but he keeps yelling over the noise. "How was your Christmas, man?"

I bite the inside of my cheeks so hard I almost draw blood.

"Nice and… quiet? Just the way you like it?"

I flex my neck from side to side, making it crack and pop.

He snickers. "Or did you visit your daddy?"

My scant amount of self-control instantly shatters, just like his face is about to.

# CHAPTER 2
# ANDIE

"NOAH! Get your butt down here! We're going to be late! Again," I mutter the last word under my breath as I stand at the bottom of the steps with my hands on my hips.

My eyes snag briefly on the items scattered up and down the stairs: stacks of clean, sort-of folded laundry, books, my Amazon subscribe and save delivery—which is super handy, by the way, and the only reason we haven't run out of toothpaste—all things Noah and I laid there with the best intentions of putting them away later. But we never did, and now they're just another reminder of my chaotic life.

Glancing once more at my watch, I sigh.

Noah appears at the top of the stairs, looking unbothered by my urgency. His dark hair tousled from sleep, and his droopy eyes telling me he just woke up. Despite me setting his alarm last night for 5:45 am.

I can't blame him, no one in their right mind enjoys waking this early. But alas, it's what I signed up for when I was pinned as a nurse. Noah makes his way down the stairs. He looks especially grouchy this morning, so instead of lecturing him, I grab the granola bar out of my scrubs pocket and hand it to him as a peace offering.

He accepts it, barely sparing me a glance of his deep brown eyes. The eyes that I adore, but also make me want to cry. Because Mom had the same ones. My heart squeezes inside my chest. I miss her so much.

Pushing those thoughts aside, I bend to pick up the back-pack sitting at my feet, and he turns so I can help him slide it over his arms. Without a word, he grabs his D.C. Eagles ball cap and heads out the door.

"Hockey practice," I whisper to myself. The Eagles hat reminding me that tonight I need to pick Noah up from the rink on my way home from work.

It's been nearly nine months since I became my little broth-er's legal guardian, and I still can't keep track of his schedule.

Nine months, and he still barely talks. (To me, anyway.)

Nine months, and this still doesn't feel real.

Maybe in another nine months, we'll have this all figured out. I doubt it.

We drive in my small car to his school, a route that's as new to me as taking care of a kid, *and* living in Washington D.C.— and literally everything else that has transpired since our parents were killed in an accident nine months ago.

I don't force Noah to talk, don't push him. He has enough going on inside that child-sized head of his. Things no kids should ever have to process. His teacher tells me he's still quiet at school—and still getting into arguments with other students in his class. But his therapist assures me he *is* making progress in therapy… so I guess that's enough for now.

I pull into the drop-off lane, which is agonizingly slow for it being this early. I'm usually the first one here.

Tightening my hands on the steering wheel in irritation, I watch the mother in front of me step out of the car. "No!" I whine, even though she can't hear me. "You never, and I repeat never, get out of the car in the drop-off line!"

I watch her unbuckle a car seat and lift her kid down. Pausing to give several hugs and kisses. Sweet, okay. But this is clearly a preschooler, and preschoolers don't get dropped off in the drop-off line for this exact reason.

"Shove your kid out, yell goodbye, then put the pedal to the metal!" I yell at the windshield, throwing my hands in the air. I'm not usually this grouchy, but I'm already running late, and I don't even have time to stop for coffee.

The mother waves goodbye one last time before sending me a steely glare. Oh, maybe she *could* hear me. "Shit."

A very small huff of a laugh comes out of Noah, who is watching me, his eyes twinkling in the same way our Dad's once did when he teased us. I smile at him, elated that he laughed. I should probably feel ashamed for yelling at the sweet mother in front of us, but I feel nothing but joy. And maybe a little hope, that we, me and Noah, will eventually be besties again.

He looks away, opening the car door and shuffling out. Right before he closes the door, he turns to look at me. "You owe a dollar to the sassy jar."

I'd forgotten about the jar. When I first moved here to be with Noah, I realized how much of a potty mouth I was, not used to being around kids. In an attempt to clean up my act, I told him I'd put a dollar in a jar every time I swore, and if it ever filled up, we'd do something extra fun. Like go to a movie… or at the rate I'm going, fly to Paris for a luxury vacation. I'm not sure I can actually afford the sassy jar. Once again, a familiar pang of regret wrenches my gut… had I not moved away, we'd be closer. Had I not moved away, we'd feel more comfortable around each other.

"Damn it," I mutter to myself.

"Two dollars," he whispers, just before closing the door. Walking toward the school without even a look, or a smile, back in my direction. But he talked to me, even made a joke.

Despite being two dollars poorer, I drive away feeling like I've won the day.

———

"You look rough," my coworker, Ronda, says to me when I slump down into a chair in the tiny break room. It's almost three and I finally have time to eat my lunch. There's no need for a large break room for ICU nurses, seeing as we hardly have breaks, anyway.

I look at Ronda, her royal-blue scrubs identical to mine. Her dark eyes that seem to sparkle like starlight against her dark skin, are half teasing and half concerned. She's twenty years my senior, and yet, my closest friend here in D.C.

I shoot her a small smile, too tired for any witty comebacks.

She tucks a silver-grey curl behind her ear, one that escaped from her neat bun. "How much sleep have you been getting?"

I scoff. "I'm a nurse. I don't even need sleep!"

Her lips purse, obviously not fooled by my sarcasm. "And when's the last time you got out of the house for something other than work?"

I look up at the drab hospital ceiling, calculating in my head how long it's been since I had a good night's sleep or got together with friends.

"And how about a date?" Ronda's voice filters through my thoughts. "When's the last time a man took you to bed, hmm?"

"Ronda!" I gasp, rising from my seat and bringing my hand to my chest.

She sighs heavily, but I know she worries about me. About Noah. "You know I'm always here to watch Noah for you. We live on the same street. All you have to do is ask, Andie."

I nod, appreciating her kindness, but quickly look away from those dark eyes that seem to pierce through my soul. I make myself busy by closing the distance between myself and the fridge, then remove my pb&j.

Ronda clears her throat, drawing my attention. Her head tilts to the side, gesturing at a Jimmy John's bag on the table next to her.

I sniff, pretending to cry. Ronda shakes her head, trying not to laugh. "Don't start."

It's too late, I'm already serenading her with my own rendition of an old Rod Stewart song. By the time my solo is finished, I'm smothering her in a hug.

She pushes out of my grasp. "Just hurry up and eat, you have *maybe* seven and a half minutes to shove that sub down your face."

"True," I concede.

Ronda rises from her seat to leave, when she passes me she grabs the pb&j out of my hand and tosses it in the trash on her way out. The break room is quiet now, aside from the beeps and quick footsteps right outside the door. I realize how little time I have to myself to think, and the quiet that once seemed normal, now feels overwhelming. Like instead of sensory overload, it's the opposite. It feels weird... eerie even. In nine months, I've grown accustomed to the small sounds of living with my much younger brother. The ball he tosses against his wall before catching it again, the sound of his footsteps upstairs when I'm in the kitchen, the rustling of papers as he does his homework.

I know I could ask for help, and I do. But Ronda already helps so much, I hate imposing on her just so I can go out and... what, exactly? Pick up men? Get a pedicure? It all feels so shallow and pointless now. Plus, I can't trust myself to take my eyes off of Noah when I don't absolutely have to. Which is why I insist on driving him to school, even though he thinks I'm super embarrassing.

My heart thuds inside my chest, the familiar feeling of overwhelming sadness. That cloud fogging up my mind, making it seem like I'll never see the sun again. I take a deep breath and think of three good things. *Noah, my job, a reliable vehicle.*

With another breath, I begin eating my lunch quickly, pushing all other thoughts aside.

# CHAPTER 3
# MITCH

"FIFTEEN GAMES?" I roar, standing from my seat in our general manager, Tom Parker's, office. I glance around at the four other people in the room, my agent (what's his face), Tom Parker (obviously), Coach Young (who's spitting mad), and some older guy I've never seen before.

I look away from the group of men staring at me and my hands fly into my hair, tugging at the strands. I do the math inside my head, fifteen games divided by 3-4 games a week… that's like five weeks of not playing. Five weeks with too much time on my hands.

"Over a stupid headache? I knew Ilya was just a giant baby." Five days ago I was happily pummeling his face, and now I'm suspended? Ridiculous.

Tom rests on the edge of his desk, his steady, calm demeanor entirely intact. His long legs are crossed at the ankles, making his slacks ride up just enough that I can see his D.C. Eagles socks peeking out from his dress shoes.

"You gave him a serious concussion, Mitch. And you're a repeat offender. Hence a longer suspension," Coach Young's voice grits out. He's in the seat beside mine. I can tell by his voice that he's pissed, at me, sure, but likely at the NHL's decision too.

But mostly at me.

Attempting to calm myself, I inhale a breath, but it comes out as a growl instead. "*And* a fine? Isn't the suspension enough?"

"You're getting off easy compared to some players," Our GM, Tom, adds, not helping my escalating temper. "But there's more, actually."

The man in the room who I haven't seen before takes a step toward me. He looks slightly older than the other men in the room, probably fifty. His hair is mostly grey, and he's dressed professionally, in navy slacks and a crisp, white dress shirt.

His golden-brown eyes penetrate my own. His stance and direct eye contact make me think of a time, I must've been six or seven. It was one of the days my dad wasn't high and actually acted like a father. One of my few good memories... the day he took me to a circus. I was enamored with the tiger trainer, watching how his movements were as he moved around the tiger, completely calm. The tiger tamer is all smooth, confident movements in front of the beast—despite the animal licking his lips—following the movements carefully before performing the trick he was trained to do, jumping through the flame-ridden hoop without fear.

This mysterious man is obviously the tiger tamer. Does that make me the tiger?

Tom continues, "As you know, in the week since your... incident... The Eagles organization had a meeting. In congruence with the National Hockey League, and since this is a repeat offense, we've decided it would be profitable..." he pauses, "for yourself, and for the team," he clears his throat, shifting uncomfortably in his seat. "To see our team therapist."

He gestures toward the older gentleman in the room, the team therapist, apparently.

The doctor extends his hand, his dark skin makes his hair look even more silver up close. "Hey Mitch, I'm Dr. Curtis. Looking forward to working together."

Staring at the extended hand, I glower. They're acting like I'm a child. Aren't the fees and suspensions enough?

"It was just a stupid fight," I say tersely, ignoring the shrink and turning my attention back to our general manager. "This is hockey, not the Rockettes."

"Actually, I've heard the Rockettes can be pretty cutthroat." The doctor retorts. I glance over to see his mouth is pulled up slightly at the corners.

I don't laugh at his joke, instead I give him a *why are you still talking* look. But I am a *little* relieved that he at least has a sense of humor if we're going to be working together. I guess. Remembering myself, I bring my gaze back to Tom, making sure to erase all evidence of humor from my expression.

He glowers right back. "It's not up for discussion, Mitch. Safety and fair treatment are important in this organization. You need to hone your mind just as much as you do your body. Think of therapy as a gym for your brain."

I barely withhold an eyeroll, but I don't argue. If I'm going to sit out fifteen games, I won't have anything better to do with my time anyway.

My agent clears his throat. I'd forgotten about him already —I can never remember his name, it's something a dog could be named, like Doug, or Buddy. He's smiling at me now with that big smile on his face, the one that never looks genuine. Maybe because his eyes are so cold.

Tom nods in my agent's direction. "Oh, and Max has a few ideas as well."

Max. Right.

My agent always strikes me as the kind of person who'd be nice to your face, but would call you an asshole the second you left a room. He annoys me… maybe because he's everywhere I am. At every event, and almost every game. The man would look totally harmless to anyone, he's probably mid-forties, dressed in business casual black pants and a simple blue dress shirt. His brown hair is cut too short, which is another source of annoyance, because I *know* I pay the man enough money for him to get a decent haircut.

"The reason I'm here." He brings a hand to his chest, his nails look clean and his hands soft, like he's never worked outside an office a day in his life. "Is to help you work on your image. *We* know you're a great guy, but we need the fans to know that too."

One of my eyebrows raises, as if to ask *does anyone here really think I'm a great guy?*

Coach Young scoffs next to me, it's subtle, but enough that I know he's thinking the same thing. I'm valuable to the team for my size and brute strength… but I'm not Weston Kershaw. Pretty sure no one would describe me as a "great guy."

"Plus…" Max rubs his fingers together like he's holding money. "Better image, better sponsorships. And seeing as your biggest sponsor called me the day after watching that stupid fight, dropping your contract… I'd take this seriously if I were you."

My eyes widen, reeling from the news that Advanced Athletics dropped me. I hadn't realized the athletic wear company ended our contract. I clench my jaw. That's millions of dollars… gone.

"Okay, so how the hell are we going to make people think I'm a great guy?" I ask Doug—er, Max, whatever.

My bluntness makes his easy facade drop for a split second, but he quickly clears his throat and straightens his spine. "As you probably know, the Eagles sponsor several youth sports teams in the district. And lucky for you, one of our youth hockey teams is in need of a short-term assistant coach."

Both of my eyebrows shoot up to my hairline. "Kids?" I look from my coach and then to Tom. They both look apprehensive about the idea too. "What makes you think that me working with children would be a good idea? I don't even like humans that are fully grown."

Max raises his hands in front of him like he's shaping a T.V. Screen for us. "Big, tough hockey player, skating around with cute little kids in their hockey gear." He splays one pampered hand across his imaginary T.V. An imaginary title I'm guessing. "Mitch Anderson: angry grizzly turned cuddly teddy bear."

I really do roll my eyes this time.

"Take this seriously," Tom says in a commanding voice.

I look over at him and see he's got his arms crossed in a defensive pose. "Coaching youth hockey? When I clearly have a temper? Are the parents even okay with this?"

I'm pulling out all the excuses, hoping they'll let me out of this. Honestly, any youth hockey kid—or parent for that matter—would probably jump up and down at the idea of an NHL player coaching their kid. Sure, I got in a fight and gave someone a concussion—accidentally—but a certain degree of fighting is expected from us. It's part of the entertainment. Or so I've heard.

"It's already decided, Mitch," Tom says, clearly unamused by my attempt to get out of this.

Coach Young pipes up from where he stands beside me. "You have the time, and it'll give your... reputation... some positivity."

"Who knows, maybe you'll end up loving it!" Max says a

little too cheerfully. Everyone in the room gives him the same unconvinced look and his smile falters slightly before he steels himself again. "Well, you start tonight. I emailed you the information and schedule. So, let's try to have some fun with it!" Max pats my arm as he walks past me and out of the room without another word.

The shock and outrage that bubbles up inside of me like a volcano about to erupt reminds me why I should never be trusted to coach children. "Tonight?!"

Tom has the wherewithal to grimace at springing this all on me at the last minute. "I'm sorry we didn't give you more warning, but the assistant coach's wife went into labor early and the opportunity arose rather... suddenly."

My head swivels to look at Coach Young, hoping a miracle will happen and he'll come to my rescue. Coach puts his hands out in front of himself, like I'd rush over and attack him. "It was Max's idea!"

I grit my teeth then shout an expletive I've been holding in. It only briefly releases the tension I feel, unfortunately. And now all the men in the room are eyeing me with caution in their eyes. Once again, it feels like my molars might crack. Just like my sanity.

Dr. Curtis chuckles, he's the only one in the room who still seems perfectly calm, and surprisingly, that makes me feel a little better. At least one person doesn't think I'll rip this room to shreds like some kind of ogre. "Mitch, I think coaching will help you develop entirely new skills... like building relationships." He doesn't flinch at the scowl still on my face, but continues, "*And* it will give you the opportunity to work on practicing control. I have several breathing exercises to help you, we'll discuss this more in our session next week."

When I don't respond, Tom clears his throat. "Alright, well, this was fun. But I have calls to make and a team to manage. So enjoy your first coaching gig, Mitch."

———

"Do you two have to follow me so closely?" I ask the photographer—Max's lackey—and Max, who are both trailing right behind me as I walk inside the ice complex.

Between two near-strangers tracking my every move and photographing it, as well as the emotions swirling around inside of me, all of my senses are heightened. And not in a good way. The fabric of my clothing feels too tight, my skin feels too itchy, the sounds inside the building are too loud, and the taste in my mouth is sour. Everything is too much as the memories of my youth hockey days fly through my mind. Some of them are good, because hockey was my break from my home life, but a lot of them... not so good.

The sour taste in my mouth is making my stomach queasy. Youth hockey was what kept me going when I was a kid, kept me motivated and gave me something positive to cling to. But this place also brings back the bad childhood memories, like when my mom left and my dad went into a downward spiral. It takes me back to late nights after practice, when Dad didn't show up, and my coaches would take turns driving me home. Until child protective services were finally called. I close my eyes and take a deep breath, willing those conflicting memories away so I can focus on this stupid assistant coaching gig.

Whatever I need to do to get back to playing. That's what I'll do.

"Sorry, Mr. Anderson. We'll try to stay out of your way," the photographer says, his voice shaky like he's nervous. "You won't even notice we're here."

I breathe out a low laugh, but there's no humor in it. We

enter a large room with benches where people can sit to put on their gear and lace up their skates. A light-haired man, probably not much older than I am, bursts through the door that must lead to one of the ice rinks. He's already in his coaching uniform, navy blue pants and a matching jacket with the team logo on the chest (which is, unfortunately, a wombat holding a hockey stick), and wearing a hockey helmet for head protection. And, of course, his skates.

"Mitch Anderson," he starts, grinning widely. "It's an honor to meet you. The kids are stoked to work with you!"

I dip my chin in response, not knowing what else to say, since I don't even want to be here.

"I'm Aaron." He extends his hand before realizing his padded hockey gloves are still on. He removes one, chuckling.

I shake his hand. He already knows my name, so I give him what I hope is a friendly grunt.

"A man of few words!" He laughs again.

Aaron laughs a lot, apparently. It's annoying.

"Your uniform is in the locker room." He points to the far left wall. "I'll let you get suited up and then meet you on the ice."

After quickly ducking into the locker room and changing, I'm now wearing the same uniform as Aaron. Dorky wombat included. Definitely not NHL quality, but I've had worse. The embroidered wombat on the chest is stiff and uncomfortable. Who would choose a wombat for the mascot? Why not something intimidating... like a dragon. At least I have my own skates, Aaron probably would've given me some with wombats on them. Max and the photographer take a few photos of me in front of the Washington Wombats banner with my uniform before I head into the arena.

Ignoring the gawking parents, clearly taking videos and photos on their phones, I skate to center ice where the entire team is huddled up. Max's email said the kids' ages range from eight to thirteen. There's even a few girls in the mix, their braids and long ponytails peeking out from under their helmets.

Aaron is on one knee, talking to the kids, when he sees me and smiles. "There's our new assistant coach!" He stands. "Wombats, let's give Coach Anderson an icy welcome!"

All the kids bang their hockey sticks against the ice and laugh, except one boy in the back who looks just as annoyed by the ordeal as I feel.

"Wow, thanks." I attempt a friendly smile. "Hopefully we'll, umm," I pause, I've never been great with words—or kids—and how do you give a pre-hockey pep talk without swearing? "Hopefully we'll have some… fun." The word *fun* comes out in a strangled sound and feels foreign as I say it.

Aaron stares at me like I'm an alien from another planet who has never spoken to children before. *Have I?*

Finally, he claps his hands together and looks at the kids. "Well, let's get started!" The kids take off, already knowing which station they're starting at.

He turns back toward me. "Tonight we separate into groups and do drills. I'm going to pair you with the most skilled kids, the ones who are part of our competitive league." He uses his stick to point to a group practicing their stick handling on the far end of the ice. Large pads separate each section, and with a quick scope of the various groupings of kids, it's obvious the group he's sending me to are more well-versed than the others. They're even wearing fancier jerseys, ones with their last names on the back.

"Alright, so what do you want me to do, exactly?" I ask as I watch the group of about eight boys skate around and shoot pucks into the net, seamlessly switching from forward skating to backward skating.

Aaron slaps me on the back, hard. "Why don't you start with teaching sportsmanship?" He winks before taking off, leaving me to my own devices.

"Okay," I say to myself, not understanding why we're practicing sportsmanship with a bunch of innocent-looking, young boys.

Skating over to my designated group, a puck comes flying towards my face and I swivel out of the way just in time. I glance over at my group to find them all staring at me, smirking.

"Sportsmanship," I mutter under my breath through gritted teeth. He gave me the most skilled kids... but also the cocky bastards of the group. Well played, Aaron.

"You gonna show us how to end up in the penalty box, Anderson?" One quips, a smirk firmly in place on his rosy-cheeked face.

The kids to his right laughs, this one has reddish hair. "*Or how to get suspended?*"

"Maybe he'll teach *how to give a concussion 101*," another one says.

"Shut up so we can get this over with." This comes from the boy with dark hair, the one who didn't participate in the stick-tapping welcome.

I swallow slowly, refusing to let a bunch of little twerps get under my skin. Noticing the flash of a camera, I look over to the plexiglass and remember the photographer and Max are watching me. I skate closer to the boys, glaring at the one with freckles before wrapping an arm around his shoulder in a vice-like grip, a warning—he's wearing tons of padding, he'll be fine—I force a smile toward the camera and freckles does the same.

Max looks pleased. I release the kid, he stumbles when I let go. Then I turn my back on the cameraman so I can look at the boys again. "Alright, you all clearly know who I am. So, why don't we start with you telling me *your* names?"

The group snickers. "What's the magic word?" A boy with blond hair asks, batting his lashes obnoxiously.

"Now?"

All of them cross their arms in unison, like they practiced this ahead of time. The thought terrifies me.

The freckled boy speaks first, he seems to be the leader here. "Listen," he starts calmly. I'm taking notes from him on how to command the group. "We'll give you our names when you've earned our respect."

I feel one eyebrow arch slowly up my forehead and my eye twitches in annoyance. "Do I need to have a talk with Coach Aaron?"

The boys glance at each other, snickering. The dark haired boy remains stoic and serious, though.

Freckles is the one to respond again. "You don't seem like a snitch to me, Anderson. Now let's get back to practice, boys."

I raise my voice just enough to get their attention back on me, "Okay, Freckles. That's enough. According to my knowledge, I'm the only one here with an NHL contract, and I'm the one in charge."

The boy with dark hair laughs for the first time, and the other boys turn to glare at him. I clap my gloved hands together to get their attention back on me. Ignoring the insolent looks on their faces, I separate them into two groups. There's only one net and one goalie, so we'll have to set a timer and switch offense and defense.

I give my directions and they skate into place, despite Freckles attempting to walk all over me at first. The first five minutes go pretty well, the group has good skating skills and work well together passing the puck. When we switch at the five-minute mark, everything starts going downhill. Freckles seems to be in the middle of every tussle, as well as the dark-haired kid who seemed so level-headed. I begin memorizing the last names on the backs of their jerseys, so I know who to yell at. Except Freckles, that's now his name permanently, whether he likes it or not.

When we switch again, Freckles and the kid with dark hair, Downsby, aim all their aggression on each other instead of the other boys. They're hooking and slashing like I've never seen before. It's a freaking battle out here.

The glares I give them after their penalties aren't working, seeing as they're not even bothering to look in my direction. I finally intervene when Downsby, the dark-haired one, high-sticks Freckles in the neck, sending him down hard on his back.

"Hey!" I yell, skating over just as the dark-haired kid jumps on top of Freckles and starts punching him over and over. I grab him by the shoulder pads and haul him off of Freckles. "What the hell, kid?! You can't just go around thrashing your opponents in the neck!"

My voice is booming, louder than I realized. Downsby stares at me, he's all dark hair and equally dark eyes. Eyes so cold and hateful... and he spits... actually spits. I think he was trying to spit in my face, but since I'm so much taller, it lands on my jersey. Disgusting.

Before I can berate him... again... I see his cold eyes go wide with horror as he eyes something behind me. I turn to see a... nurse? Walking, no stomping, toward me. She's wearing tennis shoes and she is fuming mad. As she comes closer, I notice her eyes are dark and furious like the boy whose jersey is still clutched in my fist. The blonde woman slips and lands on her butt, the boys behind me snicker until she stands back up and her angry eyes whip in their direction.

I'm so stunned by the whole situation I'm just staring at her when she finally slips, slides, and stomps her way to me. Once she's right in front of me, she juts one curvy hip out and rests a balled up fist on it. I was wrong, her eyes aren't furious, they're blazing. Blondie is pissed. *At me.*

"Who do *you* think you are? And why are you speaking to the kids like that?"

I huff out a surprised laugh. "Kids?" Surely we're not talking about the same group of disrespectful ragamuffins.

She takes another step forward and slaps my hand where it's still gripping the boy's jersey. "I don't know who kicked your puppy, sir. But yelling at these boys is highly inappropriate!"

A few of the boys behind me sniff, I glance over my shoulder and see Freckles and one of his henchmen fake crying.

"You can't be serious." I point a finger at Downsby. "Your kid high-sticked the mouthy one in the throat. The freaking throat, lady!" My voice comes out unintentionally loud again, but she doesn't back down.

Instead, she moves so close, I can smell her hair. It smells like a candy shop... more specifically, bubble gum. The sweet scent is a complete contrast to her pissed-off glare. She takes her index finger and stabs it into my chest, I notice she flinches slightly, like the impact hurts her finger.

She's little, probably ten inches shorter than me even without my skates on, but there's fire in those dark brown eyes, something that tells me she's tougher than she looks. That she could kick my butt if she really wanted to. Something that makes me a little scared but yet makes my blood run a little hotter.

"You will treat these kids with kindness and respect. I don't care if you're some kind of hockey, Ice Capades, skating expert. Or *whatever*." She waves one hand around when she says whatever.

My lips twitch at her words, and the fact she clearly has no idea who I am. And something tells me that even if she were aware she was in the presence of a famous professional athlete, she couldn't care less.

# CHAPTER 4
## ANDIE

I DON'T CARE how gorgeous, or broad, or chiseled, or... wait, where was I going with this?

Oh, right. I don't care who this big oaf is! He won't be yelling at Noah if I have anything to say about it. Or any of these cute little boys, for that matter. They'd be so mad if they knew I thought of them as cute little boys when they clearly think they're so much older than they are.

The man stares at me and has the audacity to smirk, which just makes me madder. A flash goes off and I look over to see a professional cameraman taking photos of the obnoxiously hot man. Is he a model or something? Believable. But why's he filling in for the assistant coach?

The big man opens his mouth to speak before something crosses over his face, an expression of fear, or something similar. Before I can fully analyze the look, he glides toward me in a rush and picks me up effortlessly around the waist.

I'm about to tell him a thing or two about touching someone without their consent, when two boys crash into each other right where we were just standing. The giant sets me down, his hands moving up to my shoulders to steady me before releasing me and skating backward a few feet.

The way he moves on the ice is a thing of beauty, almost as impressive as his face. Okay, so he's not *just* a model. Actually, when I really look at him, his face isn't model handsome. His face is mostly covered by his thick, dark beard, but the sharp angles are still noticeable. His features *are* handsome, but not perfect. His mouth is a little too wide, his nose a bit crooked like he broke it and it wasn't set right, and there's a scar across one eyebrow. No, he's not handsome in the typical sense of the word, but in a way all his own.

"Ma'am, you really need to get off the ice. You need skates and a helmet, at least, to be out here," His voice is getting louder and more annoyed with every word, but that deep, rumbly baritone makes me feel like I'm standing in the hot sun instead of the middle of an ice rink.

Internally, I shake his voice from my thoughts, and place my hands on my hips again for good measure. Looking as serious as I can to compensate for our size difference. "I can't speak to you through the plexiglass."

He uses his gloved hand to gesture toward the bleachers on the other side of the glass. "You have to go back to the parent viewing area." He's completely serious. Like a bunch of kids could hurt me.

I scoff and narrow my eyes at him. His arm flies up toward my head, causing me to flinch. I notice a heavy, black puck hits his gloved hand and ricochets off before tumbling to the ice, leaving me stunned.

"You're not even wearing a helmet, you're going to get a concussion at this rate," he says, squeezing his eyes shut in annoyance and shaking his head. He looks, and sounds, very put out.

I'm still in awe of his reflexes, glancing between him and

the puck that almost just rearranged my face. He groans heavily, and his eyes shift from greenish-brown to a cooler color. I can tell in that moment that he's lost all patience with me.

He removes his gloves, throwing them to the ground, skates toward me, then bends at the waist and hauls me up and over his shoulder.

I gasp and wriggle, trying to free myself from his firm grip. "Hey! You brute! Put me down!"

He ignores me, skating toward the door that leads to the parent area. "I tried asking you nicely," he says cooly.

"Have you ever interacted with people before? Your behavior isn't any better than the kids'!" I kick my legs in frustration, but his large, strong hands don't even flinch at my movements.

"I can't just let you get a brain injury. If you want to yell at me, do it after practice."

He finally puts me down, and I feel my shoes land on carpet instead of ice.

"Oh, I will," I say in a menacing tone, but he doesn't even spare me a glance over his large shoulder as he slams the door and skates away.

As I stomp back to my seat, I can still feel the warmth of his arm where it was just wrapped around my thighs. Of course someone would finally give me warm, tingly feelings, only to end up being a complete jerk. Right before I sit down, I realize all the parents are blatantly staring at me. My cheeks heat when it hits me that the big guy and myself just entertained the entire crowd of onlookers… as well as the photographer and his friend… who are also staring at me. I settle back on my spot on the bleachers and distract myself by looking for my brother on the ice.

Finding Noah in the slew of kids, I notice the entire group of boys the annoyingly handsome coach has been working with are engaged in a full out brawl. Gloves are off, sticks are flying, it's madness.

Maybe I was a little too quick to judge about the yelling? No, I won't give him the benefit of the doubt here. The man is a complete ogre! Not just with the kids, but also with me.

Releasing a heavy sigh, I try to get comfortable on the cold, hard bench. I came straight from work, and I forgot to pack a change of clothes, having left the house in such a rush this morning. The thin fabric of my scrubs isn't nearly enough of a barricade between my bum and the freezing cold metal bleacher.

I mentally make a note—for the millionth time—to keep a blanket and some fuzzy boots in the car for hockey practices. I shiver and rub my hands up and down my arms in an attempt to keep warm. Noticing a flicker of movement next to me, I slowly swivel my head to investigate. To my surprise, I find not one, but two hockey moms looking at me with wide eyes and devilish grins.

I squeak in surprise to see them so close. Neither of them was here when I sat down. And they've never even noticed me before… but then again, I'm always here late, or Ronda picks Noah up for me.

One with red hair, I'm assuming she must be the red haired boy's mom, speaks in a hushed voice. "Oh, my gosh. What was it like being carried by Mitch 'The Machine' Anderson?"

The woman with dark hair and bronze skin next to her squeals and claps her hands together excitedly. "Yeah, what was he like?"

My eyebrows pull together, I never have been good at hiding what I'm thinking. "Umm, infuriating? Aggravating? Rude?" I huff a humorless laugh when their smiles drop. "Why did you call him *the machine*?" I make dramatic air quotes when I say *the machine*.

"You mean, you don't know who he is?" the woman with amber skin asks, bringing a hand to her chest. I notice she's wearing fleece gloves and make a mental note to add some of those to my car-bag for hockey days.

"Who? The new assistant coach?"

They look at each other and giggle.

"Mitch Anderson is the top defenseman for the D.C. Eagles. AKA pro hockey player and total stud muffin," the red haired woman explains. "I'm Steph, by the way." She smiles before jutting her chin in the brunette's direction. "This is Tori."

Tori gives me an awkward little wave. "Hi."

"I'm Andie. It's nice to meet you both." I smile back. "So, if he's some famous person, why's he even here?"

"He got suspended for getting in a fight. The other guy ended up with a concussion," Tori answers casually, like it's no big deal.

A look of horror must be etched on my face, because Tori jumps in, shrugging. "It's hockey." As if that's a reasonable explanation.

Steph gives me a smile-grimace. "He has a temper, sure. But when will the kids ever have another opportunity to work directly with an NHL player?"

The two women sigh dreamily. "Plus, he's *so* nice to look at," Tori says at the tail end of her sigh, looking in Mitch's direction.

"He's pretty... but there's not much going on upstairs," I say, crossing my arms defensively. "Aren't you guys married?" I ask, remembering I've seen at least one of them here with a man before.

"I'm newly single," Steph jumps in. "And ready to mingle... especially if it's with Mitch." She sighs.

Tori scoffs. "I'm married, not dead. Just admiring God's creation." She waggles her eyebrows.

I snort a laugh, wondering if her husband would agree.

Tori and Steph turn their attention back to their boys, but my eyes are drawn to movement at the other end of the bleachers. The fancy photographer who's been taking photos of Coach Anderson this entire time is tearing down his equipment and putting it away. The man beside him—dressed in business casual attire—is not only way overdressed for a kids hockey practice, but doesn't even offer to help. The photographer continues to zip up his bags and strap them to himself like a pack mule, and then they walk past to get to the exit. The man with the short, brown hair stares at me as he passes. My skin prickles uncomfortably, like he's literally shooting daggers at me with those angry eyes. What did I ever do to him? Sheesh.

After practice, the kids file out of the rink with all of their gear. By the time I make my way through the throng of kids and parents, I attempt to find the notorious Mitch Anderson and finish our conversation, but he's long gone.

*Coward.*

I feel a hand on my arm and turn to find Steph behind me, she hands me a sticky note with numbers scribbled onto it. "Here's my number if you need anything, girl. My Declan is *really* talented… so if you'd ever like to get the boys together to skate, I'm sure he'd be happy to show Noah a few things."

I smile and thank her, trying to keep my face even. I may not know much about hockey, but it doesn't seem to me like Declan is any better than the other boys. Actually, Mom and Dad always made it sound like Noah's skills were advanced for his age, which was why they spent the money to let him take a special power skating class last year.

But I'm new to this whole thing, what do I know?

# CHAPTER 5
# MITCH

THE EVENING after my first youth-hockey coaching gig, which was a complete and utter disaster, my doorbell rings. My building's doorman wouldn't let just anyone up, so I'm assuming it's Bruce. He's really my only friend, anyway.

Normally, I'd be annoyed at him stopping by uninvited, but I'm antsy from sitting here all day. And I've already declined two phone calls from the Wisconsin Correctional Institution. AKA dear old Dad. He hasn't acted like a father for a long time, and there's nothing he can do to mend that bond now. He chose drugs and alcohol over me a long, long time ago.

Muttering curses under my breath, I toss the blanket off of my legs and pause an old John Wayne movie I've watched half a dozen times in my lifetime. Old westerns are a reminder of a time in my life that was safe, after my granddad took me in. It was always just the two of us, spending every evening after homework—or hockey practice—watching those old movies. I never even met my grandma, since she died in childbirth with my dad. But my granddad spoke fondly of her. I think the lonely old coot was kind of glad when he got custody of me and didn't have to be alone all the time.

I used to wonder what it would be like if my dad would've been more like John Wayne. A tough cowboy who'd lock up all the bad guys and make the world a better place. But no such luck. Instead, he was the bad guy.

Now these movies are just memories of my short time with Granddad before he passed. Before I was alone... again.

Hoisting myself up off of my luxury sofa, I pad across the marble floors of my penthouse apartment and open my front door. I find Bruce standing there smiling, as usual. He's dressed casual but nice in dark jeans and a brown leather jacket. "Get dressed," he says before shoving his way inside. "You look like a homeless man."

Looking down, I see my stained sweats, tee with a hole in it, and moccasin slippers. I'm sure my unkempt beard and too-long hair don't look any better. My person is a severe contrast to my modern and immaculate penthouse. "Why?"

"You're coming to the team party with me. You're my date." He smirks, sticking his hands in his pockets.

I stare at him and his eyes shift toward the hallway behind us, like he's silently pleading with me to go to my room and put on something decent.

"Last I knew, you were into leggy brunettes, Bruce. Female ones."

He chuckles. "Yeah, but I think you need me tonight more than some random puck bunny."

I cringe, hating the term used for women who throw themselves at pro hockey players. Bruce huffs out another laugh at my shudder. "Come on, Mitch. The whole team is on your side, man. We're here for you. And everyone wants you to come to the party."

I cross my arms, he and I both know that's a lie. "What if I already have other plans?"

Bruce glances behind me where my large sofa is a mess of pillows and blankets, and the artistic coffee table some designer told me would *change my life* is covered in take-out containers and a half-empty pizza box. Just to add insult to injury, the T.V. is paused on the movie *True Grit,* making it obvious I've been on a John Wayne movie marathon.

Bruce turns his attention back on me, quirking an eyebrow.

"What? This is a classic."

"Go. Change. Now." He crosses his arms.

I sigh. "I need a shower."

He brings his arm up and looks at his fancy watch. "You have fifteen minutes to shower and get dressed."

"Fine." I trudge down the hallway to my master bedroom.

"And don't use that tone with me, young man!" Bruce yells after me.

Then I hear the movie begin to play and I hear Tom Chaney say, *"Don't provoke me. There's a rattlesnake down there in that pit, and I'm gonna throw you in it."*

———

Twenty minutes later, I'm in the passenger seat of Bruce's old Chevy. Don't ask me why he refuses to give up the old clunker. Goalies are weird.

I adjust the collar of my winter coat and shift to look at Bruce. "So, where's the team party, anyway?"

Bruce keeps his eyes on the road, and his shoulders tense slightly. "Oh, I forgot to ask how coaching went last night!" He huffs out a laugh that sounds fake. "Were those kids cute as hell with their tiny little skates?"

"Well, first off, they're like twelve, not three. And it was horrible," I answer honestly. "Why'd you avoid my question?"

"I didn't." He turns on his blinker and changes lanes on the highway. "Oh hey, you wanna stop and get some coffee?"

Leaning forward, I tap the old dash clock on his pickup. "At eight pm?"

"Aw, is it going to upset your tummy this late?" He teases, bringing one arm up and shoving me.

I'm about to ask him again where the party is, when he reaches up and taps a knob on the dash. The radio blares to life with some peppy song that sounds like it was recorded in the 80s.

"Dude! This is my jam!" He starts singing along at the top of his lungs. Something about a woman needing a hero, and holding out for that hero.

I roll my eyes, giving up on prying any answers out of him. He's either avoiding my question, or has some serious ADHD. Maybe both.

He turns onto a brick street lined with luxurious, historic townhouses, then parks on the street in front of one. Our commute here was maybe fifteen minutes from my place, so it must be one of our teammate's houses, but I've never been here before. Actually, I've only been to two teammates' homes. Remy, our captain, and the jolly blond giant sitting beside me.

The old metal door squeaks as I step out of the truck and close it, as if begging for a dose of WD-40. I give Bruce a knowing look and take a few steps toward the brick path leading to the house.

"Whose place is this?" I ask.

Bruce mumbles something around a cough.

"What?"

"West's," he mutters under his breath, just loud enough for me to hear.

"Nope." I retrace my steps and grab the handle of Bruce's pickup, only to tug and find out he already locked it.

I turn to glare at him, but he's just grinning and jiggling the keys obnoxiously. "West isn't that bad. You guys just need to get to know each other."

"You purposely withheld information from me." I cross my arms and lean back against the door of the pickup.

"I'm no dummy," he says, crossing his arms too. "I knew you wouldn't come if you knew, and you needed to get out of that penthouse."

"Yeah, poor me in my fancy, spacious penthouse. Surrounded by pizza and endless John Wayne films."

Remy's voice draws our attention to the front door. "What are you two doing? It's freezing." He holds the door open a little wider. "Get your butts inside."

With a groan, I push off the pickup and follow Bruce to the door and inside Weston Kerhsaw's house. His very pretty, and equally sweet fiancee greets us as Remy closes the door behind us.

"Bruce! You're here!" She squeals and he opens his arms and gives her a big, friendly hug, like they've hung out a million times.

"Hey pip-squeak!" He lifts her off the ground in a bear hug.

"Put my woman down!" West appears in the entryway, playfully glowering at Bruce, but everyone just laughs.

Except me. My body tenses at the sight of the golden boy himself. With his perfect family home and perfect fiancee and… I bet he has a perfect labradoodle hidden around here somewhere. All the perfect people have them.

But, unfortunately, since I'm in West's house, I have to be cordial to him. I smile, at least, I try to. It must appear like I'm bearing my teeth, because West's blond eyebrows knit together.

"I'm Melanie, by the way."

My head swivels to look in the direction of the sweet, princess-sounding voice.

West's petite fiancee is smiling and extending her delicate hand in my direction. "I'm not sure we've officially met."

We've met once, back when I made a lewd comment about her just to piss off our assistant captain. Which worked like a charm, by the way. I'm distracted for a moment by her large, blue eyes. Eyes that seem to glow with friendliness and hospitality, and I wish I could take back the comment I made over a year ago.

Crap, she's one of those likable people, just like West. Speaking of her fiancé, he clears his throat loudly, and I realize I'm gawking. I grab her hand and pump it a few times.

"Mitch."

She smiles again and tells us we're welcome to use the coat rack, before disappearing into the house. West is crossing his arms and staring at me in amusement.

"Glad to see you at a team event, Mitch," he says simply. His tone is teasing, but it annoys me, nonetheless.

"Bruce kidnapped me," I offer in explanation, because I want him to know it wasn't my choice to come hang out at his house like we're old buddies. Nope. I was dragged here… against my will.

West chuckles and starts to walk past us, but waves a hand for us to follow him. We enter an open concept living space where the rest of the team is scattered about, along with Coach Young. Some are on the large couches near the T.V. playing a game on a Nintendo Switch, and others are grazing around the food table.

I withhold an eye roll when I see the mantel above the fire-place is lined with framed family photos.

The wives and girlfriends are with Melanie in the kitchen, laughing and chatting animatedly. Everyone seems really comfortable with each other. My body goes rigid watching them mingle, like this is their home away from home. Their adopted family.

I've come up with a million excuses to avoid events where the guys bring their loved ones, knowing I'd feel this way. This sense of being the odd man out, even when the other single guys don't seem to feel that way. That familiar feeling of *why can't I be normal* creeps into my thoughts.

Ugh. This is exactly the kind of crap my new shrink is going to try to get out of me at our first session on Tuesday.

West stops behind the large sectional in front of our team-mate Colby Knight, he's a good guy, minus the fact that he's West's bestie and the two act like teenage girls half the time. Speaking of girls, I think Colby draws even more attention than West in that department. Even I can admit the man's face is magazine perfection. In my opinion, he's too pretty, though. It's disarming... like he's a drawing come to life.

Before I can escape to the food table, Colby spots me and hollers, "Mitch 'The Machine!' Dude. So glad you finally came to a team party!" He lifts his beer in the air in salute. "How's the youth hockey gig going?"

Looking from him, to West, and then at Bruce and Remy... I notice they're all standing still, focused on me, waiting for me to answer. This is the last thing I want to talk about. Can't we all just ignore that I messed up and got suspended? It's embar-rassing.

Remy's eyebrow twitches, his face serious. I know I'm not getting out of talking about this. I rub the back of my neck awkwardly, feeling too hot and a little itchy.

"The kids are brats. The rink is run down. Oh, and a mom stormed onto the ice and yelled at me."

Bruce belts out a laugh, making several more heads turn in our direction. Great, just what I wanted, Bruce. *More* attention. I level a serious look at him and he sombers.

Colby has the good sense to attempt hiding his amusement, but I can tell he's biting his cheeks to keep from laughing.

Remy—as per usual—doesn't give away what he's thinking, his facial expression unchanged. "Why? Was she wearing skates?"

I shake my head once. "Nope. Just her tennis shoes. And she came to lecture me about being nice to the boys."

West's eyebrows shoot up at that. "Were you being mean to the kids?" he asks accusingly.

I glare at him. "Of course not, I'm not a monster, West." My voice comes out with more malice than I intended. I clear my throat and add, "I *was* raising my voice. But one kid high-sticked another in the throat. On purpose."

The four of them grimace.

"Damn," Bruce whispers, drawing out the word for drama. "That's intense. Maybe she didn't see that part."

"Must not have, and it was even her kid that did the high-sticking." I huff out a humorless laugh.

Colby crosses his arms, a baffled expression on his face. "Youth hockey sure has changed since I was a kid."

"For real," Remy agrees. "Good luck surviving those little savages, man."

"Thanks," I reply in an unamused monotone. "Can we eat now?"

"Anyone want a beer before I go hang with my girl?" West grins just talking about her.

Colby grins, too, and gives him a fist bump where they

pretend their hands explode afterward. I roll my eyes, but they don't notice.

West remembers asking us a question and looks at us expectantly. Bruce says, "That's alright. I'll grab one for myself after I get some food."

Then West looks at me, awaiting my answer. I glance awkwardly at Bruce and Remy. I guess no one has filled West in that I don't drink.

"Uh, I'd take a bottle of water?"

He eyes me curiously but doesn't make any annoying comments. "Sure. Hey Mel, throw me a bottle of water?"

She pulls one from the fridge and tosses it to him, he catches it easily and hands it to me. Honestly, it was a good throw. I'm impressed.

West nods at me, then scurries off to the kitchen.

He doesn't even care that he's the only guy in there, hanging out with all the girls. I'm guessing as long as Melanie is in the mix, he doesn't care who else is there. I don't understand how he can want to be with her all the time. Don't they get sick of each other? My parents sure did. Maybe other people aren't like that.

The four of us head to the food table and begin filling our plates with meat and cheese. When I glance up, I notice Colby blatantly staring at a slim blonde with short, curly hair. She's linking arms with Melanie, but I've never seen her before. Colby obviously knows her, though and shoots her a dramatic, open-mouthed wink. She flips him off with her free hand and turns away from him.

Bruce and Remy chuckle.

"Still trying to get Noel to warm up to you?" Remy asks, shaking his head.

Colby puffs out his chest, his abnormally twinkly eyes still frozen on the blonde. "She can't resist me much longer. My time is coming, boys."

Bruce must notice my confused expression and explains, "Noel is Melanie's best friend. Colby's had his eye on her for over a year, and she hates his guts."

Colby takes a big bite of salami and speaks through one side of his mouth, his words muffled since his mouth is full, "Dere's a fine wine between wuv and hate my fwiend!"

I shove his shoulder. "You're disgusting."

He grins and tosses a piece of salami on my paper plate. I wrinkle my nose in disgust and toss it into the trash can near the food table.

"Maybe she's into blonds." Bruce pumps his eyebrows up and down. "I bet she'd go out with *me*."

Colby's eyes go steely in a way I've never seen before as he glares at Bruce. I've never known Colby to glare before, even against opponents on the ice, and it's unnerving that he still looks pretty when his face is all scrunched up like that.

Bruce holds his hands up in surrender. "Dude. I'm joking."

Colby relaxes and continues adding food to his plate. Remy's eyebrows draw together, I wonder if he's thinking about how insane his teammates are and how he has to be their captain.

"Alright, let's go play Nintendo," Colby says, jutting his chin in that direction.

Reluctantly, I follow them. But I spend the rest of the party glancing at my phone and counting down until it's an appropriate amount of time to ask Bruce to take me back home.

# CHAPTER 6
# MITCH

SITTING in my car in the silence, I glance at the time on the dashboard. Thirty-two seconds until I have to get out of my comfortable vehicle and walk inside the building where my new shrink's office is located.

I don't want to dredge up old feelings, old memories. Can't we all just move on and forget about the past? Why dig up old wounds?

Freaking therapy. I scoff to myself. "What a waste of time," I mutter under my breath, opening the door of my car and stepping out.

A few cold drops of wetness hit the top of my head. Of course, it's raining today. Winter rain, the worst kind. A warm rainy day in the heat of summer is always a welcomed break from the heat, but cold rain in the middle of winter? Ugh.

I duck my head and rush inside the brick building. It's one of those that has a sign in front telling you which offices are on which floor. I pull up the email on my phone with my therapist's information on it. "Dr. Curtis, right."

Following the sign, I walk up the steps to the third floor, dread heightening in my gut with every step I take. Dr.

Curtis's name is on a plaque on the first door I come to and I take a deep breath before knocking.

The doctor opens the door, his smile is warm. "Mitch Anderson, welcome." He steps aside so I can come in. I see a coat rack and remove my now damp coat and hang it there.

"Have a seat wherever you feel the most comfortable," he tells me, walking toward a large desk in the back corner of the spacious room. Aside from his desk, there's a couch in the center of the room, and two arm chairs. Everything is in calm, cool colors. The sofas are grey, the rug is light blue. Even the pictures on the walls are of misty ocean views. I'm surprised he's not playing some stupid harp music to really top off the calming experience.

The couch looks comfy enough, so I take a seat there. Dr. Curtis rummages through some papers on his desk, then grabs a tablet and crosses the room, sitting in one of the arm chairs across from me.

"How are you today?" he asks, his voice is unnervingly calm and collected.

"Fine." Not fine. I'm annoyed, pissed actually. I could be at the gym lifting weights, using this time off to get stronger. Or at the rink, practicing drills from our coaches. But no. I'm here, in this stupid blue office, talking to a shrink.

One corner of his mouth twitches, like he can read my thoughts and is suppressing a laugh. "Tell me a little about yourself. Something I can't learn by googling you."

I sink back into the couch. "That's difficult, seeing as Google will tell you pretty much everything about me."

He chuckles. "It might tell me your height, weight and birth date. But it won't tell me what's inside."

"It kind of will. It'll tell you I'm an angry hockey player who's always in the penalty box and taking punches."

"True. But that's the public's perception of you. How do

you perceive yourself? What are your interests and hobbies? Who are your friends? Do you have a good relationship with your parents? Why do you get angry?" He pauses. "Those are the things I want to know. The real you."

"Okay," I start, getting even more irritated now than I was five minutes ago. This guy's just jumping right into it then. "My interest is hockey, my hobby is hockey, I don't like most people." I grunt. "I guess Bruce is okay, our goalie. I don't speak to my parents. At all. End of story."

He types a few notes on his iPad. "When was the last time you spoke to your parents?"

I clench my teeth, a familiar headache starting to take root in my temples. I might as well answer his asinine questions and get this over with. "My mom left when I was a boy. I didn't hear from her again until I signed a contract with the NHL. She asked me for money and I never answered another call from her after that."

He blows out a breath. "I'm sorry your mom wasn't there for you, Mitch."

I shrug. "I barely remember her."

"And what about your father?"

"He's been in prison since I was ten. I used to talk to him on the phone once a month or so, when I was in highschool. My granddad told me he wasn't worth my time, but I was stupid enough to think he was wrong. Dear old dad started asking me to pay his bail once I had the money to do so. So yeah, my grandad was right after all."

Dr. Curtis nods. "It must've been hard to grow up without your mom or your dad."

"I had my grandad, I owe everything to him," I admit. Hockey isn't a cheap sport, but he scrimped and saved to keep me in it, knowing how important it was to me.

Dr. Curtis smiles, his eyes warm. "Are you still close to him?"

"He died the summer after I graduated highschool." I drag a hand down my beard. I don't understand how telling a therapist things that happened long ago could help me now. "There you have it, my whole sob story. Happy now?"

His eyebrows draw together. "Of course not, Mitch. I'm very sorry that you've been so alone, and that you've lost so much. That's more than anyone should ever have to experience. Especially with little to no support."

"Well, doc. I'm all grown up. I eat my wheaties. I'll be fine."

His eyes, full of sympathy, look at me intently. The pity on his face makes the anger inside of me double. The last thing I need is someone's pity. I'm a professional hockey player, not a kitten stuffed in a bag and thrown in a river. I'm *fine*, damn it!

"Are we done here?" I stand up, unable to be in this room any longer. The anger and frustration is practically rolling off of me now. And if the shrink doesn't want to be in the line of fire, he better do what's smart, and let me go.

Dr. Curtis, his eyebrows still furrowed, looks from me to the clock on the wall. "We still have thirty minutes."

I want to rip the stupid clock off the wall. Leaning my head to the side, I crack my neck.

"Talking about the past can bring up a lot of difficult emotions, if you need to end the session here, we can." he says, walking toward me with an outstretched hand. I realize he's handing me a business card and I take it from him. "That has my cell number on it. If you decide you want to talk more, or need anything, you're welcome to use it."

I nod my head in response, grab my coat, and high-tail it out of there.

# CHAPTER 7
# ANDIE

WALKING INSIDE MY PARENTS' townhouse—er, mine now, I suppose—I sling my backpack onto the floor. The hooks that hang by the door are already taken, weighed down by backpacks, coats, and miscellaneous hockey gear. A large family portrait hangs above the hooks and I take a second to stare at my mom and dad's smiles. I haven't changed a thing since moving in nine months ago. Part of me wants to leave it and pretend nothing happened. That my incredible parents didn't get killed in that car accident.

But even though it doesn't feel like my home at all, I haven't been able to solidify the fact that they're gone. And the decor in this townhouse feels like the last piece of them. Looking around, I can take comfort in the paint colors my mom chose, the decor she probably hung herself while Dad was at work, the furniture they sat in. I can still picture my dad sitting on the front stoop beside Noah in the morning. Dad sipping his coffee, and tiny Noah sitting in his lap.

This isn't even the house I grew up in, and yet, I feel emotionally attached to it. After my parents had me, they tried for years to get pregnant again. Once they finally gave up, it happened. Hence the age gap between my brother and I. By the time my parents sold our house in Virginia and moved into this place so Dad could be closer to work and spend more time with me and Noah, I was already starting high school.

It would probably be good for me, and for Noah, to spruce the place up… together. To put our own stamp on it.

I'll add that to my never-ending list of things to do.

Slipping off my tennis shoes, I slide down the hallway covered in laminate wood flooring. I expect to find Ronda and Noah at the kitchen island doing homework, but instead find Ronda on the sofa by herself, a worried expression causing her eyebrows to droop.

She perks up a little when I enter the room. "Ah, Andie. You're home."

"Everything okay?" I sit next to her on the couch and she leans back into the cushions.

"Everything's fine, I think. It's just Noah seemed extra moody when I picked him up from practice. He hardly uttered a word to me. But he finished his homework."

I relax, allowing my body to sink into the sofa. Leaning my head back, I take a deep breath, and after a moment I turn to look at Ronda. "So, he usually talks to you?"

Her head leans to the side slightly as she studies me. "Of course. He tells me about his day, and always informs me how many pucks he got in the net during practice." She smiles to herself.

My eyes start to burn and I try to will the sensation away. I will not make Ronda feel bad for Noah opening up to her. I won't. It's not her fault my brother barely speaks to me.

Clearing the knot that has lodged itself in my throat, I try to huff out a casual laugh. "That's great."

She stands up and takes a few steps toward the small kitchen. "I'll warm you up some dinner. You want a glass of wine?"

I lean forward to stand up but she glowers at me. "Don't you dare. Sit down and relax."

Knowing better than to argue with her, I stay put. "You know that patient in room 504?"

She rolls her eyes. "Do I ever. Most high-maintenance patient on the floor."

"He was one of my patients today, so I don't even have the energy to feed myself."

She chuckles. "Sorry, sugar, but I draw the line at feeding you."

I laugh. "I'll muster up the energy to lift the fork to my mouth. What's on the menu tonight?"

"Tender cuts of chicken, breaded with rare italian bread crumbs. And pasta in a decadent cream sauce," she replies, grabbing a stemless wine glass from the cabinet and filling it halfway with moscato.

"So, chicken nuggets and macaroni and cheese?"

"Yep." She smiles, bringing me a plate full of dinner and the glass of wine.

I take the items from her, placing the plate on my lap and the glass on the ottoman in front of the couch. "Thanks, Ronda. For everything." I smile. "This actually looks delicious. Even though it'll go straight to my thighs."

She smacks my knee gently. "Oh, you stop that! Men like a little junk in the trunk, anyway."

I gasp. "Ronda! You are so naughty."

She rolls her eyes and walks back into the kitchen where her coat and purse are resting on a bar stool. "You guys need anything else before I head out?"

"Nah, we're good. I'll see you at work tomorrow?" I ask through a mouthful of macaroni and cheese. I wash it down quickly with the wine.

"I'll be there." She slides her coat over her shoulders just as Noah clomps down the stairs, his hair is wet from his shower and he has plaid pajama pants on with no shirt.

His shoulders slump for a second when he sees Ronda with her coat and purse. "Are you leaving?"

She ruffles his damp hair. "Yeah, buddy. I'll see you next week?"

"Alright." The corner of his mouth pulls up in a small smile. The sight of it makes my heart skip a beat.

We say our goodbyes to Ronda and Noah is about to head back up the stairs. "Hey, wait a sec!"

He stops and looks back at me. "How was practice?"

He shrugs one slim shoulder. "Alright."

"Ronda thought you seemed maybe a little… upset. Afterward." I take a step toward him, but don't move too fast. Like he's a wild animal and I might spook him away.

Noah sighs heavily. "It's not a big deal. Just that stupid new coach is… bossy."

I frown, remembering Mitch Anderson raising his voice to the boys. I can't help but wonder if they did something to deserve such a strong reprimand, but Anderson is also apparently known for being a hothead with a temper. I grit my teeth.

"Do I need to talk to him?"

His eyes widen and he shakes his head no. Then his mouth opens slightly, like he's going to say more. The way my heart leaps at the small movement is ridiculous. But maybe we're making progress here.

He clamps his mouth shut and looks down at his feet for a moment, then back up at me. "Will you… um…. be at the next practice?"

"Yeah! I'll be there." My voice comes out way too excited, but I'm desperate for this kid's approval.

"Can you maybe…" he starts but then stops, looking down at the floor again.

"Can I do what?" He's actually asking me for something, this truly is a breakthrough. My heart soars inside my chest. We're going to get through this awkward phase where he barely speaks to me and back to where he thinks I'm cool. Like before I became his guardian, in the good old days when I sent him presents from my travels.

"Can you stay off the ice next time? That was embarrassing."

My heart drops, and I'm pretty sure my face falls too. I try my hardest to school my features into a nonchalant smile. No big deal, he's embarrassed by me. Whatever. Totally cool.

"Of course." I shrug.

"Okay." He looks at me like I'm insane and I might lose my cool any second. "Well, goodnight."

"Goodnight, Noah."

———

Two days later, we arrive at the ice rink for Noah's hockey practice. I truly never realized how all-encompassing sports are for parents. The practices, the cost of the gear, the games. It takes over your entire life. But Noah loves it, and I'll do anything to see him happy.

I guess that's what keeps sports parents going, watching their kids do something they love. Although, every mother in here is watching Mitch Anderson… and *not* their kid.

I can admit it's mesmerizing watching such a large, muscled man move around on the ice with as much grace and finesse as a figure skater. Sure, his movements aren't meant to be pretty, but his skill is impressive nonetheless. And, of course, that's the only reason I can't take my eyes off of him. Not because of that dark beard, or those large shoulders. *Definitely* not the huge hands I see whenever he removes those big hockey gloves.

Mitch skates by the plexiglass right in front of me and my new-found hockey mom friends. He switches effortlessly from skating forward to backwards and raises his deep voice slightly to direct one of the boys, but not in an angry way.

The two women beside me release a collective sigh and I roll my eyes at how obvious they are.

"You guys have zero chill," I say, coining a term I've heard Noah use before. That is, when the kid actually speaks to me.

"Mitch lives rent free inside my head, and I'm not mad about it." Steph waggles her red-brown eyebrows and we all laugh.

Tori's husband walks over to join us from where he was standing. She introduced me to him earlier when the kids were putting their gear on. Tori's husband, Bryan, has blue eyes and he seems outgoing and friendly. His hair is mostly covered with a D.C. Eagles cap, but shaggy brown hair pokes out from beneath it.

Bryan glances at his wife, shaking his head and pouting before he throws a thick, plaid scarf right at her face. "Here, babe. I think you need this to clean up your drool," he teases.

Tori stands up, the ends of the scarf in both hands, then loops the middle around the back of her husband's neck, pulling him towards her for a quick peck. "No one compares to you, honey."

She pulls away from him, but not before he grabs the edges of her puffy coat and yanks her into his chest for a longer kiss. "Stop!" She gasps. "Mitch might be watching and know I'm taken!"

We all laugh, except her husband, who rolls his eyes. "You're out of control."

She winks at him in response, then looks at me. "Have you guys noticed Mitch staring at Andie?"

Steph turns a little red. She's not... jealous... is she? My shoulders tense. I've done my fair share of ogling the poor grump, but I haven't once seen him look in my direction.

"He is not. Stop that," I whisper back, glancing toward the glass to make sure he isn't nearby. Not that he'd be paying attention to me, anyway.

Bryan chuckles. "I'm a dude, and I even noticed how often he looks over here. I'm just relieved he was looking at you and not my wife, though. Given the option, she might go home with him."

Tori slaps him on the shoulder. "Oh, I would not, and you know it! Admiring God's creation is one thing... climbing it is another."

We all laugh at that, even Bryan.

Tori gives me a playful nudge. "You should ask him out, you're single, right?"

"What about me?" Steph asks, obviously offended.

"Girl, the ink on your divorce papers is barely dry." Tori turns back to me, not noticing how offended Steph is.

"I'm single... but I'm not desperate. Even the zamboni driver would be better than that jerk." I find my little brother out on the ice, his eyebrows pinched in frustration as Mitch lectures him about something. "I mean, on his first day here, I saw him yelling at the boys. That's not the kind of example I'd want to bring around Noah."

They nod, listening intently. Steph seems to have calmed down, so I continue, "If I was going to make time in my chaotic life for a man, it would be someone empathetic, caring, and... you know, fatherly." I remember the sweet man in my current romance novel that has the personality of a golden retriever and hold back a dreamy sigh.

Tori lets out a little sound that sounds like *aww*. "That makes sense. But here's my two cents: a man who's a little rough around the edges and commands authority can be just as tender and as wonderful of a father as the gentle souls." She raises her eyes to the ceiling as if thinking back on a memory before looking back at me again, her eyes full of mischief. "There's nothing better than a man with a firm hand." She says it in such a sultry, teasing tone that I gasp playfully at her comment.

Steph does a slow clap in agreement with her speech, then shivers dramatically as she says, "Yes, ma'am! A good, *firm* hand." She fans herself like she's overheating.

Tori adds, "Every time Bryan tells our kids to be quiet and speak respectfully to me, I could just drag him into the bedroom immediately."

Bryan clears his throat. "Uh, I'm gonna go back to that quiet spot over there." He walks away without another word, leaving us girls in a tizzy of giggles.

———

After practice, we're waiting by the front doors for the boys to come out of the locker room.

Steph's son, Declan, who has the same freckles and red hair she does, comes out first. A big mischievous grin plastered onto his face. The other boys file out behind him, but they go unnoticed by me because Noah's expression is furious. He's obviously upset because he walks toward me, takes the car keys from my hands, and stomps out into the parking lot.

Before I can run after him I feel someone grab my elbow from behind me. It's a gentle touch, but that large, warm hand sends a flurry of goosebumps over my skin. I'm not sure how or why, but I know it's Mitch Anderson before I can even turn to look at him.

"Can we speak… in private?" He asks in a low voice, having to lean in near my ear to be heard over the crowd.

It's annoying what that deep, baritone does to me. That voice shoots through my entire body, like one of those massage chairs that caresses you from your feet all the way up to your head.

I turn to face him. "Oh, you're not going to run off this time with your tail between your legs?"

His regular frown turns down in an even deeper frown. "Sorry, did you need to yell at me some more after that last practice?"

While he's speaking, I notice he's changed out of his coaching getup and skates, into a plain grey tee and worn jeans with sneakers. My gaze falls to his arms when he crosses them in annoyance. They're covered in tattoos. I want so badly to touch the artwork, and to study every piece of art on him, but that would be awkward.

And cool tattoos don't change someone's terrible personality.

Prying my pupils away from his arms, I answer, "Yes, in fact. I did. *Clearly* someone needed to tell you how to work with kids."

He releases a sound that's a combination of a groan and a sigh. "Can I talk to you, or not?"

"Fine," I say.

He tilts his head toward the girls' locker room, which is empty now, and not as smelly as the boys, I hope. I follow him, noticing his movements off the ice are just as sure as they are when he's got his skates on.

He holds the door for me, allowing me to step past him

inside the plain locker room. I brush past him, getting a whiff of his skin in the process. He doesn't smell bad like he should. He smells like a fresh mountain waterfall, which is really irritating. He should smell like B.O. or burning hair. Something horrible to match his grouchiness.

Taking a few steps inside the locker room I take in the large space lined with metal lockers and wooden benches in neat rows. I take a seat on the edge of one and Mitch follows suit, sitting on the bench next to mine.

"I want to explain what's going on so you don't yell at me in front of everyone... again." He quirks one eyebrow, but his eyes are serious.

I cross my arms and raise my chin. "Okay."

The grey shirt makes his hazel eyes look more brown today than when he's in the navy blue coaching uniform. Not that I'm keeping track of which side of the hazel spectrum his eyes are on a daily basis.

He nervously runs one of those giant hands through his sweaty hair, drawing my focus to his tattoos again. There's a roaring tiger on his bicep, and I want to know the story behind it. Or maybe he's one of those people who just gets tattoos he likes for little to no reason. Maybe he gets a tattoo every time he's feeling grumpy... which would explain how many there are.

"Listen, you're not completely wrong. I don't know how to work with kids. Hell, I don't even want to be here. But I have to be."

"Well, at least you're honest," I say in a clipped tone. But his admission makes me feel a pinch of guilt. Nine months ago, I had no clue how to care for Noah, and thank goodness I didn't have an audience watching all the mistakes I've made.

He clears his throat. "Anyway. The boys in our group are

teasing Noah." He pauses, looking at his sneakers. He takes a deep breath, obviously feeling uncomfortable. "They're talking about you, mostly. Which really gets under his skin. And they know it."

# CHAPTER 8
## MITCH

"WHAT? I don't understand why... or even why that would bother Noah."

Noah's mom looks genuinely surprised and confused. She obviously doesn't realize how attractive she is, and how these pre-teen boys like to tease Noah about it. It's the old Stacy's mom thing. Except... Noah's mom.

This whole conversation is really awkward. Dealing with parents is another reason not to work with kids. Thankfully, Aaron is speaking with Freckles' mom, he said she can be a bit... challenging. *Women.*

I cock my head to the side to crack my neck, a bad habit I've had since I was a kid. When I look back at her, I notice she's staring at my arms.

A rush of satisfaction pulses through my veins, making me feel a little hot. Thankfully, I'm already sweaty and gross, so she probably won't notice.

I look away from her and continue explaining the situation, "That's not what matters, really. Coach Aaron is already going to speak to the other parents. But the thing is, Noah's temper is getting him into trouble."

Her eyes widen. Maybe it's a surprise to her that Noah has a temper. "Takes one to know one," she mutters under her breath.

I glide my tongue along the front of my teeth, trying to calm myself. She's not wrong, but she could keep her sass to herself for once. The mouth on this woman makes me want to bend her over my knee and... no, that's not a good place for my thoughts to go.

I clear my throat and take a deep breath. "Noah has potential," I admit reluctantly. She's staring at me with those pursed lips and that irritated expression, and I'd like to haul the infuriating woman over my shoulder again just to wipe that look off her face. What is it about her that gets under my skin?

Closing my eyes, I get my thoughts back on track... again. "The thing is, Noah is more athletically talented than the other boys, which is probably the real reason they pick on him. But when I'm spending half of our time penalizing him for getting in fights, I can't help your son hone his skills on the ice."

What I don't say is that her son reminds me too much of myself. But seeing as the woman staring at me with those big brown eyes hates my guts, I'll keep that bit to myself. But that suppressed anger that bubbles out of Noah at the worst moments? Yeah, case in point. And I'm not sure why, but I don't want Noah to end up like me, still dealing with this pent-up anger at almost thirty years old.

"Noah is my brother, not my son," she offers before swallowing. Her skin looks a little more pale than it did before, like she's just realizing the extent of his powerful emotions and how they affect his everyday life and friendships. "He's had a hard time since our parents died. I'm not trying to make excuses for him, but I'm out of ideas to help him."

My stupid heart wars between aching for Noah that he lost his parents, and skipping a beat at the fact that she's his sister, not his mom. That's why she seems so young, because she is. Probably not much younger than myself. I can't even imagine if I'd had a younger sibling to care for on top of everything else. Suddenly, her sassy quips and defiant armor make sense.

"I know I'm not your favorite person, but maybe I can help."

Her face pinches and she scoffs. "You? What, are you going to brawl with each other and fight your anger out?"

I pin her with an annoyed expression that mirrors her own. "You talk too much."

To my surprise, she doesn't respond, just narrows her pretty eyes at me.

"If I worked with Noah one-on-one, we could focus on his hockey skills. And the extra ice time may even be good for his mental health." I look down at my feet. "It helps mine." I never usually talk this much, but sitting at home is driving me crazy. Sure, I have my practices with the team, and working out with my trainer, but without the games and the traveling, that feels like nothing. Maybe it's selfish for me to offer this, like I'm using Noah as a distraction, an excuse for more ice time. But if it helps the kid, is that really so bad?

She just stares at me again, with that stunned expression that makes her brown eyes look like two shiny chocolates. I'm not really a sweets guy, but something about those eyes makes me think I could become one.

No, no, Mitch, you cannot become one. Not one of anything. You could never be what a woman needs.

I stand abruptly, my conscience reminding me to keep my distance from anyone who makes me feel... anything. "Anyway, I have to run. But think about it and let me know at the next practice?"

I slowly inch my way toward the door and she watches me in confusion.

She stands from the bench, seeming confused. I leave before she can respond.

———

Tuesday, after practice with my Eagles teammates, I drive over to Dr. Curtis's office for my second therapy session. The room is quiet and calm again today, with the same comfortable looking armchairs and couch. Today, it's not raining, and I notice the view offered by the large window. I can even see the Washington Monument from the window.

He'll probably ask me more obnoxious questions today… questions about myself and my family, questions I didn't want to answer then, and will never want to answer. Good luck figuring out the code to this safe, doctor. I locked myself up and threw away the key a long time ago.

I'm staring out the window when he breaks the silence with a question that surprises me. "Mitch, what's something you like about yourself?"

"My charming and outgoing personality," I say dryly, looking back to the window.

He chuckles. "Alright. Anything else?"

I think for a long moment, having a hard time coming up with something I genuinely like about myself besides being good at hockey. But I don't think that answer would appease him, and if I answer this simple question it might be good enough for me to get through another session without him grilling me about my parents again. I need him to believe he's magically pried open the vault inside my chest… that I'm really opening up and making progress, or whatever.

Finally, I sigh and turn my attention toward him. "I'm a hard worker."

His face brightens. "Good, good. I can see that about you. It's how you got where you are today."

I relax a little, and try not to feel smug at how pleased he is I answered his stupid question. I tilt my chin in a barely noticeable nod.

"Can you think of anything you *dislike* about yourself?"

I scoff loudly before I can hold it back. Dr. Curtis tilts his head to the side in interest.

"Do I really need to say it out loud?"

One of his eyebrows curves in question. "Say *what* out loud?"

I throw my hands in the air, already feeling frustrated at this nonsense. "There are a million things to choose from," my voice is raised, I can feel the familiar fire of anger starting in my gut and making it all the way up to my ears. If it was scientifically possible, steam would be shooting out of them. I don't even need to look in a mirror to know my earlobes are bright red. "But most of all, I *hate* my temper."

Dr. Curtis doesn't react to my outburst, he's calmly glancing at me and writing a note on his tablet. "Thank you for your honesty, Mitch," he sets his tablet on the side table beside him and crosses his ankle over his knee, studying me. "What's interesting is you said there are a million things to choose from."

I stare at him blankly. I offered my feelings for the day. Now I'm done.

"Why do you think it's easier for you to think of negative things about yourself than positive things?"

His question genuinely catches me by surprise, causing my unaffected mask to slip. I open my mouth to speak, but no words come out. I think back to my dad and when he started using recreational drugs to numb himself after my mom left. Which quickly turned into illegal drugs. The things he said to me when he wasn't in his right mind, either drunk off his ass, or high. The things that seemed like truth to my eight-year-old self.

*You're a bad kid. Your mother would've stayed if it wasn't for you. If you weren't here, we'd still be together, and I'd be happy.*

I push the thoughts deep down, rage rising in my chest. These are the things I don't think about, the things I block from my mind and put at the bottom of my proverbial lock box. And this stupid doctor is trying to dig it all up again.

"Why don't we try some breathing exercises? You seem upset."

At the sound of Dr. Curtis's calm but concerned voice, something inside of me snaps. I can't do this. Can't sit here and talk to this man I barely know about the ghosts of my past, week after week. This is a special kind of torture. Do people actually do this voluntarily?!

I rise from my seat in the armchair and walk out of his office. I don't even bother to grab my coat.

He doesn't come after me.

The satisfaction of storming out of Dr. Curtis's office deflates quickly, because fifteen minutes later, I'm stuck in back-to-back traffic. I feel like a caged animal again, like that freaking circus tiger. Like everyone and everything is circling around me, waiting for me to either jump through that damn hoop, or go rogue and gobble up the circus performer. My knee bounces up and down with pent-up aggression, I glance over and see a popular bar. It's a Tuesday afternoon and it doesn't look busy, and for a moment, I regret the fact that I don't drink.

But I refuse to be like my father. Although, once in a while, I have to suppress the urge to numb these inconvenient things called feelings.

Feelings, emotional trauma. I'm not even sure what the

difference is anymore, I just know I don't want to feel that vice-like pressure gripping my chest and threatening to make it burst.

By the time I finally make it home and slump down onto my couch, I've calmed down.

I take my phone out of my pocket and see I have a missed call and text from Dr. Curtis. I ignore the missed call, but read the short text message.

DR. CURTIS

It's understandable to feel overwhelmed. And it's okay to be upset. But please let me know if you're not okay.

I roll my eyes, but deep down I know he's just making sure I didn't do anything stupid.

MITCH

I'm fine. At home.

I throw my phone over to the opposite side of the couch, it bounces and lands on the floor. With a groan, I pick up the T.V. remote from the ottoman and turn on a recording of the movie *Rio Grande*, featuring none other than John Wayne. This was Granddad's favorite one.

———

I'm working with my group during hockey practice. I'm actually relieved that I have a distraction and something to keep me busy after my blow up in Dr. Curtis's office yesterday. I already worked out at the team gym for three hours this morning. If I lift any more weights I'm just going to injure myself. Then I'll be out of the game even longer.

Out of the corner of my eye, I see a camera flash. I glance

over and spot Max and his minion watching me again. It looks like Max is telling him when to take photos, as if the photographer doesn't know how to do his job. And why does he need so much camera equipment, anyway?

I look around the rink and my eyes land on Coach Aaron, he's working with the smaller kids, the ones who are still cute and not sweaty mongrels. He catches my eye and salutes me with a grin.

Oh, he knows he did me dirty, and he's relishing it.

Wombats must be an incredibly aggressive and hateful animal, hence how they came up with the stupid name *Washington Wombats*. Not sure how Max and the photographer are getting *anything* useful from all this to help my image. Tonight is the same old drama, despite our conversations with the parents. Freckles—er, Declan—I learned his name from the roster Coach Aaron finally gave me, keeps muttering underhanded comments to Noah. I can instantly tell when these comments are about Andie, because of the aggressive way he responds.

I have to applaud him for coming to her defense, but the way he goes about it is all wrong. *Not that I'd know anything about that.*

If these kids weren't wearing caged helmets to protect their faces, Noah would've knocked several of Freckles' teeth out by now.

"Hey," one of the boys yells to Freckles, who's a few yards from him. "Did you see Andie's wearing *the* scrubs today? The ones that make her butt look amazing?"

Freckles nods enthusiastically. "Of course. You'd have to be blind not to notice that fine a—"

His words are cut off when Noah slams into him. Their gloves come off and fists are flying. This is their third tussle already.

All I want to do is high five Noah for sticking up for his sister to these disrespectful little pukes... but I have to remember they're kids, and I'm supposedly the responsible adult here. I skate over and pry them apart with a heavy, aggravated sigh.

"Knock it off!" I yell over the noise of the ice rink. "You guys think you're gonna learn *anything* if you're so busy penalizing each other?! You're on the same team tonight, for f—" I squeeze my eyes shut, remembering to keep my language clean around the kids. "For fork's sake!"

Freckles raises a red eyebrow. "You realize we've heard the f word before, right?"

"Sure. But you're not going to hear it from me."

One of the other boys chuckles. "We're just trying to be like you, Coach. We know you love penalties."

Freckles snickers. "Yeah, you made it to the NHL beating the crap out of everyone. We thought that must be the secret to success!"

They all burst out laughing. Except Noah, who looks at me with those big, dark eyes. His expression always seems a little melancholy, which makes me like him... maybe because that look reflects my own. I like that he doesn't talk excessively and doesn't run his mouth in smack talk like the others. He's here for one thing, and one thing only: hockey.

If only the boys would leave him the hell alone about his sister.

"Hold it together, champ," I tell him in a tone I've never heard come out of my mouth before. Something softer and more caring than usual. I withhold a shiver at how much I dislike my voice sounding like that. I clear my throat and try again, speaking in a deeper voice, "Don't let them get to you."

He dips his chin. "So, are you really going to work with me one-on-one?"

"Your sister talked to you about it?" My spine stiffens, knowing they discussed it. Discussed *me*. There was a part of me that hoped she'd forget all about the offer. But there was a larger part that hoped she'd remember.

I don't know why I wanted her to say yes to the one-on-one lessons so badly, but the feeling of anticipation annoyed me all weekend.

Noah wipes the sweat from his neck with the back of his hand. "Yeah. I told her I want to do it."

"Okay."

I inhale a deep breath that I hope he doesn't notice, then search the bleachers for Andie. She's not always here, sometimes an older woman brings Noah. But much to my stupid heart's delight, I find her easily in the small crowd. The entire place is dim and grey, worn out from all the kids and skaters coming in and out of the rink. But Andie is the bright spot in this place, shining like the sun on a dreary day.

Okay, a really mouthy sun.

"I'll find her after practice and we'll get things set up." My heart speeds up at the thought of another sparring match with the small but mighty Andie. I must be a glutton for punishment because the idea of his big sister roasting me with one of her sassy one-liners makes me way too excited.

With another nod from Noah, he skates off.

———

Once practice is over and I've changed, I leave the locker room to find a certain sassy blonde, but I don't have to search for long. Andie's twinkly, brown eyes find me instead. If you lined up twenty women in front of me and covered everything but their eyes, I'd pick Andie's out easily.

She smirks, and it hits me like the punch I got from Ilya

during our fight. The few interactions I've had so far with Andie, she's either been gawking at me like I'm insane, or yelling at me in frustration. But this small smile isn't an expression I've had the privilege of seeing yet, and that deep dimple in her left cheek makes my knees weak. She's wearing blue scrubs again, so I can only assume she works at a hospital, which explains her not being here some days.

Andie sidles up next to me, trying to match her steps with mine as she follows me outside the rink into the lobby of the iceplex. Her short legs don't stand a chance of keeping up with me. Legs I found impossible not to stare at in those black leggings she was wearing during our last conversation... Trust me, Andie is strong. Her quads give mine a run for their money, and that's saying something.

I squeeze my eyes shut, willing the thoughts away. When was the last time a woman made my head spin? Maybe never.

She starts talking as we walk, "Alright, Big Man. If I'm being honest, I'm unsure about you and Noah working together, but he seemed okay with it, so I'll give you a chance." She pauses.

*Give me a chance.* I stop once we're out of the way of the crowd that's trying to leave the rink. For once in my life, I have to fight the urge to smile. Anyone but this woman would likely sell their own arm to get an NHL player to work with their kid one-on-one. But not her.

"I mean, if the offer still stands?" she adds quickly.

I pull my phone out of my jeans pocket and ask, "What's your number? I'll save it and text you about times that will work."

Her cheeks pinken, and damn if it's not the cutest look on her. I wish she'd smile again so I could see her dimple.

Andie rattles her number off then adds, "It might be challenging with my work schedule, but I'll try to make it work."

"What do you do?" I ask before I can stop the words from coming out.

My desire to know everything about her is almost overwhelming, but I shouldn't be asking her personal questions, I shouldn't be getting close to her.

"Oh, I'm a critical care nurse." She smiles again, giving me another view of the dimples I'd easily become addicted to. "I'm PRN now that I'm Noah's guardian, so my schedule is flexible… sort of."

*Now that she's Noah's guardian.* I want to ask more questions and get a clearer idea about what happened to their parents, but I hold them back.

"Okay." I scratch the back of my head and look down at Andie's sneakers. I've always been bad at knowing how to end conversations, and I usually just abruptly walk away. But for unknown reasons, I care about Andie's opinion of me.

When I turn my attention to her face again, I notice she's looking at my bicep. Withholding a smirk of my own, I bring my arm back down to my side. She continues tracking the movement of my arm, and I realize she's studying my tattoos. I deflate a little, knowing she wasn't ogling my muscles like I thought. Andie blinks her eyes a few times and those chocolate orbs meet my gaze again.

She pops a hip out and rests a fist on it. I try not to notice the enticing curves there.

"You promise to be nice to my brother?" Her voice has that same sassy undertone that it did the first day I saw her. But I think she's *trying* to be nice to me for once.

My mouth pulls up in a smile, using facial muscles I don't normally use. It feels weird, but also nice. "One pre-teen boy is nothing after working with eight of them. I think I can handle it."

"Alright. I'd hate to come out there and mother you again."

Her eyes are fierce, but her mouth quavers like she's trying not to laugh.

"You do that, and I'll have to throw you over my shoulder again," I say, lowering my voice.

What has gotten into me? Who is this smiling, flirtatious guy and where did the intolerable asshole go? I want him back.

Her dark brown eyes seem to darken further, and the look in her eyes makes a fire burn deep in my stomach. There are a lot of things this woman makes me want to do that go further than throwing her over my shoulder.

"Are you ready?" Noah's quiet voice interrupts whatever was just happening. Andie jumps slightly, obviously surprised by his sudden presence by her side.

Feeling uncomfortable for flirting when Noah might've been watching, I draw a strict line between us in my mind. Which is why I bump my fist gently into her shoulder like a dude-bro.

"Later," I barely manage to breathe out before turning and walking out to my car as quickly as I can.

I hear Noah whisper, "Why's Coach Anderson being so weird?"

# CHAPTER 9
## ANDIE

STILL REELING from my bizarre interaction with Mitch Anderson, I slowly turn toward my brother who's brooding beside me. "Have all your stuff?"

He tilts his head toward his gigantic hockey bag on his shoulders. I don't know how he even carries that thing. It's bigger than he is.

"Andie! Wait up!" I hear Steph's voice as she runs toward us, waving me down. Dang it, all I want to do is go home, take a shower and go to bed.

I hand Noah the car keys and he walks toward the parking lot, leaving me and Steph to our conversation. "Oh, hey Steph."

Work ran late today, and I made it to the iceplex just in time to catch the end of Noah's practice. I'm exhausted. Also, I feel like we live here. Hopefully, Steph's conversation is quick, as much as I enjoy chatting with her. Tori is right behind her and they both settle in front of me. Tori smiles, but Steph's expression turns hesitant.

"Well, look who finally remembered warm clothing," Tori teases, patting my shoulder.

I laugh and flick the yarn ball on top of my head. I'm still wearing my usual scrubs, but remembered to keep a bag in the car with a fleece jacket and snow hat.

Steph clears her throat. "Hey, did anyone talk to you about the boys?"

I feel the blood drain from my face. I've just gotten sort of used to parenting and adapting to Noah's schedule. I don't think I'm ready for altercations with other parents yet.

I swallow slowly. "Um, yeah. Coach Anderson talked to me."

Steph's eyebrows shoot up. "No fair! I got Coach Aaron." She groans. "Anyway, what did he say?"

"Well, they didn't give me any names," I start off. "But I was told some of the boys are teasing Noah about…" I pause, wrinkling my nose at how awkward this is. "About me. And I guess it's been really bothering him and he's been reacting aggressively."

She snorts a humorless laugh, clearly offended, even though I didn't do anything. "This is ridiculous. Coach Aaron told me Declan is one of the boys teasing Noah. But Declan would *never* speak disrespectfully like that." Steph eyes Tori expectantly.

Tori takes the hint and hedges before adding, "Yeah… Declan is such a sweetheart."

"I know!" Steph says, putting her palms up toward the ceiling. "That just doesn't sound like him at all."

I shrug one shoulder. "I'm sure he is, Steph. I'm just repeating what I was told." I offer her a kind smile so she knows I'm not upset. I want to tell her Noah is in therapy and working through his grief and anger, but that feels like betraying him. He might be embarrassed if his friends found out.

Steph's eyebrows scrunch together, I've never seen her so

serious. "Well, I'll talk to him. But don't you think maybe Noah is exaggerating?"

It takes all my self-control to keep my face from contorting into a scowl. I'm used to working with people who are much grouchier and more difficult than Steph is at this moment.

"Thanks, Steph. I appreciate you talking to him."

They both stare at me, and I wonder if Steph isn't used to people not rolling over for her. But I won't throw Noah under the bus and make it seem like this is all his fault. Sure, Noah needs to learn to control his temper and his emotions, but the other boys need to learn to keep their mouths shut.

"Right," Steph says after a long pause. "Well, I need to get home." She walks away almost as abruptly as Mitch did.

I roll my lips together, not sure what to do in this situation. Tori gives me a sympathetic look. "It'll all get smoothed out, okay?"

"Yeah, I'm sure you're right." I force a smile.

I walk out to the car, feeling defeated. Just as I make it to my little sedan, I notice the headlights of a really nice vehicle parked a few rows over from us. The vehicle is sporty, black, and perfectly polished, so it stands out amidst the few cars still left. I wonder if it's Mitch, but don't know why he'd still be here.

Sliding inside my car, I glance at the expensive vehicle once more. It pulls out of its spot just as I'm buckling my seatbelt. Briefly, very briefly, I wonder if Mitch saw Noah come to the car alone and waited until I joined him before leaving, like he wanted to make sure Noah was safe by himself.

Nah… that doesn't sound like the man who's so grumpy and impatient with the kids. There's no way.

Plus, I'm not even sure that was Mitch, anyway.

Adjusting my rear view mirror, I start backing out of the parking spot. "Are you sure you're good with working with

Coach Anderson?" I ask Noah, who hasn't said a word yet. "I really thought you didn't like him."

Noah's shoulder shrugs, but he keeps his gaze on the passenger window. "I don't have to like him. He can help my game," he says in a cold tone.

I nod and lift my hand to turn the music up a little, but right before I do, I hear Noah quietly say, "and he's not *so* bad."

Noah doesn't speak the rest of the way home, but a warm, fuzzy feeling takes root inside of me. Noah found someone he can actually tolerate besides Ronda. A man he can look up to.

Is Mitch Anderson really the kind of man he should be emulating? I don't know. But something deep in my gut tells me there's more to Mitch than he shows to the world... that maybe, somewhere deep down, like *way* deep down, he's actually a sweetheart.

This is where being an optimist is tricky... because optimism easily leads to shattered expectations later on down the road.

# CHAPTER 10
# MITCH

I'M in the Wombat's locker room before their home game today. Max and the photographer interrupt our pregame pep talk to take a bunch of obnoxious photos of me with the kids. They don't even bother including Coach Aaron, even though he's the main coach. I notice when they're done taking photos, Max pulls a few kids aside and asks them interview questions about me.

Yeah, good luck with that. I'm sure none of them have any positive remarks.

When we make it out to the bench, the first line gets ready with their sticks and gloves. The eight boys I normally work with are the first stringers, and some of the lesser skilled, younger kids fill in as needed. We're playing the D.C. Dragons today. *I knew dragons would be a cooler name.* And the Dragons are playing a good game this season, so it's going to be a tough fight for our boys.

This being my first game ever as a coach, I'm nervous. Not even going to lie. I have a newfound admiration for Coach Young. I can't imagine how much pressure he must be under coaching an NHL team with a huge arena full of fans. It's a thousand times more nerve-racking than actually playing.

I'm standing behind the kids, along with Coach Aaron, watching anxiously as the puck drops. This could be a huge disaster since Freckles and Noah are out there together. The two of them could be great on the same line if they'd just try.

I'm trying to focus on the boys, but my eyes move toward the bleachers. I haven't seen Andie since our interaction two days ago, so naturally, I begin scanning the crowd for her pretty, blonde head. My small flurry of nerves turn into a raging blizzard when I finally spot her in the stands. I can't make out what she's wearing besides a snow hat with a big fuzzy ball on top. It shouldn't be as cute as it is. She had it last time I saw her too.

Prying my eyes away from the woman who throws off my equilibrium and captures my attention—in a way no one ever has before, I focus on the dry-erase board that Coach Aaron is holding that shows the next play.

Yeah, this definitely isn't the NHL with our giant touch screens. Here we have dry-erase boards. When I bring my eyes back to the ice, I relax slightly when Freckles and Noah appear to be working together. Noah is an excellent skater, really advanced for his age. But Freckles is the slightly better slap shot.

We're in the attacking zone when Freckles skates close to the Dragon's net, the goalie is distracted by two boys shoving each other, allowing Noah to get the puck to Freckles, who shoots it right inside the net. The crowd cheers and I fist bump the two when they make their way onto the bench, the next set of boys going out.

I realize I've never fist bumped anyone and wonder if I should feel weird about it.

My high is short lived, because when my eyes search for

Andie again, as they always seem to do, I see four burly men making their way onto the bleachers right beside her. And the reason I stop breathing isn't because I'm jealous of some other guys sitting by her, no. It's because I recognize those four sets of broad shoulders, currently decked out in Washington Wombats gear. I swear my teammates bought out the entire gift shop. They have Wombats jerseys, baseball caps, scarves, and even insulated water bottles. But all four are wearing large sunglasses, like that will keep people from recognizing them.

I groan and drop my face into my hands. Massaging my temples with my thumbs. I mutter a four letter word into my hands so the kids on the bench can't hear.

"What's that?" Coach Aaron asks.

"Nothing." I snap my head back up and try to stay focused, but my eyes glide over toward Andie and my teammates again.

The crowd is staring at them and smiling, but Andie is focused on the game, completely oblivious to the famous athletes beside her. Wow, she really knows absolutely nothing about hockey. Maybe it's because women are usually all over us—or trying to be—but the fact she doesn't know who we are, nor cares, makes my stomach blizzard return in full force. Yep, she does something to me. I'm not sure yet if it's good or bad, but it's definitely something.

I see Bruce casually make a comment to Andie, and she smiles. He leans his bucket of popcorn toward her and she takes a handful, saying something to him, and then they both laugh.

My teeth start to hurt and I realize I'm grinding them as I watch Bruce and Andie laughing together. It's *not* jealousy, I have no reason to be jealous. I focus on the game instead, not wanting to dive into whatever I'm feeling.

The rest of the game is okay, Freckles seems too intent on

winning to bug Noah today, and the two of them don't cause any unnecessary drama. In the end, it's a pretty uneventful game and we win 1-0.

———

We exit the locker room after Coach Aaron congratulates the boys on a job well done. When I walk out the locker room door, I'm hesitant, worried my teammates will be there waiting to raz me and drawing a huge crowd. But they're not anywhere in sight. My shoulders relax, happy to have avoided an overwhelming scenario, and also glad the guys didn't take the attention away from the Wombats after their win.

But I don't make it out of the arena before Freckles' mom sidles up next to me, a little too close. She bats her lashes as she says, "Great game, Coach."

"Uh, thanks."

She giggles in an obviously flirtatious way. "The strong silent type. I like it."

She's not an unattractive woman, her red hair is pretty, I guess. And although she's older than me, her skin is nice, she has freckles along her nose just like her son. But I like to be the pursuer and not the pursued. Maybe that makes me old fashioned, or maybe women throwing themselves at me all the time just gets old.

I nod my head once toward the woman, a dismissal. Hopefully an obvious one, then walk out to the parking lot. I spot Andie as she and Noah are getting inside her car, and she glances up and catches my gaze. She pauses before giving me a faint smile. I bring a hand up and give her a salute. My people skills are top notch, as usual.

When I look toward my car, I spot my teammates and roll

my eyes. Remy, Bruce, Colby, and West are all grinning and leaning against my Tesla.

"What the he—" I stop myself from swearing in case any kids are nearby. "What the heck are you guys doing here?"

They chuckle and I roll my eyes.

"And did you really think the sunglasses would do anything?"

Remy takes his sunglasses off. "The shades were Colby's idea."

Colby shrugs. "You didn't have any better suggestions!"

Bruce steps forward and pounds a fist into my shoulder. "Dude! Great job tonight."

"It was cool seeing you coach the kids, man," West adds, his face serious, like complimenting me is painful.

"Uh, thanks. But you guys really don't need to come to the games."

"We got back early from the road and thought we'd come show our support," Colby says, tugging on the brim of his Wombats cap. "But who decided on the team name?"

I huff out a laugh. "Yeah, that was my first thought too."

Bruce stares at the cuddly, furry wombat on the front of his jersey. "They could've at least made them look more tough. Like razor sharp teeth or something."

West studies the wombat. "Oh yeah, you're totally right. That would be a huge improvement."

"Have their people call my people," Bruce says to me. "We'll get it taken care of."

I roll my eyes again.

"Hey, which kid is the one who likes high-sticking like you?" Colby teases, earning another glare from me. He cringes and adds, "Too soon?"

"Number 55 is an incredible player," Remy changes the subject. "Sweet power skating."

The guys nod their heads in agreement. Bruce whistles. "Yeah, I loved watching him."

"That's Noah," I tell them, then turn to Colby, "the high-sticker, actually. I'm going to work with him one-on-one a bit."

They all stare at me with blank expressions.

"What?"

West lifts his eyebrows and smiles. "You're *willingly* coaching this kid one-on-one? I think we're all just surprised."

"It's not like I have anything better to do with my time." I shrug, then lean against Remy's SUV that's parked beside my car.

"Is it because his sister is hot?" Bruce asks, causing me to bristle. He sits beside her one time and talked to her enough to know she's Noah's sister? Now I know how Colby felt when Bruce teased he was going to get that blonde at the party to go out with him. My teammates share amused glances.

"Interesting," Colby says, bringing his hand to his chin and rubbing it conspiratorially.

"You guys are ridiculous. I'm not working with Noah because Andie is hot." I push off the car and unlock my vehicle with the key fob in my hand.

"Oh, we know her name, do we?" Bruce teases. "I sat next to her during the game. She's a sweetheart."

I scoff. "Are you kidding me? Sweet is the last word to describe her."

Bruce's eyebrows shoot up in surprise.

"She's the crazy lady who yelled at me on my first day of coaching!"

All four of them erupt into laughter. Bruce and Colby have literal tears streaming down their faces.

Remy shakes his head, smirking. "Mitch 'The Machine' Anderson." He pins me with a serious look. "I think you've met your match."

# CHAPTER 11
# ANDIE

NOAH IS quiet on the drive home after the game. But his shoulders are straight and proud, and a very faint smile pulls at his mouth. It's not a bad quiet, I think he's just reflecting.

When I pull into our designated parking spot in the garage and we begin walking down the street to our townhouse, Noah surprises me by starting up a conversation.

"So," he starts.

"So… what?" I tease.

"Do you have any idea who those guys were?"

I look down at him. "What guys?"

He gives a subtle shake of his head. "The four guys who sat by you at the game. The ones you were chatting with."

My brows knit together as I think about it. They were all broad shouldered, I assume from muscle, and quite good looking. Especially the one with dark hair and dimples. But pretty boys aren't really my type.

"No. I guess I thought they were there watching their kids."

He laughs and it's the best sound I've ever heard. I want to bottle it up and listen to it over and over. It sounds just like my dad's laugh, except not as deep.

I nudge his shoulder playfully. "Are you going to tell me who they were?"

He rolls his lips with his teeth, contemplating. "Nah. I'll let you figure it out for yourself." Then he takes off in a run toward the front door of our house.

"Hey! Not fair." I chase after him, huffing and puffing when I catch up to him. I really need to start working out again, I miss feeling strong.

I unlock our door and we tumble inside. Noah is smirking, obviously amused by my ignorance.

"Give me one clue."

"Hmm." He looks up at the ceiling as he shrugs out of his coat and hangs it on the hook. "Hockey."

"*That's* my clue? That's worthless!"

Noah chuckles a low laugh under his breath. "Whatever you say."

I smile at my little brother. "This is nice."

He wrinkles his nose, then turns and walks down the hallway into the living room. "What's nice?"

I follow him and we both sit on the sofa. "This." I gesture between the two of us. "Us talking. I like when you talk to me, it feels like old times. You used to be so chatty during Face-Time, but now you're so quiet around me."

His shoulders tense and he looks away from me. Of course, I ruined the moment. Why can't I just keep my mouth shut?

"It's just that," Noah starts, but slams his mouth shut and runs a hand through his dark hair.

"Yeah?" I encourage him to continue, but try not to come across as desperate.

"You look so much like her."

Tears fill my eyes, knowing he's referring to Mom.

"Sometimes it's hard to look at you, it just makes me miss her so much." His voice is barely above a whisper and his admission absolutely breaks my heart.

"I understand," my voice breaks. "You remind me so much of Dad, Noah. This is all so hard." I squeeze his shoulder and he doesn't pull away. "I miss them too. So much."

He nods and one lonesome tear streams down his face. His shoulder leans into my hand so slightly, I almost think I'm imagining it. I want to hold my brother, to hug him. But he's not a little boy anymore, and I'm scared to push him, scared that he'll retreat from me again. So I keep my hand on his shoulder until he excuses himself to take a shower and head to bed.

Once Noah's room is quiet and I'm sure he's asleep for the night, I run a hot bath for myself. I need to relax my body and my mind after this day. I'm in a weird mood, like I'm feeling everything at once. I feel *hopeful* after my interaction with Noah and him finally opening up to me. I feel *broken* that it's hard for him to look at me because it makes him miss Mom. I feel an *ache* in my chest at how much I miss Mom and Dad and wish they were here. I feel *exhausted* emotionally and physically from work today.

It's all too much.

Pouring my favorite bubble-gum-scented kids' bubble bath into the hot water, I inhale the scent and take a deep breath. Bubble gum may not be the most relaxing scent, but it sure makes the best bubble. The only tub is in the master bedroom, *my* master bedroom, I remind myself. Even though my parents' belongings still fill the space. This is my home now, I need to stop thinking of it as just my parents' place. I love that their memory will always be here, but part of me still feels like a visitor just passing through. I know Mom and Dad would want me to feel at home here, so I need to make more of an effort to make it feel that way.

Starting with moving my crap up here to the master and turning my old room downstairs into a home gym. All I'd need is a squat rack and weight bench and I'd be set. Lifting was always my stress release during the long work weeks that come with being a travel nurse. Not to mention difficult patients or weeks where we dealt with a lot of death. It's part of the job, but that doesn't make it easy... physically or emotionally. I need to be strong, not just for myself and my job, but to be a good example to my brother.

But tonight, I'm sliding into this bubble bath, turning on a mind-numbing audiobook, and relaxing. Tomorrow, things are changing.

Tapping on my phone, I find my audiobook app and press play on the book with the golden retriever of a hero, Prince Romeo. I slip into the water and an embarrassing amount of bubble-gum-scented bubbles. A good bubble bath is *almost* as good as a strenuous workout when it comes to stress relief.

This book is a Bachelor style romance where the prince has to find a wife, and a bunch of girls have been sent from different kingdoms. Prince Romeo is clearly in love with Alexandra already, and in his mind, none of the others even come close.

I sigh and sink deeper into the tub, closing my eyes as I listen to the story unfold. The hero is about to kiss the woman he loves, *finally*. But they're interrupted a split second before their lips meet, by Jezebel, the book's drama queen.

"No! Why??" I yell at the phone. I've yelled at this book more than I usually do. "I'm here for mindless relaxation and swoony kisses!"

Jezebel is fake crying and Prince Romeo takes her aside to see what's wrong, leaving the woman he loves behind. I resist my urge to throw my phone across the room. *Yeah, weight lifting is definitely the superior stress relief option.* I grab my phone off the side of the tub, pausing the book. I can't handle Romeo's idiocy tonight.

Instead, I pull up Instagram and start mindlessly scrolling. The Washington Wombats page has a new post, it's a graphic of the Wombats logo, the final score of tonight's game, and the background is a photo of Mitch talking to the boys on the bench. I smile at the sight of him towering over the boys, wearing his track pants and zip-up jacket. Too bad the sleeves aren't rolled up to show off his tattoos.

I tap the photo to see if he's tagged in it, and sure enough, he is. My heart leaps when I tap again and the gram takes me straight to his profile so I can cyber-stalk him. I'm left disappointed when he doesn't even have a profile pic, and he only has one post. It's a picture of him signing with the D.C. Eagles eight years ago. His young face is clean shaven, and his arms don't appear to have any tattoos yet. I smile at this version of Mitch, he might look younger, but his expression is still the same grouchy one I've grown accustomed to.

I glance at the followers and see he has ninety thousand, but he's not following a single account. I snicker, unsurprised by any of this. Mitch Anderson doesn't strike me as someone who enjoys being in the public eye, or who thinks of posting on social media.

My stalking session reminds me I haven't set up a time for Noah and Mitch to work together, so with a deep breath, I scroll to find the text he sent me after I gave him my number.

It's short and not sweet, with only two words.

BIG MAN

It's Mitch.

I type out and erase several different messages, unsure

whether to be friendly, snarky, or funny. In the end, I choose simplicity, because he's doing us a huge favor.

ANDIE

Hey, It's Andie. I was wondering what days you could work with Noah this week? My days off are Monday, Wednesday, and Thursday.

I stare at the screen for two whole minutes. No response, and no typing bubbles. I set my phone back on the ledge of the bathtub. I should've just kept listening to my stupid book.

Closing my eyes, I attempt to put the text I sent him out of my mind. Maybe he's busy, maybe he went out with friends. Maybe he has a girlfriend! Oh, my gosh. Of course the famous hockey man with arms of steel would have a girlfriend. Probably several. And how's he going to have time with all these girl-friends of his if he's helping Noah? My texting him was utterly ridiculous. Picking my phone back up, I type out another text.

ANDIE

No pressure, though.

ANDIE

I'm sure you're busy.

Still nothing.

ANDIE

Let's just forget about it!

The more texts I send, the more anxious and weird I feel. Setting my phone back on the ledge again, I sink down into the tub until my head is completely immersed. Can I just stay here and forget I ever sent all those texts to Mitch Anderson?

I feel the vibration of my phone through the tub and pop up through the surface of the water… and bubbles. Bubbles that taste really bad, by the way.

Reaching for my fluffy yellow towel that's hanging a few feet away on a towel rack, I dry off my hands and face before glancing at my phone screen. Two texts from Mitch. I grab my phone so fast, heart racing, that I almost drop the phone into the bathtub.

BIG MAN

Sorry I was in the shower.

I scoff. "With all your girlfriends?" I mutter to myself in a stupid voice.

BIG MAN

I can do Wednesday. What time?

I take a deep breath.

ANDIE

Are you sure you're not too busy?

BIG MAN

Blondie, I'm the opposite of busy. Now, what time?

ANDIE

Let's do 4PM.

"Blondie." I scoff. "How original."

But I can't help the smile that tugs at my lips. I wonder what it would sound like when he says Blondie out loud, all deep and rumbly and annoyed. He's always annoyed, actually. Brow always scrunched. Realizing I'm smiling at the thought, I quickly make my expression neutral, even though no one's here to see me.

Mitch is nothing like the sweet-as-a-cinnamon-roll hero in my book. But then again, Prince Romeo in said book keeps pursuing the other contestants in his search for a wife, when he already knows he's in love with one of them.

Something tells me a guy like Mitch wouldn't do that. No, if he was really into someone, he'd be all, *this is my woman. No one touches her.*

And hell if he wouldn't sound really sexy being all alpha and possessive. Goosebumps graze my skin under the hot water in my bath.

*Pull yourself together, Andie.*

————

"So, I was thinking," I say the next morning to a bleary-eyed, messy-haired Noah. "What do you think of helping me spruce this place up a bit?"

I study his face from my seat next to him at our small table next to the kitchen. His features are the perfect mixture of Mom and Dad's, whereas I look like a clone of my mother. He has our Dad's thick, dark hair and eyebrows, but our Mom's warm brown eyes and full mouth. I don't think he realizes how handsome he is, I wonder if all the girls in his class have crushes on him.

His eyebrows raise as he chews his mouthful of sugary cereal—Saturday mornings are the only time I'll allow it—then they furrow slightly, like he's deep in thought. Noah swallows. "Yeah, okay. Sounds good."

"Really?" That was too easy. "Of course, I don't want to change too much. And I want all the photos of Mom and Dad to stay up."

He nods, surprisingly calm about this. "I think it would be... nice." Noah looks at his cereal like it's the most interesting thing in the world. "The house has seemed really sad, you know, without them. Maybe changing things up would help." He scoops another bite of cereal into his mouth.

His honesty makes my eyes burn with tears. I choke them back, not wanting to ruin the moment.

I clear the lump in my throat. "Yeah, I feel that way too." I pause, biting my bottom lip while I think. "I thought about moving my stuff to the master and turning my old room down here into a gym."

His eyes widen and a small smile plays on his lips. "Really? That would be awesome. I'd like to strengthen my legs." He pauses. "But I think *I* should get the master bedroom."

"Nice try." I reach over and muss his hair. "Do you have any decorating ideas?"

He smooths his hair back down, stands, and walks over to the kitchen sink. He's thoughtful as he rinses out his now-empty cereal bowl. His back is to me, but I hear him say, "Could we paint?"

"Yeah! Which room?"

He turns and glances around the open kitchen, living area we're in. It's currently painted a light green color. "This room."

I nod. "Green was Mom's favorite color."

"I know. It makes me kind of sad."

Again, I hold back tears. After losing a loved one, every small change seems bigger somehow, like the world is just moving on without them, even though your heart isn't.

"What color are you thinking?" I ask, my voice thick with emotion again.

"How about D.C. Eagles red?" He says it with such a straight face, it takes me ten whole seconds to realize he's joking, and I burst out laughing.

"You had me there for a second."

Noah smirks.

Standing up, I set my hands on my hips and survey the room. "How about a pale blush color?"

He scoffs and shakes his head. "I have no clue what that means."

"Grab your coat, we're going paint shopping."

Thirty minutes later, we're at one of those giant stores that smells like lumber, perusing the paint swatches. We decide on a happy yellow color and spend a small fortune on paint supplies. This could be a complete disaster, seeing as neither of us have ever painted before.

But the last nine months have been the two of us against the world, both of us learning how to do life without our parents. Balancing the hardship of moving forward with bitter-sweet remembering. Painting is no different than anything else we've conquered, and it's probably the easiest new thing we've attempted together.

If it ends up terrible and we hate the color, or we splatter it everywhere…

We can fix it. We can learn from it, we can conquer it.

# CHAPTER 12
# MITCH

BETWEEN EAGLES PRACTICE, therapy, working out, and coaching... I've managed to stay pretty busy during this suspension. It's going by faster than I thought it would. One week down... four to go.

Monday morning I'm lacing up my skates for practice with my Eagles teammates. Last week I worked with a trainer by myself since the guys were on an away stint for most of the week. Even though it was obnoxious that they came to the Wombats game over the weekend, I'm disturbed by how much I'm looking forward to everyone being around today.

The noise, chatter, chaos, friendly smack-talking. Did I actually *miss* it? Surely not. I'm just out of sorts from spending so much time at home.

We're working with our power play coach today, which I love. My position as a defenseman means I keep my eyes on the puck at all times. It's my job to ensure the offense doesn't get anywhere near the net with said puck. Keeping the other team from scoring is just as satisfying to me as getting the puck in the net myself. I think it's why I connect with Noah, because his defensive skills take me back to when I was twelve. When I lived with my granddad, until he passed.

Colby tries, unsuccessfully, to zoom past me. He has the puck and I'm in front of him, skating backwards. With my stick, I steal the puck from him and pass it to West. Colby catches up to him, trying to steal the puck back, but West does one of those fancy moves of his to fake him out, then shoots the puck to me.

I'm surprised at first, usually West would just put it in the net. He's a puck-hog.

And since I'm unprepared, it flies right between my legs. I spin and catch it quickly, taking it across the ice and shooting it towards the top right corner of the net. Bruce reaches up and nearly catches it in his glove, but just barely misses and it goes in.

I glance at West and he winks at me. I'm not sure what's going on today, did we slip into some portal to a magical fantasy land? First, I'm enjoying being around people, and secondly, I don't want to punch Weston Kershaw's face in. I blink a few times and West skates off.

Bruce whistles low through his goalie mask. "Man, all this rest is upping The Machine's game!"

Remy slams into me from behind, almost knocking me to the ground. He's the one guy on the team who's even bigger than I am.

I shove him off and he chuckles. "Ahh, there's that grumpy face we all love. When's the next Wombats game?"

"I'm not telling any of you that information." I remove a glove with my teeth and play with the tape on my hockey stick.

Bruce, who's leaning against the net a few yards away from us, yells, "I already got their schedule online!"

I swear under my breath, causing Remy to chuckle again.

West shoots a puck into the net easily since Bruce isn't paying attention. "Forward it to me! Mel wants to come next time."

Colby perks up and skates over to join the conversation. "Is she bringing Noel?"

West shakes his head. "You're hopeless."

"Hopelessly in love," Colby says with a dramatic sigh. West hooks his leg with his stick and sends him flying across the ice on his stomach.

Bruce laughs, settling back into the net and blocking shots the rest of the team is sending at him. I skate over to the bench and grab my water bottle and guzzle half of it, Colby, West, and Remy following closely behind.

"When do you start coaching that kid? Noah?" Remy asks before taking a swig of his own water.

"None of your business," I answer.

Colby and West share a look.

"What was that?" I ask, looking between the two of them.

"Will, um, Andie be getting one-on-one lessons too?" Colby asks, somehow managing to keep a straight face.

I shoot him an unamused glare.

"You could give her a different kind of one-on-one lesson," Colby offers. "Something a little hotter than ice skating?"

My eyes narrow and I'm about to lunge for him, but he's smart enough to see the blaze in my eyes and skates off quickly, laughter rumbling from him the whole time.

And here I was thinking I was actually enjoying my team-mates for once.

———

The next morning, I walk inside Dr. Curtis's office for our weekly session. He looks up from where he's sitting behind his large oak desk and smiles, his glasses resting at the tip of his nose like he was reading something before I walked in. As usual, he's wearing slacks and a dress shirt.

I'm in an Eagles tee and jeans, I wonder if other people dress up more for therapy... but I also don't really care.

"Mitch, good to see you," he says calmly.

I grunt and sit in my usual spot, the large couch. Closing my eyes, I inhale a deep breath and hope he doesn't make me talk about what happened last week. I hear his footsteps as he moves across the room, then the rumpling of fabric when he takes a seat across from me. When I open my eyes, he's typing on his tablet—a picture of cool, calm, and collected.

He finishes whatever notes he's making and looks up at me, those warm brown eyes making me feel just a little more relaxed. The brown makes me think of Andie's eyes, but hers have gold flecks throughout the brown. Mesmerizing. I blink a few times, wishing away thoughts of the woman I can't seem to keep out of my mind no matter how hard I try.

"I realize you're not ready to talk to me, Mitch. And that's okay, you'll talk when you're ready." He sets his tablet on the side table and crosses his legs. "But I want to give you some tools to calm your racing thoughts, if and when the situation occurs."

"Are you going to hypnotize me?"

Dr. Curtis's cool facade cracks and he laughs, it's a warm, hearty sound. "I'm sorry. I've never been asked that. But no, no hypnosis."

I breathe a sigh of relief, which draws another laugh from my shrink.

"We're just going to work on some breathing techniques, and it doesn't require any talking. Sound good?"

I exhale an annoyed breath, but it's better than talking about my family history, so I nod my head once.

"Alright." Dr. Curtis uncrosses his legs, leans forward and

rests his elbows on his knees. "So, this is the 7/11 method. It's very simple, first you inhale for seven seconds, then exhale for eleven seconds. You can count fast, no Mississippi or anything. Go ahead and try it."

He waits expectantly. I roll my eyes but oblige his request, and count while inhaling and exhaling. I look out the window while I'm breathing, wishing I was outside enjoying the sun.

I glance back at him when I'm done and raise an eyebrow as if to ask, *what next.*

He chuckles. "Good, good. Now let's try it again, but this time, think of a scenario that could cause you to feel angry, and think about the consequences of reacting in anger in such a situation."

I narrow my eyes at him, knowing he tricked me here. I might not be talking about my past out loud, but now I have to actually think about it. Dr. Curtis is unfettered, waving his hand in a silent decree for me to begin again.

Looking out the window again, the first thing that pops into my mind is, of course, my dad. The day he got arrested, leaving me without a mother *or* a father. If it wasn't for my granddad, I would've ended up in foster care. The rage starts to burn deep down in my gut and moves up to my chest and shoulders, I tense.

"Don't forget to breathe," Dr. Curtis says quietly.

I inhale, counting to seven. I think of what the anger makes me want to do: punch anything or anyone in sight, or drink myself into oblivion. All of which would ruin my career. That's the consequence. And the reason I *don't* drink.

Exhaling for eleven seconds, I feel my shoulders relax a little and the feeling in my chest start to ease. Not completely, but enough to make me realize this stupid breathing thing may actually work. Not that I'm going to admit that to the shrink.

"Great work," Dr. Curtis says. He has his tablet again and starts typing. "How do you feel after that?"

I grunt and shrug one shoulder.

Dr. Curtis smirks, like he knows it helped and that I won't admit it.

# CHAPTER 13
# MITCH

WEDNESDAY, I'm at the ice rink where the Wombats practice. I reserved one of the rinks for me and Noah, I don't care about the cost as long as I don't have to deal with a bunch of fawning NHL fans.

I have a net set up for us and a dozen pucks. I'm waiting for Andie and Noah to arrive, and it's embarrassing how many times I've glanced at the door to the rink. It's also embarrassing how much time I took on my hair this morning, even though I have my helmet on.

I tell myself I'm just excited to work with Noah and to see what he can do without the other boys here to tease him, but deep down, I know I just want a glimpse of Andie's brown eyes, and maybe that dimple too.

When the door finally opens, it's not Andie who appears at Noah's side, but an older woman with salt and pepper hair, brown skin, and eyes that seem to see straight through me.

I skate toward them and the woman's eyes rake over me slowly… not in the way someone would check me out, but more like how a bodyguard would survey a threat. She takes in my beard, my probably narrowed eyes, then my shoulders and down my tattooed arms, which are on full display since the sleeves of my grey henley are rolled up to my elbows. Her eyes continue all the way down to the laces on my skates, not missing a thing.

She allows her eyes to drift back up and she meets my gaze, her own eyes cold and calculating. Noah skates onto the ice, smiling, and I can't stop the smile that dawns on my own face. I'm not used to seeing him smile, but it seems to brighten up the entire rink. A trait he has in common with his sister.

"Hey, Downsby," I say as he skates past me, he tries to body slam me, but I don't budge. Instead, I laugh and give him a playful shove. The laughter makes my throat feel warm and rumbly. It feels almost foreign to me, and I wonder when was the last time I really laughed?

Noah heads straight for the pucks and starts shooting them towards the net. While he's preoccupied I skate over to where the woman who brought him is standing.

"Someone called in sick at work today and Andie took their shift at the last minute," she explains, giving me a hesitant smile. "I'm Ronda, by the way."

I tip my chin to acknowledge her introduction. "Mitch."

One side of her mouth pulls up in a humorless smile. "I know who you are, young man."

"Ah, I see my reputation precedes me."

"Indeed it does," she says simply, then turns and takes a seat on the bench nearby.

Wow. This woman who is probably a hundred pounds lighter and a foot shorter than me, somehow made me feel small. I have an inkling her cold attitude isn't because she thinks she's better than me, so much as a silent statement that she will find me and kill me if I do anything to hurt Andie or Noah. And I can respect her for that.

I blow out a breath and catch up with Noah. He shoots me

a puck and I shoot it into the net easily, seeing as we don't have a goalie.

"Ready to work?"

"Always," he says, then quirks his lips like he's deep in thought. "Well, when it comes to hockey, anyway."

I chuckle. *Since when do I chuckle?*

Me and Noah spend the next half hour going through defensive drills, Noah acts as defenseman and I try to get the puck past him.

Then we work on his slap shot, which is more challenging for him. In only half an hour, I've discovered he's much chattier one-on-one. Another thing we have in common, I suppose. After a full hour of drills, I can tell he's starting to get frustrated.

He enjoys the defensive work way more than scoring goals. Finally, I hold my gloved hands in a T for timeout. He rolls his eyes and skates toward me.

"You wanna know something I learned… recently?" I catch myself before I say the words *in therapy*.

He quirks an eyebrow, but I continue anyway.

"When you start feeling pissed, like all you wanna do is give someone a bloody nose… inhale for seven seconds, and then–"

"Exhale for eleven seconds." He looks at me like I'm a moron. "I already know that. Learned it in therapy."

My eyes widen, not because he's *in* therapy, but because he's talking about it. Here I am, almost thirty years old, and even I'm embarrassed for anyone to know I'm in therapy. "You're… in therapy?"

He huffs out a laugh at my surprised reaction. "Yeah. It's not a big deal. Andie says everyone needs therapy… She found a therapist for me right after our parents died."

He sombers, like he's thinking back to that day. I wonder how long ago it happened, *how* they died, but I don't push.

"Everyone needs therapy though, right?"

He skates away and starts working on his shot again. "Right," I mutter to myself, feeling like an idiot. Noah is braver and more mature at eleven than I am at twenty-eight.

I study him with a newfound respect and... affection? This boy still has his whole life ahead of him, and he lost his parents. They won't get to see him graduate, possibly make it to the AHL or NHL if he keeps working hard, and he's processing grief similar to what I had to.

Something deep inside me aches for him... not my heart though, that thing has been dead for a while.

"You're not going to start crying are you?" Noah asks, pulling me out of my stupor.

"No," I scoff.

"It's okay if you do, I won't laugh," Noah offers, then adds, "That's what Andie always tells me anyway. But *I* might laugh a little if *you* cry."

I shake my head and he grins. "So, what else have you learned in therapy? Anything good?"

His grin widens. "Oh, young grasshopper, I have so much to teach you."

That brings another smile to my face. Who needs Dr. Curtis when you have Dr. Noah?

# CHAPTER 14
# ANDIE

I ARRIVE HOME from work later than usual and know Noah will already be asleep. I'm a little disappointed I can't ask him how his first lesson with Mitch went. I'm even more disappointed—and annoyed with myself—for being bummed that I missed seeing the giant brute today. Don't get me wrong, the guy has issues, and I'm totally not into him. But I can still enjoy the view, the same way I'd enjoy looking at a pretty waterfall, or a great book cover.

But when I made my schedule a month ago, I'd forgotten about Noah's birthday. Huge sister fail. I'd been trying for weeks to find someone who could switch days with me, and this was my chance. Sara didn't mind working for me next week if I covered for her today. Now I just need to find something special to do for Noah's birthday. Maybe I'll finally use those D.C. Eagles season tickets my Dad got.

When I open the front door, Ronda is standing in the entry-way, her arms crossed, her right foot tapping on the laminate flooring, and her stare drilling into me.

"Why do I feel like I'm about to be grounded?" I ask, screeching to a halt the moment the door closes behind me.

"You never mentioned that Mitch 'The Machine' Anderson was the guy working with Noah."

"I didn't know it was a big deal?"

"Mhmm. Mitch is awfully young and awfully handsome."

"Ronda, Ronda" I say in an innocent tone. "I mean, he seems a little young for you... but get it, girl."

She narrows her eyes. "That's not what I meant, and you know it."

Sighing, I slide off my sneakers and walk past her down the hallway and into the kitchen. She trails right behind me, arms still crossed, I'm sure. I open the fridge and pull out a container of leftover Chinese takeout.

"When I told you you needed to go on a date, I didn't mean with a roguish professional athlete whose temper could rival the god of the underworld."

I pop the Chinese into the microwave to warm it up then turn to look at Ronda. I was right, her arms are still crossed. "Hades?" I laugh. "I'm not dating him, Ronda, I don't even like the guy. I'll admit... he's easy on the eyes," I offer, opening the silverware drawer and taking out a fork. "But I'm not interested in him. He never even smiles!"

Ronda's eyebrow quirks. She looks unconvinced.

I roll my eyes. "He has time at the moment to help Noah. That's it." I shrug just as the microwave beeps, giving me an excuse to turn away from Ronda's intense stare.

She heaves a heavy sigh as I remove my food from the microwave and stick my fork inside the container. "Alright, whatever you say. Just..." She pauses and I turn back to look at her. Her expression conveys her concern. "Just be careful with your heart, okay?"

Trying to lighten the mood, I tease, "What happened to Miss 'when's the last time you took a man to bed?'"

She smirks and steps forward to pat my shoulder. "You can't take just anyone to bed, sweetheart."

"So no hot, tattooed, muscular athletes? Just double checking the rules here."

She laughs. "How about a nice, clean-skinned, boy-next-door type instead?"

"Booooooooring."

She throws her hands up in defeat. "You're impossible."

"Don't worry. I'm not into broody-angry guys." I take a bite of rice and talk with my mouth full, too hungry to care. "But if you find any hot, muscular, *nice* guys, let me know. Preferably ones with tattoos."

"I'm gonna head out. You behave yourself." She waves me off, then walks down the hallway to let herself out the front door.

I yell, "Well-behaved women rarely make history, Ronda. *Or* get to ride off into the sunset with a hot, inked manly man!"

"I'm ignoring you!" she yells back, then I hear the click of the door.

Chuckling, I finish my Chinese leftovers then head upstairs, shower, throw on my rattiest tee shirt, and *finally* fall into bed.

Let's face it, life is better horizontal.

The fact that the word *horizontal* instantly makes a fantasy of Mitch Anderson pop into my mind? Yeah, I'm probably going straight to the underworld for that.

As hard as I try, I can't get Mitch out of my stupid head. Curiosity about his time with Noah today is eating away at me anyway, so I might as well just text him about it. It's totally not a big deal. It's like texting one of Noah's teachers.

Except I don't have his teacher's cell phone numbers, and don't picture any of his teachers horizontal. I'm contemplating sending him a message and lecturing myself for having a dirty mind, when my phone pings.

BIG MAN

Had to work today?

The tiny bubbles of satisfaction and giddiness that erupt inside of me are nothing short of mortifying. And here I was just convincing Ronda that Mitch isn't my type, blah, blah. Yeah, she saw right through that. Mitch is everyone's type. Except Ronda's, apparently.

ANDIE

Yeah, sorry about that. Noah's birthday is next week and I'd been trying to switch days with someone. How'd today go? Were you a bully? Do I need to come over there and pummel your ass?

Oh, the things I'd like to do to that man…

BIG MAN

It went fine.

Wow. That's all I get? I should've known. A rock has better communication skills.

BIG MAN

What are you doing for his birthday?

My eyebrows shoot up to my hairline. I wasn't expecting him to ask, or care.

ANDIE

There's some lame team in town that my parents purchased season tickets for. Huge waste of money, if you ask me. But it's Noah's birthday, not mine. At least their ugliest player is suspended right now.

I snort with laughter then instantly sober and wonder if I went too far. Why do I always say too much?

BIG MAN

Funny.

ANDIE

*GIF of Ron Swanson giggling*

BIG MAN

I've seen those guys in the locker room, trust me, there are way uglier guys than me.

ANDIE

So who's the handsomest one? I'll keep an eye out.

Three bubbles appear and disappear several times before a response comes through.

BIG MAN

Colby Knight. #27.

I giggle, who is this and what has he done with the big man who barely speaks? Maybe he's better at texting.

BIG MAN

But he's a pretty boy.

I burrow deeper into the blankets on my bed, and bite my bottom lip as I think of how to respond.

ANDIE

Maybe I'm not into pretty boys.

BIG MAN

A pretty boy could never handle that mouth of yours.

My blush spreads from my face to my chest. What is happening right now… is Mitch… flirting? I glance at my bedroom door, which is closed, and I wonder if Ronda is going to pop inside my room any second and yell 'gotcha!'

ANDIE

I'm a lot to handle.

BIG MAN

That's an understatement.

I stare at the text, trying to read between the lines. I honestly can't tell if he's flirting, or if he's genuinely irritated by my personality. Mitch starts typing again. Then stops. Then starts typing. Over and over again. I don't know how many minutes tick by when another text finally comes through.

BIG MAN

What day is Noah's birthday?

Once again he surprises me. Why does he even want to know?

ANDIE

Friday.

BIG MAN

Too bad you don't know someone who could get you box seats for Friday's game.

ANDIE

Are you offering…?

BIG MAN

Trying to get a favor from the ugliest player on the D.C. Eagles?

ANDIE

Oh… no. Of course not. I was totes talking about someone else in my earlier text.

BIG MAN

Really? I didn't know anyone else was suspended.

ANDIE

Yeah… that one guy. He's not very well known. I'd never refer to YOU as ugly! You're a beaut, Big Man! Like a big, growly, hairy grizzly bear.

BIG MAN

Hairy?

ANDIE

Referring to the beard.

BIG MAN

What's wrong with beards?

ANDIE

I LOVE beards. I'd grow one if I could.

I cringe. Why am I so weird?

BIG MAN

Please don't.

> **ANDIE**
>
> Let me start over…

> **ANDIE**
>
> Mitch Anderson, largest, most beautiful bearded man in the NHL, would you ever find it in your big, strong heart to hook me up with great seats for Noah's 12th birthday?

> **ANDIE**
>
> I'm not above groveling.

My cheeks feel sore and I realize I've been grinning at my phone like a fool this entire time. I open my mouth wide to stretch my facial muscles then try to scowl the way Mitch would. No more grinning.

> **BIG MAN**
>
> Only if I can tag along.

> **ANDIE**
>
> You want to come with us?

> **BIG MAN**
>
> Not really. But if I go with you, I can introduce Noah to the team. And if I was turning twelve, that would probably be the ultimate birthday.

> **ANDIE**
>
> Liar. You want to come with us.

> **BIG MAN**
>
> Do you want the tickets or not?

> **ANDIE**
>
> Yes.

**BIG MAN**

You're racking up a lot of favors, you know.

**ANDIE**

How will I ever repay you?

I could offer him several ideas. Including, but not limited to unlimited abdominal massages. I just *know* he's got a killer set of abs. The typing bubbles appear and disappear several times again. Maybe my comment was too blatantly flirtatious.

**BIG MAN**

No need to repay me. I'll text you the details when I get the tickets from our GM.

My cheeks heat once more, this time from embarrassment. I spooked him with my whole repayment comment. Well, he's still coming to the game with us, so I must not have freaked him out too much with my personality. I know I'm a lot, he's not wrong that not just any guy could handle me.

**ANDIE**

Thank you, Mitch!

**BIG MAN**

No problem. Goodnight, Blondie.

**ANDIE**

Goodnight.

———

I drop Noah off at school the next morning and when I arrive back home, the front door is nearly barricaded with boxes.

"The gym equipment," I say to myself in a half groan. It

arrived earlier than I expected. Now my peaceful morning has unfortunately been interrupted. I'm suddenly regretting the energy and inspiration I had last week with revamping the town house and making an in-home gym.

When will I even have time to workout? Oh well. I can sleep when I'm dead.

It takes me half an hour just to get the boxes inside my door. They're freaking heavy. And I'm currently out of shape from not strength training in the last nine months.

Sweat drips down my back by the time I've moved the boxes inside. And by inside, I mean right inside the door. I haven't even pushed the boxes down the hallway and into the guest room yet.

I stare at the boxes for five straight minutes before deciding I'll do the rest another day. Right now, I need caffeine. Then hopefully, I'll have newfound energy to finish taking apart the bed in the guest room and clearing it out for the gym equipment. Glancing at the watch on my wrist, I calculate how many hours I have to clean this room out and do laundry before getting Noah from school and taking him to hockey practice. I turn in the slim hallway, which is awkward since there are boxes everywhere, and gaze at the photo of me and Noah with our parents. A wave of emotion and exhaustion hits me like a slap in the face.

I'm so busy that I don't often have time to acknowledge the feelings swirling around inside me at the loss of them. These two amazing people I adored, who Noah adored. Who were the most amazing parents.

Mom never complained about Noah's hockey schedule, and here I am completely overwhelmed most of the time.

"How'd you do it, Mom?" I ask the picture, her deep brown eyes staring back at me.

And I wish, so much, that she could answer me. That she

could talk to me right now. Give me some of that epic, wise advice she always had.

I wish we could have coffee together, that I could ask her how she likes the pale yellow color we painted in her living room last week, or that I could just wrap my arms around her shoulders one last time.

But she's just… gone.

Here I was, so looking forward to having a quiet day to myself today, but suddenly the quiet makes my thoughts feel too loud. I sniff and realize I've been crying, my shirt is damp from the tears streaming down my face. What a picture this must be, a sweaty woman standing in a hallway, barricaded with boxes, crying her eyes out.

Sighing, I place a kiss to my index finger then tap it against her forehead in the photo. I clear my throat and set my shoulders.

"This is your life now, Andie, live it, and live it well," I say to myself, thinking that's probably what my mom would say to me at this moment.

Walking into the kitchen, I pour my coffee inside a travel mug, and set out to build my stupid gym. Because I don't give up and wallow in self-pity, and neither would Mom.

I'm going to thrive, and I'm going to be strong. For myself and for Noah.

I last one hour before I'm on the guest room floor sweaty, sore and crying again. The pieces of my new squat rack are strewn about the room along with weights and nuts and bolts. It's chaos.

This home gym is now a reflection of my life. I'm laying on my back staring at the ceiling when I yell, "I give up, okay!? I can't be you, Mom!"

I instantly feel guilty… and childish.

So I'm not a travel nurse anymore? Big deal. So I can't go

out whenever I want? Whatever. So I don't even have time to date and I'm flirting with my little brother's coach? Okay, that one's borderline desperate.

But none of it matters when my parents are gone. I'd give up a million more freedoms if I could have them back... for Noah to have them back.

There's no feeling more desperate, more gut-wrenching... than being completely and utterly overwhelmed in life, and having zero options to change the circumstances to make things easier... lighter. The fact is, this is heavy. This is hard. And I just have to learn to deal with it all gracefully.

When all I really want to do is lay here on the floor and cry and feel sorry for myself. I don't want to be strong and resilient... I want to live out my days as the fun, carefree sister who travels all over the country doing the job she loves.

And yet, here I am... forced into being strong and resilient.

Slowly, I force myself into a sitting position and then stand up. I groan at the mess around me, turning and walking out of my bedroom—er, guestroom. Wait, it's now the home gym. Okay, 'home gym' is a major exaggeration in its current state—then close the door firmly behind me.

When I'm back in the kitchen, my eyes go straight to the bright pink container labeled *sassy jar*. It sits there in its glittery bedazzled glory, mocking me. I want to smash it on the ground into a million little pieces and curse at it.

*Yeah, I know... the irony is not lost on me.*

With a deep breath, I think of three things I'm grateful for today: Ronda, audiobooks, and my gym equipment. (My feelings on that last are iffy).

I *can* do this. Me and Noah? We've got this. A few swear words and an unfinished home gym won't stop us.

———

That evening at hockey practice, I sit alone. The perfect end to my day full of emotional breakdowns. *We're allowed one of those days every once in a while, right?*

Tori smiled at me when she walked in, but Steph has avoided eye contact. I sit there, watching Noah—and Mitch—wishing I knew how to handle the Steph situation. And feeling melancholy and alone.

I've never wanted a hug so badly in my life.

The only thing that brings a smile to my face today, is watching the familiarity between Noah and Mitch tonight. It's like they went from mean coach and annoying student, to big brother and little brother… in their own subdued, broody way. I never realized before how alike their personalities are. Maybe that's why they butted heads at first. Or perhaps, they just really bonded during their one-on-one time.

But tonight, Mitch seems softer somehow, kinder. Like this coaching gig is teaching him just as much as it is the kids. Like he's learning right along with them.

Mitch glances over at me and catches me staring. I'm too emotionally and physically exhausted to jerk my eyes away and pretend I wasn't looking at him, so I pull a Mitch and nod my head once. He gives me a barely perceptible smirk back, something so small I wouldn't have considered it a smile a few weeks ago. But the more I interact with Mitch, I notice the small things that most people wouldn't.

It's like my Mitch-related senses are heightened because I have to really look, really pay attention, to notice his reactions. The shine of his eyes when he's teasing, the twitch of his mouth when he's smiling, the clench of his jaw when he's irritated—which happens frequently—yeah, Mitch 'The Machine' isn't a robot at all. Everything besides his temper, and the sheer size of him, is just understated.

# CHAPTER 15
# MITCH

ANDIE'S PUFFY, sad eyes make my chest ache. My chest that's supposed to be a locked-down, barricaded monstrosity. Somehow, my stupid therapy is making me feel things, even though I haven't really opened up to Dr. Curtis that much. Or maybe it's Andie that's making me feel things.

The problem is, I don't want to feel this way. But at the same time, it feels good.

No, good isn't the right word. It feels terrifying, but in a not-bad way, like getting your first tattoo.

I notice Noah glancing at his sister a few times as well, his brows scrunching together in concern.

Finally, I ask, "Is your sister okay?"

He quirks a brow, probably surprised I'm asking about her, and I hope he doesn't think I'm just like the kids who tease him and think about how hot she is. I definitely think about the latter, but I'd never tease him about it.

"I don't know. I think she's upset about the gym."

"The gym?" I ask, feeling more confused.

Noah's working on backwards skating exercises, so I flip around and skate backward beside him while he explains,

"She wanted to start lifting weights again, so she ordered equipment for a home gym." He pauses, concentrating on his movements. "She said she wasn't tall enough to get the squat rack assembled." He stops and glances over at his sister again. "She seemed really upset about it."

"I'm tall," I blurt before I can stop myself. Not wanting to sound desperate, I clear my throat and add, "and I have lots of tall... friends." The word friends feels weird on my tongue. Like eating Pop Rocks and drinking soda at the same time.

"You think you and your... friends," Noah says the word friends with a smirk like he realizes how uncomfortable it makes me. "Could help?"

I shrug my shoulders. "Probably."

He nods slowly. "Alright. Maybe then she wouldn't be so sad. I guess she *really* wants to work out."

I almost chuckle at his comment, there has to be more going on inside that head of hers. And I want to know what it is. I want to be the person she confides her deepest thoughts to. And I'm the last person she should *want* to do that with.

"So, what's your address?"

Noah's mouth slowly pulls up in a wide smile.

———

Not even twenty-four hours later, I'm standing in front of Andie and Noah's front door, about to ring the doorbell. I pause when I hear tittering and whispers behind me. I turn to glare at Bruce and Colby, who are being obnoxious. What was I thinking, bringing them in on this?

Remy shares my look of annoyance and elbows Colby in the side. West had a date night planned with Mel, so at least that's one less annoying hockey player.

"Would you guys shut up?"

"Sorry!" Colby whisper-yells. "I just can't believe you have a crush."

"I don't have a crush," I respond a little too quickly and they start quietly laughing again.

"Riiiiiight," Bruce says with a wink.

Remy groans.

Closing my eyes and taking a deep breath, I turn toward the door and ring the doorbell.

After a beat, the door opens and Noah stands there, his eyes are wide as he takes in the four of us. I can tell he's a little starstruck. More by my teammates than myself. He's wearing a red Eagles jersey with Remy's number on the shoulders.

I make a note to get him one with my number instead.

"Hi," he breathes out nervously. "C-c-c-ome in."

The four of us step inside the small entryway, we're shoulder to shoulder in the tight space. I notice a family photo of Noah and Andie, with who I assume are their parents. I can see similar features between him and his dad, but he has his mother's eyes. Andie is an exact replica of her mother, though. Just a younger version. I look away from the picture, feeling like I'm intruding somehow.

"Noah? Who is it?" Andie yells from another room.

Noah starts to turn toward her voice, waving his arm for us to follow him. We walk down the skinny hallway single file since that's the only way we'll fit, and enter an open living room and dining room area. It's painted a cheerful yellow color. The kitchen is messy with lunch boxes and water bottles, dirty dishes still in the sink. But it's a nice home despite being lived-in.

Andie stands from the sofa, remote in hand, and gapes at us. "Uhh," is all she can say as she takes us in, which is fine, because that also gives me time to look at her.

She's wearing little pink shorts with hearts on them,

showing off her incredible, muscled legs. Her tank top says, *I like big books and I cannot lie*, with a picture of a book stack on it. Her blonde hair is in a crazy pony-tail right on top of her head, and she's wearing white, fuzzy socks that come up over her knees.

She's the prettiest thing I've ever seen.

Andie finally finds her voice. "Noah... why are there four giants in our home? Is there a magical beanstalk nearby I don't know about?"

I glance over my shoulder at the guys. Remy's eyebrows are high on his forehead, most likely surprised she doesn't recognize them. Remy isn't cocky, it's just that the Eagles are a big deal in D.C., it's nearly impossible to go anywhere without being recognized.

Bruce is biting the insides of his cheeks, trying not to laugh, and Colby looks like he's about to burst from holding in his own laughter. I give them a look of warning, then turn back to Andie.

"Noah didn't tell you we were coming?" I ask.

She crosses her arms over her book shirt and glares at Noah, who's now standing beside her. "Nope." She pops the p for extra impact and her brother takes a step away from her.

I scratch the back of my head, feeling suddenly very weird about this. "We're here to help with the gym."

Andie looks from me to the guys behind me again and lifts her hands up to mess with her hair. The movement makes her tank top ride up just enough for me to notice that her belly button is an outie.

I gulp. That might be even cuter than her dimple.

"You seriously don't need to do that. We'll figure it out." Her hands settle on her hips now, she can't stop fidgeting.

I feel bad that we invaded her space. But in my defense, Noah was supposed to give her a warning like an hour ago. I should've just texted her about it, but I knew she'd come up with excuses or just flat out say no. But she needs height, and we have that in spades.

"Where's the gym, blondie? We're not leaving until your equipment is safely assemble—"

"What's a sassy jar?" Colby interrupts from behind me. My eyes follow Andie's to a hot pink glass jar that's been bedazzled with fake gems and has a huge label on it that says *sassy jar*. The jar is stuffed full of cash. Almost overflowing.

She runs over to the kitchen counter and grabs the jar off of it, sticking it inside the nearest cabinet. "Oh, that's nothing."

"Andie has a potty mouth. She has to put a dollar in the jar every time she swears," Noah tells us, ratting out his poor sister.

She gasps and pins him with the meanest look she can muster. But it looks more like the face of a cute, angry kitten. "Have you no loyalty!?"

Noah tries to hide his grin, unsuccessfully. Remy, Bruce, and Colby chuckle. I try to hide the smirk that's trying so hard to creep up, but it's difficult.

"But she says when we have enough we'll do something fun," Noah adds, trying to get back into his sister's good graces.

She harumphs and crosses her arms.

Bruce says, "Looks to me like you already have enough to do something pretty fun."

Remy clears his throat. "So, where's the gym?" he asks Andie, then turns to me. "We should get started."

She sighs in resignation. "Noah, show them where the gym is." She glances down at her fuzzy socks and turns a bright shade of pink, somewhere between a strawberry and a tomato. She must've just remembered she's in her PJ's. "I'm going to change."

She darts across the room toward the staircase that's across from the kitchen. The woman moves so quickly up those stairs, you would think someone was chasing her.

"This way," Noah says, leading the way again.

Ten minutes later, we're all stuffed inside the downstairs bedroom. Bruce is holding up the top piece of the squat rack while Remy screws in the bolts. Colby and I are assembling the dumbbell rack, and Noah is holding a container full of screws, handing them to us when we ask. We already have things well in hand, it won't take us more than an hour to get everything put together.

Andie walks through the doorway looking calmer now. She's changed into dark pink leggings and a white hoodie... but I'll never get the image of her bare legs out of my head.

"Sorry about earlier... I was a little caught off guard. What are your names again? I'm Andie." She smiles and looks at my teammates.

Remy smiles politely back at her and says, "I'm Ford, but everyone calls me Remy. Nice meeting you."

She squints, looking at the three men more closely. "Oh my gosh. I'm so dumb! You guys were at the game."

Bruce chuckles. "Hard to recognize us without the sunglasses, eh?"

She laughs. "You're... Bruce, right?"

"That's me!" He grins. When she turns her attention to Colby, Bruce looks at me and waggles his eyebrows.

"And you are..."

"Colby, ma'am. At your service!"

"Colby..." She scratches her chin and taps her foot, her toe nails are painted hot pink with white daisies. "Why does that sound so familiar?"

"Hockey," Noah whispers.

Andie's eyes widen and her head snaps toward Noah, then to me. "Are these your teammates??"

"Wow. You catch on quick," I jab.

Andie smacks a palm against her forehead. "You guys must think I've been living under a rock."

Bruce and Colby snicker, but Remy looks unconvinced that anyone could really be this clueless.

"So you really don't know anything about hockey?" Colby asks.

"Zilch," she answers, not even having to think about it.

Remy's eyes squint and I can tell an idea is brewing inside that quiet head of his. "How about a little game of trivia? Just to confirm your lack of hockey knowledge."

Andie crosses her arms and widens her stance. "Game on. What are the stakes?"

"For every answer you get correct, I'll put a dollar in the sassy jar," Remy explains. I'm not sure if he doesn't believe her, or if he's just playing around.

When you're in our position, it's difficult to trust people.

Colby slaps his knee. "I'm in! I'll throw a dollar in for every correct answer too."

"Me too!" Bruce says with a smile.

Andie grimaces and looks at her brother. "Noah, I apologize in advance for how disappointed you're about to be with me."

I smile and shake my head. Remy finishes screwing a bolt into the top of the rack and takes a step back. "Question one. It's easy. Who's the all time top goal scorer in the NHL?"

Andie stares blankly back at him, it's obvious she has no clue. I stifle a laugh.

Colby tries to help her out and offers a clue, "It rhymes with *lame pretzky*."

"Umm." She bites her bottom lip. "Blane Letzky?"

Bruce, Colby, Noah and Remy all groan in unison. I can't stop the laugh that thunders out of me, drawing everyone's attention. My teammates, Andie, and even Noah gape at me like I'm a unicorn or something.

"How is me laughing crazier than Andie not knowing who Wayne Gretzky is?" I ask no one in particular.

Bruce closes his eyes and starts massaging his temples. "There's too much weird stuff happening right now, my brain can't comprehend."

"Don't be so dramatic," Andie teases. "How was I supposed to know who this Wayne guy is?"

"*Everyone* knows who Wayne Gretzky is," Noah tells her.

She throws her hands up in the air dramatically. Remy and Bruce grab another iron beam for the squat rack and start attaching it to the sides. Remy looks deep in thought, probably trying to think of a question that might be easier for her. Colby still looks like he's in shock, as does Bruce.

Finally, Remy speaks again, "Okay, question two. In hockey, what's an announcer referring to when he says *biscuit*?"

Andie's shoulders slump. "Biscuit?" She repeats it like it's from a language she's never heard. "Is it like... the team dog... or a mascot?"

Bruce makes a whimpering sound like he's about to cry. Colby's mouth falls open in shock. Noah and Remy just shake their heads.

"The biscuit is referring to the puck, Blondie," I explain.

She glares at me, then turns back to Remy. "Okay, the first two don't count. Give me another one."

He eyes her skeptically, but asks, "Who's currently the team captain for the D.C. Eagles?"

Myself, Noah, Bruce and Colby look directly at Remy,

trying to convey that she's literally speaking to the team captain.

But she doesn't even notice, completely missing our silent clue. Andie groans, "These questions are way too hard!"

The room erupts in laughter. We're all laughing so loud it must sound like thunder to her neighbors. Even Remy has tears in his eyes... or maybe that's from disappointment and not humor.

"Sorry Blondie," Remy uses my nickname for her. "You're a lost cause."

"Ask me what a hat trick is!" She raises her voice defensively. "I know that one! Or, or the colors of the jerseys!"

Colby scoffs. "I'd rather drop a hundo in your jar right now than suffer through any more of this."

"Same," Bruce admits.

"Fine. But I'd like to see you guys try to place an I.V." She sighs heavily and shifts on her feet. "Well, can I get everyone something to drink, at least? I was about to make myself a piña colada before you all got here."

Colby looks up from the instructions he was reading and says, "I'm down!"

"Me too," Bruce says, then starts singing the old song about loving piña coladas.

Remy nods. "I need something stronger after that... but I'll settle for a piña colada."

Andie meets my gaze, and I swear her eyes soften. It's like they went from dark chocolate to melted chocolate. There's a silent question in her eyes. Her look conveys more than *do you want a piña colada*. Maybe I'm reading into her look, convincing myself she's feeling something she's not.... but I'd like to tell her I'd like a helluva lot more than a piña colada.

Being overwhelmed by her looking at me like that, I blurt, "I don't drink."

"Oh," She starts, looking a bit surprised, but recovers quickly. "How about pink lemonade?"

I feel a now familiar tug at the corners of my mouth, like my body is willing me to smile. Holding back smiles used to be easy... until Andie. The girl who has pink lemonade and piña coladas in January.

"Yeah, that'd be great."

She smiles and widens her eyes at her brother. He understands her meaning and follows after her to help with the drinks.

Colby grabs the front of his t-shirt and starts tugging at the collar of it. "Dang, is it hot in here? Or was that just the steam from Andie and Mitch's heated eye contact?"

"Oh, it was definitely from the eye contact," Remy states matter of factly. I glare at him, he's supposed to be the mature, level-headed one of the group.

Bruce whistles. "The chemistry between you guys almost makes up for the fact that she's never heard of Wayne Gretzky."

"Almost," Colby agrees.

# CHAPTER 16
# ANDIE

"YOU'RE JUST GIVING our address out to strangers now?" I whisper to Noah in the kitchen as I assemble the piña coladas… and pink lemonade.

"Mitch isn't a stranger," he whispers back. "And you've met the other guys too."

"Once!" I say a little too loudly and lower my voice again. "Meeting someone once doesn't mean we give them our address. Didn't Mom and Dad teach you about stranger danger?"

"Mitch wanted to help, and you *needed* help."

I huff, unable to argue with that point. I thrust the little paper umbrellas into the tropical drinks a little too forcefully and almost knock one of them over.

Noah rolls his lips together, trying not to smile. I realize he's smiled and spoken more since the guys got here than he has in a long time. That realization melts my irritation. A little.

"At least give me some warning next time? I was in my PJs." I widen my eyes for effect.

"I didn't think you'd care." He shrugs. "Oh…" His

eyebrows shoot up as if he just solved a riddle. "You have a crush on Mitch."

My mouth falls open with a gasp, but I snap it shut. "I do not."

Noah studies me closely, making me feel uncomfortable. I look at the ceiling, the drinks, my feet, anywhere but at him. "Then why are you all red?"

Ignoring his question, I take the tray of drinks off the counter and thrust it into his hands. One of the piña coladas sloshes over the side and onto the tray. "The drinks are getting warm, we better take them to the guys."

"Right." Noah turns and walks toward the guest room without another word.

Gripping the edge of the counter, I inhale a deep, calming breath. Closing my eyes, I release it slowly. I stare at the tall glass I filled with pink lemonade and add a little umbrella to it, so Mitch won't feel left out. Am I curious why he doesn't drink? Of course. But it's not really any of my business. Maybe it's to help his athletic performance… although, the other guys don't seem to be against it.

Pushing down my persistent curiosity about Mitch, I take the glass and head back to the guest room, which is now almost a gym thanks to the big man himself… and his teammates.

———

The rest of the weekend, I worked and didn't get to use my amazing new gym. I have to admit, the guys did a much better, and faster job of putting everything together. I need to find some way to say thank you, besides piña coladas. But what does one do for a group of men who have the money to buy themselves anything they could ever want? Make them a homemade card? Lame.

I drop Noah off at school, something he's still annoyed about me doing. But sending him off on the bus makes me worry. I don't even know the driver, I don't know if they're cautious, safe. And I've already lost too many people I love. So, I'll continue driving him to school and back on the days I'm off. When I'm working, he has to take the bus on his way home... but I hate it.

Today, he made me drop him off two blocks away so his friends wouldn't see. I roll my eyes as I walk into the downstairs guest room and admire how it turned out. The floor is now covered in thick, black mats, the far right wall is covered in back-to-back mirrors, the squat rack is centered on the mirrored wall, and the dumbbell shelf is across from it. And the best part? I hooked up some speakers so I can workout *and* listen to my audio books. The master bedroom is a gigantic mess from me moving my stuff in there, but oh well. One thing at a time.

I'm already dressed for my workout in leggings, sneakers, and a long sleeved tee. I press play on my book and get to work. Prince Romeo now thinks he's confused between two girls. Alexandra and Jezebel. Literally everyone but the prince knows Alexandra is the love of his life.

There's tension, and there's stupidity. *This* is stupidity.

I almost don't want to even finish this ridiculous book, but I've wasted hours of my life listening to it and I can't stop now that it's almost done.

Setting up my bar and weights, I get to work squatting. Feeling my body move and my muscles strain hurts so good. I missed this. When I was traveling, I worked out every night after work. Always making sure there was a gym in the short-term apartments I rented. This is a small piece of my former life I can work into my new one.

I wonder what else I could do to merge the two? Perhaps, dating?

I can't remember the last time I went on a date. Even when I was a travel nurse I didn't date much, what with moving to a new location every month or two. Mom used to lecture me about how I needed to settle down, plant some roots. And sometimes I think she was right. What if I would've bought a house here in D.C. and worked here? I would've been closer to my brother, had friends to support me... maybe even a boyfriend.

But now, nowhere feels like home. And besides Ronda, and apparently, Mitch, I don't have anyone to lean on.

Not that I lean on Mitch. Him helping me with my gym doesn't make us friends... Does it? I suppose he is helping my brother out, and getting us great seats to Friday's game. But that's all for Noah.

Abruptly, I stop squatting and rack my bar. What if all those stolen glances and comments I deciphered as flirtatious, were just Mitch being nice? What if he just wants to be buds with Noah and he doesn't see me that way at all?

I scoff and pick up the bar again.

"Good riddance. He's super annoying, anyway," I say to myself in the mirror. But even my reflection knows that's a lie.

## CHAPTER 17
# MITCH

TUESDAY AFTER PRACTICE, I head to my weekly sesh with Dr. Curtis. I'm not dreading it today like I usually am, and I have to wonder if Noah's bravery is rubbing off on me a little. It's like he's my coach, instead of the other way around.

If this not-quite-twelve-year-old boy can deal with his crap in therapy, can't I at least try? We'll see how it goes, anyway. I don't want to give my shrink a heart attack by suddenly pouring out my deepest darkest fears or anything.

When I walk inside the neat office, I notice Dr. Curtis is already seated in an armchair waiting for me. I hang my coat on a hook by the door and take a seat across from him. He smiles in that serene way he always does, and I hate that it's actually soothing somehow. Like black magic or something.

"How are you, Mitch?" he asks.

I grunt in answer, then remember Noah's advice during our training sesh... *if you don't talk about stuff, it'll stay trapped in your head forever and you'll go crazy.*

Reluctantly, I speak real words following the grunt. "I'm doing... okay." I can practically hear Noah cheering me on inside my thick skull.

Dr. Curtis's eyes widen so slightly that I think I may have imagined it. But he corrects his expression quickly, going back to that cool and unaffected expression he always keeps in place. "I'd love to hear how the coaching is going, if you want to talk about it."

I take a deep breath. "At first, I hated it."

Dr. Curtis smiles. "And now?"

"There's this kid," I start, but then feel weird talking and absently bring my hand up to scratch the back of my neck. "He reminds me of myself. When I was a kid. And, even now, sort of."

Dr. Curtis nods subtly, like if he makes a sudden movement I'll clam up and stop talking… and honestly, I might. "How does he remind you of yourself?"

"He gets angry and makes stupid decisions," I admit.

"Ah, a miniature Mitch 'The Machine,' then?" Dr. Curtis teases, relaxing in his chair.

I smile, thinking how annoyed Noah would be if he heard someone say that. "He's a good kid, though. And a talented skater."

Dr. Curtis nods, his expression relaxed as he listens. Probably relieved I'm actually speaking, for once.

"He lost his parents," I continue. "Not even a year ago. So, I know hockey is the only thing he has… besides his sister. Who's great." I clear my throat, I hadn't meant to say anything about Andie.

"And that's how you feel? Like all you have is hockey?" Dr. Curtis frowns.

I huff out a humorless laugh. "I know it sounds stupid. Poor professional athlete, woe is me—"

Dr. Curtis cuts me off. "Don't make your struggles seem small. Our careers are important, of course, but humans are meant to have deep, personal relationships. Without that piece of the puzzle, anyone would struggle."

My throat feels thick as I soak in his words. The more I think about them, the more my nose burns. *I will not cry in therapy. I will not cry in therapy.*

I think of Noah's words again… *it's okay if you cry. I won't make fun of you.*

"I've pretty much been alone since I was eighteen. My mom left when I was eight, but she was never around much to begin with. Then my dad self-medicated after she left. Which escalated into more, and he managed to land himself in prison shortly after I turned ten." I swallow the lump in my throat not wanting to go down. "I think I could've been alright, if my granddad hadn't passed right after I graduated highschool." My eyes blur with tears, but I choke them back. "He was all I had left… and then he was just gone. And I had nothing."

Dr. Curtis is silent for a moment, like he's allowing me time to process my own words. "I'm sorry you had to face so much loss, Mitch."

I do the fancy breathing thing, in for seven, out for eleven, to calm my racing heart.

"Is it your Grandfather's passing that makes you feel the most anger?" He asks softly.

"I think it's just what tipped the iceberg, so to speak. Like I could hold it together… until the last thing I had was ripped away just like everything else."

He nods. "Often, when we face hardships, we feel angry. But anger is a surface-level emotion. Usually, it's just covering up another, much deeper, emotion. We have to ask ourselves, what's happening deep down that's causing us to feel angry?"

I rub one hand down my beard, pondering his words. I never thought it could be so challenging to identify emotions, to know what I'm feeling. But it's hard to label.

Dr. Curtis makes a few notes on the tablet he's holding then looks back up at me. His brown eyes study mine, there's no judgment in his expression… but maybe, empathy? When I don't say anything, he continues. "Do you think your experiences have made you avoid building relationships?"

I breath out a quiet laugh. "Um, yeah."

He smiles slightly, since we both know the answer to the question he's about to ask. "Why's that?"

"I lose everyone I love."

Silence falls over us. I bend forward and lean my elbows on my knees, looking at the ground and relishing in the quiet of the room. Allowing my words to wash over me. To soak in my thoughts for once instead of fighting against them. It feels… heavy. Those five words I've never dared speak out loud.

*I lose everyone I love.*

*I lose everyone I love.*

*I lose everyone I love.*

I'm not sure how long we sit in silence before Dr. Curtis speaks, it could be a minute, or an hour. But I appreciate the silence he's giving me, and I think he senses I'm done talking for the day.

He finally breaks the silence, pulling my eyes away from the carpet and back to his face. "I have some homework for you, Mitch." He pauses and smiles. "I want you to find something that you enjoy, that's *not* hockey related, and not on a screen. It can be a small thing, but just find something that's relaxing that simply makes you feel happy."

"That's it?"

He laughs. "Yes, that's it."

"Okay, I'll try," I say slowly, already trying to think of something besides John Wayne movies or hockey that I'd enjoy.

———

The following afternoon, I'm at the rink waiting for Noah. It's more than a little embarrassing how nervous I am to see whether Andie brings him, or Ronda. Not because Ronda terrifies me... because she does, but because I really freaking hope it's Andie's blonde head and warm brown eyes that appear when that door opens.

A few seconds pass, and Andie walks through the doors, Noah trailing right behind her. I release a deep breath. I hadn't noticed I'd even been waiting with bated breath, but I had. I can't even breathe correctly when it comes to Andie.

She spots me and smiles, throwing me an awkward, very Andie-like wave. I smile back, but I'm sure mine isn't as brilliant as hers.

Noah flies onto the ice and skates a few circles around me. I can see Andie laughing from the opposite side of the plexiglass. I wish I could hear her laughter from here, that bubbly, happy sound that reminds me of popping a champagne bottle.

Andie crooks her finger, gesturing for me to come closer. That little finger crook could get me to do just about anything. A fantasy pops inside my head... Andie in those little heart shorts, and fluffy, white socks... crooking that finger at me with hooded eyes and a *come hither* expression.

*Lord, have mercy.*

I skate over to the door between the ice and the bleachers, still a little light-headed from my daydream.

She's leaning against the doorway waiting for me. "Hey, I was going to run and grab groceries, is that okay?"

"You trust me to be nice?"

She smirks. "I have a feeling you're a soft, squishy teddy bear under that big, tough exterior."

I snort... not an attractive sound, but she surprised me. "Oh, really? So, now I'm hairy *and* squishy?"

Her eyes rake over my arms, focusing on the tattoos for a

moment, then they glide back up to my face and she looks at me through her long, dark lashes. "I never said there's *anything* soft and squishy about your exterior."

My whole body stills. It takes all of my willpower not to grab her and kiss her... to see what those pink, sassy lips of hers taste like... to kiss her until she can't think of any more ways to drive me crazy.

Andie smirks and spins on her heel. She's walking away from me, leaving me stunned. But she surprises me again when she stops, glances over her shoulder, and says, "but you *are* hairy."

She waves, probably at Noah, who's now by my side, and he waves back.

"What's wrong with you?" Noah asks once his sister exits the rink.

I look down at him and notice he's staring at me with concern. Likely because I'm standing there gaping at the interaction I just had with Andie.

I clear my throat. "Nothing, I'm fine."

He glances back at the door his sister just walked through. "I think my sister has a crush on you."

"Really?" I say a little too loud and a little too eagerly.

Noah glares. "Don't be so happy about it, sheesh."

"I'm not." My tone sounds defensive, even to my own ears. Noah purses his lips and crosses his arms, still holding his stick in one hand. "I'm just curious why you'd think that."

He laughs through his nose. "You don't know much about girls, do you?"

My face twists in annoyance. "And *you* do?"

He nods slowly. "I know that when a girl's face gets all red when they're around you, that means they have a crush on you."

My eyes widen and Noah's expression tells me he's quite

pleased with himself. "And Andie's face is always red when you're around."

I feel my own face growing warmer. "Probably because I make her mad."

His eyes look up and he quirks his lips, pondering my words. "Yeah, you're right. That's probably it." He skates away from me toward the net, leaving me there gaping at him. The ability to leave me stunned and at a loss for words must be a family trait.

Noah and I spend a half hour going over drills, practicing our shots from various positions, and he even shows me some of his speed skating moves. I replicate the moves easily, but I definitely couldn't have when I was his age.

We're taking a water break when I remember my homework from Dr. Curtis for therapy. I thought hard about it last night, but couldn't come up with a damn thing to help me relax.

"So, my shrink gave me homework," I say, then take a big gulp from my water bottle.

"Yeah? What was it?" Noah squirts water into his mouth from his water bottle, then wipes his mouth on the back of his hand.

"Finding something to help me relax. Any ideas? Something non-hockey related and not on a screen."

He wrinkles his nose. "What else is left?"

I huff out a laugh. "My thoughts exactly."

Noah rubs his chin with the hand not holding onto his water bottle. He's deep in thought when his eyes light up with an idea. "Andie relaxes after work by taking bubble baths and listening to books."

"Really?" I ask, trying to mask the fact that his big sister in a bubble bath is extremely interesting to me. "I never thought about listening to books… and I do have a giant bathtub."

"She'd be so jealous," he says, smiling to himself. "The tub in my parents' master bathroom is tiny. Well, I guess it's Andie's now… not my parents'." His face falls, and my hand moves of its own volition to his shoulder.

I go with it, gripping his shoulder tightly in a comforting gesture. It's not something I'm used to doing, comforting people, but I think it's what I probably needed when I was his age. Even though I never would've admitted it. My granddad was my favorite person, and he did his best, but he definitely wasn't affectionate. I'm not even sure I can recall the last time someone hugged me, like *really* hugged me. A big, full-on, bear hug.

In my youth, right after being drafted, I did my fair share of dallying with the ladies. I'm no innocent little angel, alright? But having someone *know* you, someone to talk to, someone to comfort you? That's different. And I never thought I'd want that, never thought I'd crave someone's touch in that way… and maybe therapy is just completely and utterly ruining me… but it's starting to not sound so bad.

"Why do you always look like you're about to cry?"

My head whips over to look at Noah, who's studying me intently. I'm not sure how long he's been staring at me while I thought about hugs. "I'm not crying. And I thought you said you wouldn't make fun of me if I did?"

"I won't. But you gotta give a guy some warning." He stands on his skates and starts making his way onto the ice.

"I wasn't crying!" I yell after him. He ignores me.

# CHAPTER 18
# ANDIE

STEPPING OUT OF MY CAR, I see Mitch and Noah sitting outside the iceplex chatting. It's a brisk January evening and they're both bundled up in their coats. Mitch is all big shoulders and chiseled jawline where Noah is slight, his face still rounded in that youthful way. Not quite a man, not quite a child.

Seeing the difference they make in each other amazes me. Like they both just needed someone who understood them. Noah needed someone after we lost our parents, and I can't help but wonder what happened in Mitch's past that made him need someone too. And made him feel kinship with Noah.

Their heads pop up when I put the car in park and they start walking my way. Noah has his giant hockey bag, as always, the one with that dorky wombat on the side.

I pop my trunk via the lever inside my driver's side door, then walk around to the back to make sure the groceries are out of the way.

"Hey, guys. How'd it go?" I ask before bending down to grab Noah's bag and hoist it inside the trunk.

Mitch's eyebrows knit together when he spots my hand on Noah's bag.

Noah, who's oblivious to his look, responds, "Good. See ya, Coach Anderson." He strides to the passenger door and plops down in the seat, closing the door behind him.

Mitch's face is still sour, and he's still glaring at my hand. He places his hand over mine, sending warmth shooting up my arm. The sensation of his rough, warm hand is something I've never experienced, something new. Sure, I've held hands with men before, but this contact is unique... it's *more...* somehow.

The distraction of his gigantic, calloused, manly hand covering mine keeps me from noticing that Mitch is still silent... and glaring. When my wits come back, I stare at him, feeling utterly confused. Did I do something?

"Did Noah piss you off, Big Man? Why the sour face?"

He nudges my hand with his, and I realize he wants me to remove my hand from the bag. Feeling embarrassed, and a little offended, I remove my hand quickly. This whole time he was completely unaffected by the feel of my hand. Meanwhile, for me, the feel of his hand on mine will linger for *days*. I'll dream about that big, grumpy hand. And wonder how those calluses would feel against my cheek, or running through my hair? Really freaking nice, I bet.

"Noah should carry his own bag," the big guy finally speaks, his voice doing that low, grumbly thing that makes me want to curl into it, to nuzzle my face against his stubbly throat and see what his voice feels like. "He shouldn't make *you* do it."

He lifts the huge bag like it weighs nothing, making me think back to a few weeks ago when I saw Mitch for the first time... when he lugged me over his shoulder like I weighed no more than a stuffed animal. He doesn't step aside after lifting the bag inside the trunk, but stays put. He's no more than a foot away from me. So close that I can smell that *hiking in the mountains and stumbling upon a waterfall* scent that always lingers on his skin. Sweat, paired with whatever deodorant he uses. It shouldn't be enticing… but it is. I want to climb him like the mountain he smells like.

"Oh," I mutter, my brain clearly not working. "But it's so big." I'm talking about the bag, not the man right in front of me… I think.

Mitch's hazel eyes, an even mixture of blue, green, and brown today, find mine. He doesn't look away, but just calmly looks at me. "If he can wear the gear, he can carry the bag. It's a rule in hockey. Everyone carries their own bag," Mitch's voice is even deeper now, with a raspy edge to it.

"Huh," I breathe out. "I suppose that makes sense."

I can feel my body trying to lean into him, to get closer. But I resist the urge. Especially since Noah is sitting a few feet from us. If his friends teasing him about me makes him upset, I can't imagine he'd be good with me and his coach getting frisky.

Mitch's mysterious, color-changing eyes look away from me. He must find something interesting in the trunk of my car, because those mood-ring eyes widen and his mouth quirks. My head whips to the side to see what's so amusing, and I notice that my bubble-gum-scented bubble bath has slid out of the grocery bag. It's the kid stuff, the one that makes the *good* bubbles. And I'm not ashamed.

"Captain Bubbles, huh?" He smirks, giving his eyes an evil twinkle.

It hits me then, as this man towers over me, smirking… Mitch 'The Machine' Anderson is the real-life lovable villain that everyone loves to hate… or hates to love.

"It makes the best bubbles," I admit, placing my hands on

my hips. A pose I've come to depend on around Mitch. A pose that makes me feel tough, like I can resist him.

His eyes land on my hips and rest there for a moment. The way he's looking at me isn't helping me feel like I can resist him. "Don't knock Captain Bubbles until you try him."

Mitch's eyes meet mine again, and one of those dark, roguish eyebrows arches. "You don't think I'd take a bath with Captain Bubbles?"

My mind goes back to when we were texting and he'd just gotten out of the shower… the picture of him in just his towel. In my head, the towel dips low enough to see his abs and he's still glistening a little with steam.

"I can't picture you taking a bath at all. You seem like a shower guy," I rasp, then regret my words instantly. I'd do anything to push them back inside. But it's like toothpaste… easy to squeeze out, impossible to get back inside the tube.

"Ah, so you picture me in the shower?" He brings a hand up to rub his beard thoughtfully. "That's weird, since I'm so ugly and hairy."

My mouth gapes open. "That's not what I said!"

His throat makes a noise that sounds like a strangled laugh. "Sure…"

I open my mouth to defend myself, but Noah appears beside Mitch, he glances between the two of us with a strange expression on his face. "Are you two done arguing? I'm starving." He glances between us again before turning and going back to his spot in the passenger seat.

Mitch is still smirking. I want to wipe that stupid look off of his stupid face. Instead, I glare at him.

"See you, Blondie," he says before strutting off toward his fancy vehicle.

I watch him walk, not because his butt is incredible—

because it totally is—but because I'm internally willing for him to trip or do something dumb.

But of course, he doesn't stumble, or trip, or anything. He struts away like a magnificent peacock.

With an annoyed huff, I slam the trunk of my car closed, stomp around to the driver's side door, open it and slide inside.

Noah is smirking at me, similar to the way Mitch just did. "Your face is all red again."

"Shut up."

———

On the drive home, Noah talks to me. Not just occasional sarcastic comments, but he *really* talks to me. This has been happening more and more since Mitch started coaching. I may be reading into this, or seeing what I want to see… but I don't think so.

I think Noah felt so lost without a strong male influence in his life, and now he has someone to fill that role. But I worry that when Mitch's suspension is over and he goes back to his insane schedule with lots of traveling, we'll barely see him anymore.

What if Noah clams up again when Mitch is too busy for him? Ugh, I'm not cut out for this parenting stuff.

"So then I told Mitch he should try bubble baths because that's how you relax." Noah pauses and looks at me expectantly. I realize he's been talking this whole time, and he's waiting for a response.

I say the first thing that pops into my head. "Why does he need a bubble bath?"

Noah releases a heavy sigh. "You weren't even listening, were you? His therapist told him to find ways to relax.

Anyway, he said he might try it because he has a huge tub that he's never used."

"Mitch goes to therapy?"

"Yeah, he lost his parents too. And his grandpa. Well, his parents didn't die, but he says there are many ways to lose people."

I'm at a loss for words. Something inside me crumples at this information, but it also puts together so many pieces to Mitch Anderson that had been a mystery. Sure, a person isn't defined by losing a loved one, or multiple, but it makes sense now why he's closed off. And the kinship between Mitch and Noah definitely adds up now. They have this huge thing in common, this thing that has shaped both of them, this history of trauma and loss.

"Really?" I ask quietly, not knowing what else to say. "I didn't know that."

I just want to give them both a big hug. Noah definitely won't let me… but Mitch might. Maybe the man just needs a good hug. Goosebumps break out along my arms just thinking about wrapping my arms around him… it's like my senses are screaming, *we volunteer! We volunteer as tribute!*

"You enjoy hanging out with Mitch, huh?" I glance over at him quickly, then return my eyes to the traffic in front of me.

He's quiet for a few seconds, contemplating his answer. "Yeah," he says with a small laugh. "I hated him at first. But I guess he's grown on me."

I smile to myself, turning on my blinker to turn onto the street that leads to our townhouse.

"And he's grown on you too," he says. It's not a question, it's a statement.

Willing myself not to blush, I decide to change the subject to something safer. "So, you have homework tonight?"

He huffs a laugh, seeing right through my subject changing tactics. "Just a division worksheet. No sweat."

I pull into our designated parking spot and peek over at my little brother. His head is turned slightly, looking out the window. But he looks so relaxed, and so happy, it breaks my heart a little.

Because a month ago, I wondered how we were going to deal with Mitch Anderson being in our lives... and now I'm wondering how we're going to survive without him once he's gone.

# CHAPTER 19
# MITCH

THE REST of the week goes by quickly. I had practice with the Eagles Thursday morning, coached the Wombats Thursday evening, another Eagles practice this morning, and in a few hours… the Eagles game with Andie and Noah.

As I prepare for the game, I realize it feels strangely similar to getting ready for a date. I know it's not a date, but there's no denying the attraction I feel for Andie. Therefore, the desire to impress her—or at least, not disgust her.

Which is why I'm trying out the whole bubble bath thing. I even added Captain Bubbles bubble bath to my weekly grocery order. I got the wild berry scent, thinking Andie might notice if I smelled like bubble gum.

A man has to have some secrets.

My giant, free-standing tub is filled to the max with hot water and a good dose of bubble bath. And Andie wasn't wrong, this stuff really does make some serious bubbles.

Now, per my homework from Dr. Curtis, I need to decide on an audiobook. I already set up a subscription to a company where I could check out audiobooks. I didn't even know that was a thing until today. Noah said Andie listens to romance, but I'm not so sure that's for me. I type the word *hockey* into the search bar. Surely, listening to a book about hockey wouldn't break Dr. Curtis's rules? There's a biography about Wayne Gretzy that pops up, but I'm pretty sure I already know everything about him.

I keep scrolling and come across a book titled "Mighty Pucks." I read the first sentence of the description and discover it *is* a romance, but it's about a professional hockey player... so how bad could it be?

I tap the play button on my phone and it starts reading to me through my bathroom speakers, which are connected to my phone's audio. I adjust the volume and set my phone on the bathroom counter.

I'm ready to relax. Looking at the prissy bathtub filled with pink bubbles, I second guess this entire thing.

"What the hell," I grumble, removing the towel draped around my waist and letting it fall to the floor. I step one leg inside the tub, then the other. Okay, not so bad. I allow myself to sink into a sitting position.

*I am one with the tub. I am relaxed. This is my new hobby.*

The audio book gets past the beginning credits and starts reading to me from the man's point of view. He's on the team's private jet, flirting with the coach's daughter.

I snort a laugh. "A coach's daughter would never travel with the team."

I keep listening, and they keep flirting. The coach's daughter invites the player to meet her in the plane's bathroom in five minutes.

"What the... what kind of book is this?"

It continues and he's trying to figure out how to slip into the bathroom with miss-hot-pants without his teammates, or coach, noticing. This would literally never happen. I don't know whether to laugh, or to jump out of the tub and stop the audiobook from continuing.

But I decide to stick it out and give this thing a chance. Hopefully, it'll turn around soon.

It doesn't. He magically sneaks past all the guys on the small plane and they shut themselves inside the tiny airplane bathroom.

"That's unsanitary," I whisper to myself.

I try to stay relaxed and close my eyes, thinking someone will come knock on the door and interrupt them before this book gets a little too wild for me. But no... the two of them start making out and removing clothing. Things are progressing *very* quickly—there's no way a large hockey player could accomplish all this in an airplane lavatory—I fly out of the tub to stop the book.

Hot water and bubbles splatter all over the floor as I run for the phone, yelling, "No, no, no!"

I can't move fast enough, not wanting to slip and land on my butt, and things start happening in this book that I'm wholly unprepared for.

Finally, I reach my phone and stop the book just as the hockey player tells the coach's daughter she's a *good girl.*

"If she's such a good girl, why's she doing *that* two feet away from her dad? And in a lavatory? Gross."

I slip and slide back to the tub and get back in the hot water, this time with my phone in hand. Scrolling through the options of books, again, I find a John Wayne biography and start playing that one instead. I breathe a sigh of relief when the first chapter passes without anything steamy.

Pretty soon, I'm interested in the book, enjoying the narrator and the details about John Wayne's life. I think of my granddad, and the time we spent watching John Wayne's films together. He would've enjoyed this book. I find myself sinking deeper in the tub and smiling to myself.

My eyes open when it hits me… I'm thinking of my granddad and *smiling*. Normally, when thoughts of my family slink into my mind unbidden, all I feel is that tightness in my chest. That old feeling of bitterness and anger. That over-whelming loneliness that takes over my body and makes me want to break something.

But today is different.

I know my anger and resentment won't heal in one month, or even one year. But for the first time in years, I feel some-thing new.

Something that seems a lot like *hope*.

———

"Mitch 'The Machine'! Good to see you in the house," Tom Parker says, his face genuinely happy—and maybe a little surprised—as he reaches a hand out to me.

I shake his hand and he pats my shoulder. "I was thrilled when you reached out for tickets. I thought maybe you didn't miss us at all." He winks. "Looking good, by the way."

Tugging at my tie nervously, I grunt my thanks. It's been a month since I wore one of my custom-tailored game-day suits, and it feels a little weird. Tonight, I selected the one that is the most fitted, showing off my muscled arms (Andie seems to like my arms… or maybe it's just the tattoos). The suit is a dark forest green with a subtle gold pattern, and the golden, silk tie matches. I admit, "I didn't want to draw attention by coming to the games."

Tom shrugs. "You'll have to be back in the limelight sooner or later. So tell me, how are the Washington Wombats? I bet they'll miss having you around when you come back to us in a week."

"I doubt that," I say dryly. "But... it hasn't been as bad as I expected."

Andie and Noah enter the box just then, and Noah's face lights up when he sees me. It's enough to completely shatter what's left of that lockbox around my heart. I fight the urge to run to them when Andie smiles at me, tugging at my tie again instead.

Tom turns to see what I'm looking at and I don't miss the curious glint in his eyes.

Noah strides over to where we're standing, his eyes are huge... like two brown pucks resting below his eyebrows. "Hey, Coach... I can't believe you hooked us up with these tickets." He's wearing the same worn-out jersey he had on when me and the guys were helping with Andie's gym.

I reach out and mess up his shaggy, dark hair. Out of the corner of my eye, I see Tom shift on his feet, watching us with interest.

Andie ambles over to join us, looking as delicious as ever. Her bubble gum scent fills the space between us, making my mouth water. She does a quick intake of my person from top to bottom. She seems pleased with what she sees, just like I hoped.

"I feel underdressed." Andie rubs her hands over her legging-clad thighs like her palms are sweaty. Her black leggings show off those powerful legs of hers. She paired the leggings with bright white sneakers, and a denim jacket over a white tee. She's an absolute vision.

"You look fine," I say, not feeling comfortable complimenting her in front of Noah. Or Tom. Oh, right... Tom is still beside me. "Andie, Noah, this is the team's general manager, Tom Parker."

Tom steps forward and shakes both of their hands. "Great meeting you both." He looks down at Noah. "So Noah, I'm assuming you're one of Mitch's youth hockey kids?"

"Yeah," he says dryly. "He was a real pain at first, but he's getting better."

I roll my eyes but Tom bursts into laughter. "I like this kid," he says.

I gesture to the two bar stools in front of us, there's a present for Noah on one and a present for Andie on the other. It's easy to distinguish one from the other because Andie's is in a pink, sparkly gift bag and Noah's is in an Eagle's gift bag.

"You knew it was my birthday?" Noah asks, barely able to contain his excitement.

"Of course. Go open your present," I tell him, crossing my arms and leaning against the bar to watch.

He doesn't waste any time, leaping toward the D.C. Eagle's bag that I found at the arena's gift shop. He tosses the tissue paper to the floor, and Andie laughs. Noah gasps when he pulls out a jersey. It's new and pristine, making the one he's wearing look even older. He flips it over to look at the back and grins when he sees my last name on it. He gasps again, even louder, when he notices it's signed by the entire team.

"This is sick," he whisper-yells, like he's trying so hard to play it cool.

I stifle a laugh and Tom snickers behind me. "You like it?" I ask, already knowing the answer.

"Like it?" His face changes and he looks down at the jersey, then at the bar stool that has a direct view of the ice below. "This is the best present I've ever gotten."

His eyes get that shiny glint to them as if he's holding back tears and Andie places a hand on his shoulder. He shrugs out of her grasp and clears his throat, sticking his hand back inside the bag. He pulls out an Eagles tumbler, and a baseball cap with Remy's number on it.

"Thanks, Mitch." He smiles up at me before focusing on his sister. "Open yours, Andie!"

Andie grins, showing off that little dimple. Then she glances at me, her smile faltering. She looks unsure and a little annoyed. Her look says, *why did you get me a present, and is it something awful?*

Slowly, she picks up the pink bag, her eyebrows raise when she discovers how heavy it is. She glares at me, cautiously removing the tissue paper like a live snake is going to pop out of the bag and bite her. When she pulls her hand back out, she laughs and holds up her very own jersey. This one also has Anderson on the back, because I'd die before I saw this woman wear anyone's jersey but mine.

It *is* signed by the entire team like Noah's, but that's where I draw the line.

She smiles at me, looking relieved, then reaches in for the other item in the bag, along with a note. "You have got to be kidding me." Her head falls back and she releases a booming laugh. When her head pops back up, she holds the yellow book in front of her for all of us to see. "Hockey For Dummies?"

Tom looks between the three of us again. "I'm assuming there's a story here?"

Andie grabs the thick book in both hands and whacks my shoulder with it. Chuckling under my breath, I instinctively bring my hands up to protect myself, grabbing the book until my hands are covering hers. The skin-to-skin contact jolts something in both of us and our eyes snap to meet the other's gaze.

I've heard people talk about electricity between themselves and another person, an electric current. But until now, I'd never experienced it. I think I've spent my entire life in the dark, until Andie stomped her way in and lit up my entire world.

She slides her hands out from underneath mine and steps away from me in one smooth move. Andie exhales a forced laugh as she reaches for the note that was attached to the book and has now fallen to the floor.

She looks it over for a second and then reads it out loud, "Andie, your hockey knowledge needs some work. Do the world a favor and read up. There's a whole section in here about Wayne Gretzky. Sincerely, Bruce, Colby, and Ford Remington (AKA the current team captain of the D.C. Eagles)."

Popping a hip out, she rests a hand on it. Her signature pose.

"I hate you guys," she tells me, but there's no mirth to her tone.

"I think what you mean to say is, thank you?" I tease.

"Mhmm. Thank you, Big Man."

Tom chimes in from behind me, "Noah, why don't you come over here and sit by me? I have the inside scoop on the team, after all."

"Cool," Noah says before rushing over and sitting on the tall stool beside Tom. The two of them start chatting animatedly as Tom points out different features inside the arena to him.

When I look at Andie, I see her eyeing the two stools left and I gesture for her to take a seat next to her brother. The only available seat now is the stool at the end... right beside her. I conveniently scoot my chair slightly closer to her before sitting down. If she notices, she doesn't say anything.

I place her Hockey for Dummies book in front of her on the table top overlooking the arena and hear my phone ping.

Wondering if it's the guys asking how she liked her present, I take out my phone and look at the screen.

TOM PARKER

I see coaching is going very well, indeed. You sure this is a good idea?

MITCH

As of Wednesday, I'm not the coach anymore.

TOM PARKER

Max isn't going to be thrilled.

# CHAPTER 20
# ANDIE

HOCKEY FOR DUMMIES. Those clever idiots. I roll my lips together, trying not to smile at the hilarious, if not offensive, present. And the jersey with Mitch's last name on the back? Why does that gift feel so... intimate?

Is wearing a guy's jersey sort of like wearing a guy's letter jacket... or class ring? Mitch and I are barely even friends, right?

And is it me, or is Mitch's scent different this evening... not his usual waterfall in the mountains smell... but something more fruity, with a subtle hint of bubble gum.

Mitch interrupts my thoughts, leaning towards me. His lips are right next to my ear when he asks, "How's the home gym?"

I don't think he's trying to flirt, it's just loud in the arena and if he didn't say that directly into my ear, I wouldn't have heard him. But my body responds anyway, sending a shiver down my spine. And it's not even cold all the way up here, so I can't blame it on the ice. I take advantage of his nearness and attempt a subtle sniff.

Yep, definitely a hint of bubble gum.

"Great!" I answer, pulling back slightly to put some distance between us. "I even got my speakers hooked up for my audiobooks."

His eyebrows shoot up to his hairline and his cheeks turn red. He shakes his head slightly as if trying to remove thoughts from his own brain. Then he grunts instead of responding.

What was that all about?

Before I can say anything, someone starts announcing the opposing team over the speakers. A few people clap and cheer politely, but the real fun begins when a booming voice announces the Eagles. Classic rock music blares through the speakers and red fog comes out of machines near the ceiling. I glance over at Noah, who's having the time of his life.

He smiles and says, "This is awesome!" I nod, agreeing with him. I may not be a hockey fan, but there's no denying they know how to put on a good show.

The announcer says the names of several players I don't know, and the crowd goes wild. I don't recognize any of them until the goalie skates onto the ice, waving and grinning. It's Bruce. I cheer loudly and clap for him, even though he can't hear or see me.

Colby comes out next, and the female fans go absolutely berserk. There's whistling and whooping. He eats it up, skating around for the crowd and blowing kisses. I shake my head and look over at Mitch, who's watching me instead of his teammates.

Probably just wanting to see how I react to my first NHL game, nothing more. I look away quickly.

Weston Kershaw, the assistant captain apparently, is announced next. I recognize him from Noah's game. I remember he has a fiancee, but he gets his fair share of female fanfare from the crowd too. It must be so weird to be engaged to a man so beloved by the female population.

Lastly, the team captain is announced. Which, of course, is Remy. He gets the biggest applause and the loudest cheers. Everyone clearly loves him, but he's more humble about it. He gives a faint smile and a big wave to the arena before skating to center ice for the puck drop.

But before the referee drops the puck on center ice, the announcer starts up again. "Tonight we have a special guest with us! Ladies and gentleman, give it up for Mitch 'The Machine' Anderson! We've missed you, man!"

The crowd erupts again, mostly cheering, but a fair amount of booing too. The Jumbotron zooms in on Mitch, and I lean as far away from him as possible, so as not to be on the Jumbotron. No, thank you.

Mitch's face is stoic as he looks at the camera and gives it a small salute. No smile, no kisses, no attention-seeking behavior. Just the same stony face I've come to expect. And hell if it doesn't make me smile all the same.

Thankfully, the camera doesn't slide over to me, or to Noah, and the arena quiets down for the puck drop.

Throughout the game, Mitch calmly explains what's happening, not in a condescending, mansplaining way…. but just filling me in on the rules of the game. Some of it I've figured out from watching Noah's games, but a lot of the information is new, and helpful.

With each bit of commentary from Mitch, I swear he scoots closer and closer to me. When one of the Eagles forwards gets sent to the penalty box, I swivel on my stool to look over at Mitch, meaning to ask why the player was penalized… but I hadn't realized how close he'd scooted to me and the movement makes my knees bump against his. He doesn't move away, and I don't either. I have the overwhelming desire to rest my palm on his muscular thigh, I can practically feel my hand itching to move in that direction.

Instead, I focus on his face, which is a mere six inches from mine. My eyes quickly steal a glance at his lips. They're set in a straight line, of course, but at this close distance they look softer and more full than I expected. I've never kissed a guy with a beard, and my mind can't help but wonder what it would feel like. I allow my eyes to dip down to his suit too. He looks so dapper, so perfect, practically edible. But I have to admit I miss those long-sleeved tees he wears when working with Noah, the ones he scrunches up during practice to show off those incredible tattooed forearms.

I blink a few times and look back up to his hazel eyes. His gaze is on my lips and a little thrill runs through my body at the idea. When his eyes flick up to meet mine, I note that his eyes are more green than brown today. The hunter green of his suit brings out the green flecks in his eyes in a way that makes it difficult to breathe.

We sit like that for a moment, looking at each other in a blatant way we haven't allowed before. Like in this moment, we're both silently acknowledging our attraction, that we don't *actually* hate each other. The noise in the arena and Noah's conversation with the Eagle's general manager fade into the background. All I see is Mitch, his kissable lips, his eyes piercing straight through mine like he can read my every thought. All I feel is his knee against mine. All I hear are his quiet but steady breaths.

Quiet and steady, just like the man.

If we were truly alone at this moment, I'm 99.9% sure he would kiss me. And if he didn't… I'm 100% sure I'd kiss him. I imagine how I'd do it: my hand on his thigh, my chin tilting upward, letting him know my intentions. I'd pause, allowing him the chance to say no. But he wouldn't. He'd close the distance and take over, kissing me fervently.

At least, that's how I imagine it would go.

"Andie," Noah tugs on my sleeve. I close my eyes and take a deep breath before turning away from Mitch's searing gaze and his warm knee against mine. I plaster a smile on my face and pretend I wasn't just about to drag my little brother's hockey coach into the storage closet—if this room even has one of those. "Mr. Parker says we can meet the team after the game."

"Haven't we already met most of them?" I ask in a teasing tone.

Tom Parker chuckles. Noah's jaw drops in offense. "Not even close. I've only met four of them!"

"You've met the most important one," Mitch says, leaning in so Noah can hear him. His chest grazes against my shoulder in the process and I struggle not to flinch with the contact.

Noah scoffs. "Whatever."

Noah goes back to his conversation with Tom and I excuse myself to the restroom to compose myself after… after what? Grazing shoulders with Mitch Anderson? I'm pathetic.

When I come back to our box, I feel normal again. Until I spot Mitch, who's now in Tom's spot beside Noah. They're leaning into one another, chatting about the game. One of the Eagles players scores a goal and they both clap and cheer. Tom must've left for general manager duties, but I'm grateful for the break from sitting next to Mitch. I can't handle the arm grazing, and the knee touching, and the silent glances any longer. A woman can only take so much.

I sit down and notice the bar is lined with food now. There's nachos, sodas, popcorn, cotton candy, and corn dogs. Whew, something to do with my hands—and mouth—besides running them all over Mitch Anderson.

Speaking of Mitch, he's not partaking in the junk food. Instead, he has a grilled chicken salad in front of him with a bottle of water and a protein shake. He looks up at me when I sit down and sees me eyeing his food.

"My suspension is over soon, I need to eat for peak performance," he explains.

If the Mitch I've seen over the last month *hasn't* been at peak performance, how am I going to resist him when he's *at* peak performance?

I nod, not trusting myself to say words at the moment. Grabbing a corn dog, I take a big bite, extra incentive not to speak and say something stupid about his peak performance.

Noah's attention is back on the ice, happily watching the game. He's also chowing down on nachos and soda. I foresee a late night. But it's his birthday, after all. I've been freaking out all week that he'd be so upset today. His first birthday without Mom and Dad. But thanks to the big man sitting with us, his birthday was amazing.

Mitch keeps surprising me and helping out when I least expect it. If someone would've told me a month ago that Noah would make friends with a pro hockey player and start actually enjoying life again, I wouldn't have believed them. And if they would've told me he'd be our biggest source of support, besides Ronda, I would've laughed in their faces.

Mitch 'The Machine' Anderson is a good man. A damn good man. But something tells me he doesn't see himself that way.

*Three things I'm grateful for today; Mitch Anderson, his goofy teammates, and surprisingly enough… hockey.*

———

"Right down this tunnel is the locker room, but let me warn them so you don't walk into a bunch of naked hockey players," Tom tells me as he leads us toward the Eagles locker room.

I laugh and don't bother telling him that that would be most women's dream come true.

He scans his I.D. on his lanyard on the door scanner and it unlocks, he slips through the large, heavy-looking door, leaving me standing there with Mitch and Noah. Noah has wide eyes and looks nervous, and Mitch is standing stiffly, seeming uncomfortable. I wonder if it's really weird for him to be here visiting instead of in the locker room cooling down with the rest of the team. I imagine Noah would feel that way too. Noah looks at me and I offer him what I hope is a comforting smile.

Noah releases a slow breath. "I'm nervous."

Mitch relaxes slightly and smirks. "Why? Just a bunch of sweaty, smelly athletes."

"Sweaty, smelly, professional athletes. Athletes literally living my dream," Noah says with a shake of his head.

Mitch roughs up his hair with one of those giant hands of his and Noah shoves it away and tries to smooth his hair out.

The heavy door opens and Tom waves us in. "Alright, everyone's decent."

We walk inside the spacious locker room, sweaty guys grin at Noah and give him fist bumps and high fives. I take a second to look around, because this is a really fancy locker room. Polished wood separates each player's locker/cubby area. Name plates with each guy's name are secured onto the wood. A giant eagle light sprawls across the ceiling, and awards and trophies are displayed on the walls opposite the lockers. Locker room isn't even a fitting term for this sweat-palace.

But it still reeks of sweaty boys, just like any other locker room.

Bruce waddles toward me on his skates, his torso bare, but still in his gear from the waist down. "Blondie! How'd you like your present?"

I try holding back my smile, but it's impossible with Bruce grinning at me with that ornery smile of his. I manage to keep my eyes plastered firmly on his face, because if I look down, I know I'll see nothing but muscles on muscles on *more* muscles. And I don't need that image in my head. The only guy in this room I'd like to see shirtless is the grouchy one behind me.

Colby ambles up beside him, also shirtless (and also spectacularly fit), with his padded shorts still on. He slings a sweaty arm over Bruce's shoulders. "Did you read the book during the game? Or were you too busy watching me?"

Bruce shoves him and he teeters on his skates. "I was too busy eating nachos and corn dogs. Sorry, I didn't really pay attention to the game." I shrug.

Colby brings a hand to his bare chest, feigning offense. "I'm hurt."

"Me too! I had some sweet saves you missed," Bruce says in a pouty tone.

I laugh and spot Remy across the room from us, he sees me and gives me a brief wave. There are two reporters, one connecting a mic to Remy's shirt and the other connecting one to Weston Kershaw's. They're ushered out of the room, I assume for an interview. I wonder if Remy enjoys interviews and press? He seems so quiet and reserved. Actually, he and Weston were part of the few guys in here who still had shirts on.

Bruce and Colby sidle over to chat with Noah and their other teammates and I smile at the excitement on my little brother's face.

Realizing Mitch hasn't made a peep this whole time, I glance over my shoulder to look at him. I can tell Mitch is standing right behind me because my body is humming the way it always does when he's nearby. I can also still smell the very faint scent of berries and bubble gum coming from him, which is a welcome reprieve from the locker room's other smells.

Mitch's expression is not amused at all. He's glaring at his teammates. The man practically has laser beams coming out of his eyeballs.

"Why the sour face?" I ask in a low voice.

He crosses his arms. "The guys could've had a little respect and stayed dressed for five more minutes."

"Whoa, I didn't realize you're a prude, it's not like I've never seen a man's chest before." I pause, leaning in slightly closer to him. "Plus, there's only one person I'm interested in seeing shirtless."

His gaze falls to my lips and lingers there for a second before glancing back up. "Is it Colby?"

I snort, very unattractively, and give him a shove so he has to take a step back. "You're clueless, Big Man."

# CHAPTER 21
# MITCH

"THERE YOU ARE!" My agent, Max, says, walking into the locker room of the Eagles practice rink. He looks aggravated even though his usual fake smile is firmly in place. "You're a difficult man to get a hold of."

I'm freshly showered from practicing with one of the coaches this morning and standing by my locker in just a towel. My hair is still wet and dripping down my back. I swear, this guy finds the worst times to bug me. But then again, I'm the one who's been ignoring his phone calls since last night.

"Oh, hey Max," I say dryly, grabbing the towel from around my waist and using it to dry my hair. If he wants to chat with me right after my shower, that's his problem.

He quickly looks down at his shoes. "I wanted to talk to you about how much positivity has come from your hockey coaching."

I nod, but I'm only half listening. I barely slept last night, and have been distracted all morning. But with my suspension almost done, and my first game back on Wednesday, I've gotta get over this brain fog. Or, Andie fog.

This *does she hate me, or does she want me* game is about to drive me insane. There were at least five different times last night I wanted to pull Andie in for a kiss. Five agonizing, gut-wrenching moments that I craved her so badly I could hardly sit still.

But last night wasn't about me or Andie, it was about Noah. And he was within a two-foot proximity to us the entire evening. Don't get me wrong, as kids go, Noah is the greatest. He's quiet, not obnoxious, and just an all-around cool guy. But when all I want to do is kiss his big sister? Yeah, having him nearby is an issue.

"Mitch?" Max's voice pulls me from my thoughts. I look up and see him staring at me, which is okay since I'm fully dressed now. I hardly even remember putting clothes on, that's how consuming my thoughts of Andie are. All I can think about is how to have some time alone with her.

"Yeah, I'm listening." I'm not.

Max clears his throat and leans against the lockers. "So anyway, the comments on the Wombats social media page, and the article where we interviewed the boys before their game a few weeks ago were amazing. Everyone loves you!"

I close my locker and toss my damp towel in the large hamper in the center of the room before looking at Max and seeing his stupid, smug smile.

"Glad to hear it." My voice isn't very convincing. I really haven't minded coaching the kids, it was more tolerable than I expected. But I feel cringey about using it as a way to get people to like me.

"However, photos are circulating. They're of you and the youth hockey mom… from the game last night."

My jaw twitches. I want to protect Andie, not drag her into my stupid media circus. "She's not a hockey mom. She's Noah's sister."

He rolls his lips together as if trying to hold back what he really wants to say. "Hockey mom, or hockey sister. Whatever causes the most drama is what people will cling to. He runs a hand through his too-short hair. "I'd just stay away from her, to avoid getting mixed up in the drama… because I have good news!" Max's demeanor changes from annoyance, back to his fake grin. Then he annoys me further by making an ear piercing drum-roll sound on the metal lockers. "You have a new company interested in collaborating! This is a big one. They're offering even more than Advanced Athletics."

"Really? What company?" I ask, ignoring his comment about avoiding the one person in this world who makes me smile. It's none of Max's business who I date. He's my sports agent, not my babysitter.

"Franklin Distilleries," he says excitedly.

My shoulders slump, but he either doesn't notice, or ignores it completely.

"They're creating a new bourbon blend, and they want *your* name on it!"

I sigh heavily. "I don't drink."

He waves his hand in the air as if shooing my remark away. "Doesn't matter! They don't care if you drink it, they just want your help promoting it. They want to call it *The Machine*. Catchy, huh?" He pumps his eyebrows a few times.

"Not interested." I grab my car keys from the locker and brush past him.

Max leaps in front of me, holding his hands out to stop me. When I look down at him with a scowl, he changes his mind and moves out of my way. "Mitch, come on! Just listen to me."

"I don't have anything against people drinking or whatever. But it's not for me, and I wouldn't feel right about having my name on a bottle of bourbon."

I keep walking, but hear his voice from behind me. "This is

a huge payday. And after losing your other big sponsor, you'd be a fool not to take it."

Stopping in my tracks, I turn to face him. "My personal boundaries aren't up for discussion, Max."

"You're making all the wrong choices," he mutters as he stands there gawking at me. His look says he thinks I'm crazy not to take this deal. But I'm not going to promote a product I know nothing about and would never use. When I draw a line... I don't cross it.

Okay... I *usually* don't. But I've definitely toed the line I drew with Andie. And I can't stop crossing it. I've pretty much used my shoe to completely scuff the line and erase it. I keep walking until I'm outside in the parking lot. I find my car and get inside, still bristling with restrained anger.

If he thinks the right choice is promoting a product I'm personally against and avoiding a person who brings me joy, then maybe *he's* the one who needs therapy.

I reach for my phone, the reminder of a certain blonde makes me itch to text her.

Things I'm not crossing the line on: alcohol.

Things I'm *definitely* crossing the line on: Andie Downsby.

Pushing Max and his bourbon proposal completely out of my mind, I think of how best to get Andie alone so I can spend time with her. Most men would just ask the girl on a date, easy peasy. But dating a high-profile athlete is no small feat. And Andie isn't the kind to seek the public's attention. There's also still a small part of me that's not sure she's interested in me like that. So I'm going to play it cool.

Finally, I think I've thought of the perfect plan. I type out a text that she'll probably see right through, but oh well. I'm shooting my shot.

MITCH

> Hey, could we get together and schedule my last session with Noah?

I smile down at my phone as I hit send. Smooth, Mitch, smooth.

ANDIE

> We can't schedule it via texts?

I knew she'd make this difficult.

MITCH

> We could... but I thought it might be easier in person.

ANDIE

> Suuuuure, Big Man.

MITCH

> Isn't Ronda taking Noah out for his birthday tonight?

ANDIE

> Yes...

MITCH

> Perfect. Come over here, and we'll eat dinner and schedule me and Noah's session.

ANDIE

> Dinner? At your place?

MITCH

> I'd meet you somewhere, but I don't want to deal with fans... since we'll be busy scheduling.

ANDIE

Scheduling, huh? Is that what the kids are
calling it these days?

I sigh heavily. She's impossible.

MITCH

Would that work or not?

ANDIE

Is this a date?

MITCH

Stop answering a question with a question.

ANDIE

You're bad at this.

MITCH

Andie Downsby, would you please do me the
honor of coming over to my penthouse for
dinner this evening?

ANDIE

Why yes, Mitchell Anderson, I would love to.

Rolling my eyes, I correct her.

MITCH

My name isn't Mitchell. It's just Mitch.

I text her the address and time before ordering dinner for
us online, soup and sandwiches from one of my favorite
restaurants. I would've gone for pasta, but I've eaten too many
carbs, and too little protein during my suspension. I need to
get back on track.

———

Half an hour later, I'm walking into my building. When I see the receptionist at the front desk, I remember one more thing I need to take care of and walk over until I'm standing right in front of her.

"Hey, I'm in the penthouse… Mitch Anderson."

The young woman looks up at me and her eyes widen with recognition. "Yes, sir. How can I help you?"

I attempt a slight smile because she looks a little terrified of me. "I'd like to add Andie Downsby to my list of approved guests."

"Okay, I can do that for you, Mr. Anderson. Is Andie Downsby just approved for this evening?" She asks, then starts typing on the computer in front of her.

"No, indefinitely."

She pauses and peeks over the computer screen, then snaps her eyes back down and starts typing and clicking again. "Yes, sir."

"Thank you." I nod, then walk toward the elevator. Once I'm inside the elevator I allow a wide smile to spread across my face. A smile that's been threatening to appear since Andie agreed to come over tonight. I think my facial muscles may be getting used to smiling, actually.

I rub my palms together. It's all coming together. I will finally get Andie all to myself.

# CHAPTER 22
# MITCH

THAT EVENING, my doorbell rings. I look in the large mirror in my bathroom one last time to make sure I look okay. I went simple tonight with a soft black t-shirt and dark-wash jeans.

Rushing out of my room and down the hallway, I take a calming breath before swinging the front door open. Andie's wearing jeans, her usual white sneakers, and a long-sleeved wine-colored top that stops right at the waistband of her jeans, so when she moves, a sliver of her stomach peaks out.

Suddenly, I remember her little outie belly button and have a difficult time prying my eyes away from that sliver of skin on her abdomen. I blink a few times and look away, opening the door wide and stepping aside to make room for her to come in.

Andie comes in and holds her arms out at her sides. "Sorry, I wasn't sure how casual one dresses for a little-brother-scheduling-conference non-date."

Tilting my head, I pin her with an unamused stare. She laughs and takes a few more steps into my penthouse. I run a hand through my hair, then rest it on the back of my neck, feeling nervous now that she's here and we're alone… for the first time. Ever.

"Nice place, Big Man. Fancy." She spins in a slow circle, taking in the entire open living room, dining room, kitchen area. Her stare lingers on the huge chef's kitchen. "You don't strike me as someone who loves to cook."

I huff out a laugh. "I don't mind cooking, but I usually order meals for the week since my NHL schedule doesn't allow me much free time."

She nods. "Yeah, I feel you there. Not the NHL schedule, but the ICU one. So, are you going to give me a tour? I wanna see the giant bathtub."

"Noah told you?"

She smiles. "Yes, and I'm jealous."

Thankfully, my housekeeper came this morning and everything is clean and tidy. I guide her down the hallway to the bathroom. Is this a weird thing to be showing her? Probably.

When we walk inside my master bedroom, Andie gasps. "Oh my gosh! Your bed is gigantic."

"As you like to say, I'm a big man." I shrug and point to the open door leading to the bathroom.

She follows my finger and rushes over to see the large standing tub in the center of the bathroom. On one wall is a long vanity with two sinks, and on the other wall is a tiled shower with five waterfall shower heads. That shower is the reason I rented this place, actually.

Andie bursts out laughing and walks over to the vanity, grabbing the bottle of Captain Bubbles off of the counter. "Ah-ha! I knew it."

Dang it, I forgot to put that bottle away when I took a bath earlier.

In one quick step, I'm next to her, grabbing the bottle out of her hand. She reaches up, trying to snag it from me, but I lift it above my head. Oh, and there's that gorgeous outie, peeking out from under her shirt as she reaches up for the Captain Bubbles.

*Thank you, Captain Bubbles.*

Andie gives up and looks at me through slitted eyes. "Why do you have Captain Bubbles after making fun of mine?"

I sigh and put the bubble bath away inside the cabinet. "Well, I kind of… go to…"

"Spit it out, I don't have all day."

"I'm in therapy," I blurt. Her expression changes from annoyed to something softer. Not pity, I couldn't handle pity. But something that feels like a warm hug. Not that I've really had one of those. "He recommended I find a way to relax that didn't involve screens… or hockey."

"So, you tried a bubble bath?"

I throw my hands up, not wanting to talk about this anymore. "Noah told me to, okay? He said you take baths and listen to books to relax. I thought I'd try it."

I exit the bathroom and my bedroom and wait for her in the hallway. She follows quickly and stands by my side. "And you loved it? Didn't you?"

"You're annoying."

"You did!" She lifts her index finger to my nose and boops it.

I think she's the only human on this planet that could boop my nose and get away with it. I just stare at her in shock.

"Alright, come on. I'm starving." She starts walking toward the kitchen, waving an arm for me to follow her.

The woman has been here five minutes and is already acting like she owns the place. Surprisingly, it's not annoying. She can own this place—and me—if she wants to.

Andie spots the soup and sandwiches at the bar, along with

the plates and glasses I set out, and makes an *aw* sound. "Did you set this for us? I love soup."

I scratch the back of my neck and look at my feet. "Oh, yeah. Same." Smooth, Mitch. Really smooth. When I bring my head back up and see her staring at the arm that's behind my head, I gain a little confidence back.

Her eyes snap to meet mine and she blushes adorably. "Tell me about your tattoos." She scoots one of my mid-century modern chairs out and takes a seat.

I sit beside her, basking in that bubble gum scent for a moment. "The tiger is a memory of my dad. My last good memory."

She asks, "Did he pass away?"

"He's in prison," I say bluntly, then remove the lids from our salads and soup.

I can feel her staring at me. "I'm sorry, Mitch."

Andie never says my name, it's always Anderson, or Big Man. I relish in the sound of my name on her lips, playing it over a few times so I remember what it sounded like. "I'm sorry about your parents, too. What happened to them?" I immediately regret prodding and add, "You don't have to tell me if you don't want to."

"Head-on collision with a semi truck. The driver fell asleep and crossed a median," she says softly.

"Wow, that's awful." I think of her and Noah finding out the news all those months ago, and my heart tightens inside my chest. The same heart I didn't think worked anymore.

"It's been hard, I just feel so bad for Noah. I miss them like crazy, but they got to see me grow up, you know? Prom, college graduations, starting my career. But they'll miss all of his milestones. I think that hits him really hard."

"That sucks." I clear my throat that suddenly feels too thick. "I can relate to that. My parents are alive, sure. But my mom left when I was little and my dad's been in prison since I was ten. I don't *know* them. My mom has called me *once* since she walked out of my life, it must've been five years ago. I'm not even sure how she got my number... but she didn't even ask how I was doing. Just said she needed money. I blocked her number. And my dad, I don't even accept his calls anymore."

Andie studies me, a question in her eyes. I tilt my chin in a small nod, giving her permission to ask whatever it is she wants to know. Something I've never allowed anyone else—unlimited access to my mind, my soul, my heart of stone.

I wonder if she understands how much I'd give her.

Everything.

I'd give her everything.

But nobody wants a heart of stone, do they?

She finally asks her question, "Why don't you answer his calls?"

"I used to," I answer honestly. "I used to hope we could be fixed... put back together. But every call ended the same way... him blaming me for Mom leaving. Then, when my NHL career was well on its way, he only called begging me to pay his bail." I pause to take a drink of water, trying to clear the knot in my throat. "They haven't been my parents for a long time. Maybe in blood, but not where it matters. They only wanted me for what I could do for them."

Andie's small, warm hand comes to rest on my leg. It's comforting and exhilarating all at the same.

"You're pretty amazing, so it's too bad they're missing out. Your parents really suck," she says, looking up at me with those big brown eyes.

Surprised by her response, I laugh. A real, throaty laugh that shakes my whole body. This girl and her sassy mouth.

I can feel her staring at me as my laughter fades, smirking

up at me with a twinkle in her eyes. "If I knew where they lived, I'd toilet paper their houses."

"Well, my dad lives at the Wisconsin Correctional Institution, so please don't do that."

This time, Andie laughs, then stops abruptly and brings her free hand to her mouth. "I'm so sorry. I shouldn't have laughed at that."

Sliding my hand over the one she has on my leg, I tell her, "Weirdly enough, it's kind of nice to laugh about it. Better laughing than being angry, right?"

Andie gives me a little smile and I find myself rubbing the back of her knuckles with my thumb. Back and forth, tracing the shape of her hand, enjoying the smoothness of her skin. She surprises me yet again when she flips her hand over and twines her fingers with mine. The way our hands fit together sends a warmth through my body, like déjà vu. Like I've dreamed of this girl, this moment, my entire life and it finally came to fruition.

"I wanted to do this last night at the game," I whisper.

"Do what?"

"Hold your hand."

# CHAPTER 23
# ANDIE

I COULD SPEND days just sitting here, holding this man's hand. The way he looks at me, touches me, is so reverent, so tender. I almost can't face the intensity of it. I should've expected it; everything Mitch does is with passion and intensity.

But when all of that is poured into something as simple as hand-holding?

I am undone.

Eventually, he slides his hand out of mine and tells me we should eat. The loss of his hand in mine feels like the loss of a limb. It just felt so right there.

We start eating our soup and sandwiches, which are delicious, and I notice Mitch's turkey panini is *loaded* with meat. Like probably three times the amount in mine.

"Geez, did you order double meat or something? You can barely fit that thing inside your mouth."

He nearly chokes on his bite at my comment. He takes a drink of water and pounds his chest a few times like he's dislodging food that got stuck there. "Triple meat. I have to get a certain amount of protein each day. Helps me build muscle and gives me energy for the games and practices."

I make a show of looking him up and down. "Yeah, glad you're back on the protein bandwagon, you're practically wasting away, you're so scrawny."

His eyes drop to my jean-clad legs and then back up to my eyes. "I'm trying to keep up with you, I can't have your quads out-doing mine."

"Mitchell Anderson," I say with an obnoxious, fake southern drawl. "Have you been looking at my quads?"

He closes his eyes for a beat, like he's trying really hard not to be annoyed. "It's just Mitch." He looks down at my legs again. "And yes, I have."

Heat rushes to my face. "Your legs are pretty impressive too."

He pretends to be shocked. Sarcastic Mitch might be my favorite Mitch. "Andie Downsby, did you just compliment me?"

"Yeah, yeah. Don't get used to it."

"Too late," he says smugly. "From this moment on, I expect you to shower me with compliments. It's the least you can do since you called me the ugliest Eagles player."

"Sorry, what I meant to say was the *grouchiest* Eagles player."

His perfect mouth pulls up into a slow, mischievous grin. It's absolutely devastating. He leans in closer to me, his face mere inches from mine. It takes every ounce of self-preservation I have not to move, and not to look down at his lips.

He whispers, "I think you're into grouchy guys."

Mitch leans in with an aching slowness, closing that last bit of space between us. This moment that has built up over the past month, this moment that I can't stop, can't deny myself of.

He's going slow, giving me the chance to stop his lips from meeting mine. But I couldn't even if I wanted to.

And then he kisses me, swiveling in his seat so my knees are trapped between his own. His powerful thighs are warm against mine, making me feel secure... safe. One of his hands lands on my waist, and the other comes up to caress the side of my neck. His lips on mine are hot and soft, contrasting perfectly with his rough beard and calloused hands. I scoot to the end of my seat, trying to get as close to him as I can. And his hand on my waist seems just as desperate, his large fingers squeezing the dip in my waist. One of his fingers dips under my shirt, feeling so warm against the skin on my torso. Thank goodness for cropped shirts.

Our lips move against each other in perfect tandem, like we've been kissing each other all our lives, but I've never had a kiss like this. So tender and yet so desperate. His hand moves along my neck and then into my hair, along my scalp. Normally, I don't like it when people play with my hair, it doesn't feel soothing to me... but when Mitch does it? Yes, please. Soothing isn't the right word for the gentle tugging I feel on my hair, titillating is probably a better description.

He pulls back just long enough for me to see his hooded hazel eyes, and to whisper, "Kissing you is even better than I imagined."

Bringing my hands to his black t-shirt, I grasp it with my fists and pull him back to me, kissing him again. I flatten my palms against his broad, defined chest and enjoy the feel of his muscles beneath my hands. I trail them down, longing to feel if his abs are as chiseled as I've pictured, but his hands gently grab mine and I feel him smile against my lips. "Are you trying to undress me?"

"I just want to touch your abs, please," I beg.

"Am I just a piece of meat to you, Blondie?"

I whimper. "Yes. Girls need protein too, you know."

I feel his body start to shake as he tries to stifle his laughter, but he fails. A thunderous laugh comes out of his mouth, and it's music to my soul. Making Mitch 'The Machine' Anderson laugh will never get old. I wield this ability like the rarity it is, because I know not just anyone can make him laugh. You have to work for those laughs, you have to earn them.

Finally, he shakes his head. "I never know what's going to come out of your mouth."

"Isn't it great? Stick with me, Anderson, and you'll never get bored."

He opens his mouth to speak just as my phone rings from my back pocket. It's Ronda's ringtone. I give Mitch an apologetic glance, then pull it out and answer it. "Hey Ronda, everything okay?"

"Hey, Noah started feeling sick at the restaurant so I brought him home. We're watching a movie and he's sipping water. I just wanted to let you know," Ronda says, her voice serious and concerned.

"Oh no. Do you think it's food poisoning?"

"I'm not sure, sweetie. If you're out having fun, don't worry about rushing home! I've got it under control."

I glance up at Mitch, he's close enough to hear the entire conversation. I know I'll feel horrible if I leave Ronda to deal with my sick little brother. I give Mitch a sad smile and he rubs my knee gently as if to say *it's okay, I understand.*

Ronda and I say our goodbyes and Mitch gets up from his seat before taking my hands and pulling me up too. Hand in hand, we walk slowly toward his front door. So slowly that I know neither of us wants this evening to end.

We stop in front of the door and he turns to me. "I'd like to do this again," he says, pinning me with those serious eyes of his.

"Make out?"

He shakes his head in dismay, but he's smirking, so I'll count it as a win. "I'll see you Monday? It'll be my last time coaching. Oh, and we never set up a day for my last one-on-one with Noah." Mitch releases my hand so he can slip his arm around my waist. He pulls me closer to himself. "My first game back with the Eagles is Wednesday, but I could work with him Thursday?"

"I work Thursday, but let me check with Ronda and see if she can drop him off." He nods solemnly and a wave of sadness washes over me. I will the feeling away, not wanting to ruin how wonderful this evening has been… minus Noah's sickness. "I'll kind of miss seeing you at his games and practices."

Mitch's free hand comes to my chin and tilts my face up, he stares into my eyes like there are a million things he wants to say, but doesn't have the time to say them. "I want to see you. I know my schedule is about to get crazy, but I want to keep seeing you."

"Okay. I'd like that."

He bends down and I close my eyes, expecting him to kiss me goodbye. But his lips land on my left eyelid with a kiss as soft as a butterfly's wings. He repeats the movement with my right eyelid. I don't want to open my eyes, I don't want this to end. But I picture Noah laying on the sofa, feeling miserable. And with that, I open my eyes and say goodbye.

———

Sunday, I called in to work so I could stay home with my sick brother, and by Monday, he's all better. It must've been something he ate at the restaurant. Just the perfect amount of time to ruin my almost-perfect evening with Mitch.

Little brothers, man. But I *am* relieved he's feeling okay now.

We head to practice Monday evening and I'm practically giddy to see Mitch. We've texted the past few days, fighting and flirting like we usually do, but it's so much more satisfying now that I'm certain he likes me.

*Likes* me, likes me… as Noah would say.

When we walk inside the iceplex, I'm trying so hard to play it cool, but as soon as I see Mitch standing there in his coaching gear and hockey skates, a huge grin spreads across my face.

Yeah, I have no chill. I feel a little better when he smiles back at me, in a way he doesn't smile at anyone else. I amble up to him like an awkward teenage girl, tucking a piece of hair behind my ear so I have something to do with my hands, and biting my bottom lip to keep myself from kissing him in front of everyone. I've gone two days without his lips, and am dying to kiss him again.

Mitch's hazel eyes, looking more blue today, twinkle as he says, "Hey, Blondie."

Two words. That's all it takes for me to melt. "Hey, Big Man."

"Uh, what's happening?" Noah asks, looking back and forth between us with a furrowed brow. "Why are you guys being nice to each other?"

Mitch tousles Noah's hair. "I'm always nice to your sister."

"Okay, but she's not usually nice to you."

I cross my arms and glare at him. "That's not true."

"Yeah it is," Mitch argues, still with that gleam in his eyes. "I'm just an innocent soul, constantly being bullied by you. You're vicious."

He says it with such a straight face, I almost laugh. Noah

narrows his eyes, looking at me through slits. "You're taking his side?" I ask, allowing my jaw to drop dramatically.

"Of course he is, you've been yelling at me since day one," Mitch says, crossing his arms to match mine.

"You know," I say. "I liked you better when you spoke in grunts and growls."

Noah looks between us again and rolls his eyes, walking off toward the locker room to get ready.

Mitch takes a step closer, angling his head down to look at me with that intense stare of his. His eyes are dark and hooded now as he looks into my eyes like we're the only two people in the room... or in the world. Then he makes a low, growly sound in his throat. That sound pulses through me like a heart-beat. "Is that better?"

"Is what better?" My eyes are half closed and my voice comes out in a whisper.

Mitch chuckles deep and low. "Growling instead of talking."

"Yes, much better."

Mitch smirks then steps away from me, and I instantly miss being in his towering shadow. Like when you're having the best summer day but then the sun sets and it's all over too quickly.

"I gotta help Coach Aaron get set up for practice, I'll find you after." He gives me a faint smile, then turns and walks through the doors leading to one of the ice rinks.

How a man can sexily swagger away like that with hockey skates strapped onto his feet is a mystery I will never solve. I would certainly look like a penguin trying to walk for the very first time, but not Mitch.

"You guys looked awfully cozy." A voice comes from behind me.

I look over my shoulder to find Steph and Tori standing a

few feet away. Tori smiles but Steph still appears to be sour about the altercation between Declan and Noah.

"Oh, hey guys. How have you been?" I ask, giving them both a friendly smile.

Steph crosses her arms. "Not as good as you, apparently."

"Steph, come on," Tori whispers, looking annoyed at her friend.

Steph ignores her and continues, "So, this is how you get the coaches to take Noah's side?"

"Steph!" Tori gasps and steps away from her.

Steph's accusation feels like a physical slap. I'm not sure whether to cry or slap her back. I clench my hands at my sides, just to be sure I don't actually slap her. After a beat, I decide there's no use in arguing or fighting with someone who's opinion clearly cannot be swayed.

"I'm sorry you think so little of my character, Steph," I tell her with no anger, no mirth, then turn and walk away. Because oftentimes, walking away is the best thing you can do.

During practice, I watch Mitch intently, noticing how different he is a month into coaching. Not only is he more patient with the boys, but I think he's earned their respect… a little. I mean, they're still getting into fights, but I haven't seen any of what Mitch calls *hooking*. And when he speaks—with authority but not anger—the boys stop and listen to him. I'm impressed by how far the boys have come, *and* how far Mitch has come. At times, I can see him struggling not to get angry and yell at them, I can see him close his eyes and take a few deep breaths, possibly practicing his breathing.

I'm curious to see if they'll stay in line when the other coach is back at the end of the week. My stomach sinks at the thought of not seeing Mitch at practices. This whole month we've been forced into seeing each other several times a week, and now we'll have to be intentional about it. Choosing to make time for each other. And will he make time for me? Can he make time for me?

My thoughts are interrupted when Noah slams Declan into the boards, steals the puck and passes it to his teammate who scores a goal. Declan rushes over to Noah and shoves him, making him fall on his butt. Noah gets back on his feet, his eyebrows drawn, and skates after Declan. He shoves Declan from behind and he stumbles on his skates. Both of them pull their arms back as if they're about to punch each other, but Mitch skates over in the nick of time and places himself between the two boys. Using his large hands, he holds them as far away from each other as he can. They both calm down, but are still scowling at each other. Mitch's face is red and he looks irritated, but he doesn't yell or lash out at them. Instead, he says something to them sternly. They both skate off toward the bench and quietly sit down. Noah and Declan sit there with their backs toward each other while they cool down.

Okay, things aren't perfect. But they're better… I think.

# CHAPTER 24
## MITCH

EARLY TUESDAY MORNING, I'm at the rink for team practice, except I arrived an hour before everyone else. I'm so amped up for my first game back tomorrow, I couldn't sleep anyway. I've been to all the Eagles practices during my suspension, but without the games, I don't feel like I've really used my strength and agility the way I should be. There's something about the arena, the music, the cheering crowd, that makes you work harder and power through the games.

I'm enjoying the quiet rink, doing skating drills on my own, when I spot the bane of my existence, Max. He's standing behind the bench and waves a hand, gesturing for me to come over and chat. Why he's awake, bright eyed, and dressed immaculately in a dress shirt and slacks at seven in the morning, I have no idea. And why he wants to talk to me? Also no clue, but I don't like it.

I skate over and he greets me, "Mitch Anderson, just the person I was hoping to see." He waits for me to come to a stop, eyeing me with a stern expression punctuated by his crappy haircut.

"Max. What did you need?" I ask, glancing back at the ice as if to silently tell him I have work to do.

He sighs heavily. "Well, you see, the whole reason I had you coach a youth hockey team during your suspension was to rebuild your image."

"I remember."

"Well, another photo of you and hockey mom is circulating." His expression doesn't change with the accusation, he just stares at me blankly.

"Hockey *sister*. And I guess it's a good thing I'm not coaching anymore." I stare at him with the same blank expression he's giving me. He obviously doesn't know much, because Andie isn't even a mom. But whatever. I really need to find a new agent.

"Mitch, you know the press will link her to the Washington Wombats and make all kinds of crazy accusations. You've been around long enough to know this."

"We haven't even gone on a date." *Yet*, I think, but don't say it out loud. "I'm done coaching the Wombats, my mental health is better… I don't know what more you want from me."

"I'm going to be straight with you, you're not getting any younger. And the only company who has reached out to collaborate with you is Franklin Distilleries. Which apparently isn't good enough for you. Just stay out of trouble until I can get you some new opportunities. After you gain a few sponsors, you can hook up with all the hockey moms you want to."

I clench my teeth and take a deep breath. I will not lash out at this infuriating man. "Hockey *sister*. And there's only one. Thanks for the chat, but I gotta get back to work."

*In for seven… out for eleven.*

His jaw clenches. "Alright. Have a good day, Mitch."

I grunt, starting back on my drills, but I'm fuming. I've watched guys on our team sneak women into their hotel rooms for years, even with a different girl every night. And I get berated for seeing a mature, responsible adult that I genuinely like. Max can kiss my butt, along with all of his *sponsorships*.

Of course, I'd love to have sponsors, but I won't give up Andie for it. I have plenty of money saved up to retire someday. I might not be able to live the same way I do now, but I'll be okay.

"You trying to steal my position, Anderson?"

I look up to find Remy skating toward me. He's usually the first one here on practice days, being the team captain and all. "You and I both know I'd make a horrible team captain."

He huffs out a laugh. "You know, exhausting yourself isn't a great way to get ready for a game."

"Just dusting off the cobwebs."

"How's Andie?" He abruptly changes the subject.

I think for a second, not one to talk about my personal life. But I respect Remy, and it's just the two of us. "Funny you should ask. I just got a lecture from my agent about her."

His eyebrows raise in surprise. "Really?"

"Apparently, hooking up with the legal guardian of a kid I was coaching is bad for my image."

He laughs out loud. "Wow. Well, as team captain, I'm all for players having a good image and helping the team. But Andie is good for you. I don't know what's going on between you two, exactly, but you come out of your shell around her and act like a real human."

"Gee, thanks," I mutter, but he just laughs again. "So, you don't think it's an issue?"

"Nah, I like this new Mitch who's not such a grumpy old man."

I shake my head. "She's too good for me. I don't deserve her," I tell him honestly. Saying it out loud feels even worse than thinking it. The knowledge that I'll never be good enough for her and Noah reverberating around my brain and my body like the words are a real, living thing.

"In my experience, men are seldom deserving of the women they're with," he says, a flash of something like grief or regret passing over his face.

Our conversation is rudely interrupted when the rest of our team appears, skating onto the ice with a ridiculous amount of energy and commotion. West and Colby are chatting about something but skate over toward me and Remy. Bruce changes direction from the net to our group when he spots the four of us.

"My boys!" he yells as he flies toward us in all of his giant goalie gear. "How's my girl, by the way?" He directs the question at me. "Or is she *your* girl yet?"

"She's mine," I practically growl the words at him.

The guys erupt into laughter and West gives me a hard smack on the back. "Welcome to the smitten kitten club, man."

Coach Young whistles from the box and glares in our direction. "Get your giggling asses over here, we have work to do."

———

I'm sitting in Dr. Curtis's now familiar office after practice. I feel calm as I wait for him, no feelings of dread coursing through me. Me and Doc have a rapport now, he knows when not to push me to talk and I feel more comfortable actually talking… a little.

"Alright, so how'd the homework go?" he asks, typing a few notes on his tablet, then meeting my gaze.

"I took a bubble bath."

His eyebrows raise and his mouth quirks. "Good, good. Was it relaxing?"

I shrug. "The bath wasn't really my thing, but I listened to an audiobook during the bath, and I was surprised how much I enjoyed it. I'm on my second book now."

"Wonderful," he says, placing his tablet on the table beside him and crossing his ankle over his knee. "I love audiobooks as well. What gave you the idea... for the bath and audiobook?"

I hesitate. "Remember the boy I told you about, Noah?"

He nods.

"He said his big sister enjoys baths and books, and I like her... so I gave it a try." Once again, words bubble out of my mouth about Andie Downsby. I can't seem to *not* talk about her.

Dr. Curtis smiles. "Are you and Andie seeing each other?"

I drag a hand through my hair nervously. "Kind of. I mean, I'd like to be..."

"But?"

That coiling sensation of steel wrapping itself around my heart starts up. That feeling of shutting down, of hiding behind my barrier. But if I want anything with Andie, if she'll even have me, I have to relearn how to talk, how to process things in a healthy way.

*What would Noah do?* He'd be brave.

"I just feel like it's hopeless to try, like I'll never be good enough, anyway. Or worse, I'll get attached and she'll leave. She'll figure out I'm not worthy of her and leave me in the dust. Just like everyone else."

Dr. Curtis is quiet for a beat, maybe thinking about how insane I am, or maybe giving me a moment of peace to reflect on the words I just said. Maybe both.

When he finally speaks, his voice is calm and steady. "Mitch, it's understandable that you fear people leaving you, given what you've been through. And, of course, love is always a risk. There are no guarantees when it comes to love and relationships. But despite what anyone has told you before, they didn't leave because of you, they left because of themselves. They left because of their own selfish desires, or perhaps some internal struggle they had. But it had nothing to do with you. The things people say and do usually have everything to do with themselves… and nothing to do with us." He pauses, his eyes laser focused on mine. "You, Mitch Anderson, are a good person. You are worthy of love, and worthy of happiness. And you should chase after it."

I sit there for a long time, looking down at my hands, contemplating what he just said. Letting myself feel the weight of his words, and trying to let them sink in. But as much as I want to take them to heart and really believe what he said, I have a lifetime of negative thoughts to regroup from. It's going to take longer than five minutes for my heart to accept this new information.

But I *want* to believe them. I really do.

# CHAPTER 25
# ANDIE

TUESDAY during my lunch break at work—AKA stuffing food down my throat as fast as I can before returning to my patients—I check my phone for the first time since I woke up this morning. My heart leaps when I see I have three missed texts from Mitch.

BIG MAN

Hey Blondie. Want a ticket for tomorrow's game? I can get Noah a ticket too, if you want.

BIG MAN

I know you're not really into hockey… so, no pressure.

BIG MAN

But I heard the Eagles' ugliest player will finally be back tomorrow.

I laugh as I read the texts.

ANDIE

I'd love to come watch the Eagles' hairiest player. Let me see if Ronda can hang out with Noah. It'd be fun to come cheer for you without Noah judging me.

BIG MAN

Sure. Just let me know.

BIG MAN

P.S. I'm not hairy.

I burst out laughing and one of the other nurses in the break room, who's currently trying to have a phone conversation, gives me a funny look.

I mouth the word *Sorry*.

Ronda strides into the break room in her confident way and slumps down in the chair next to me. "I'm getting too old for this," she mutters.

"Oh stop it. You're healthy as an ox." I take the last bite of my peanut butter and jelly sandwich, licking my fingers for good measure, when I muster up the bravery to talk to Ronda about the game tomorrow. "So, umm."

She pins me with a knowing look. I straighten my spine and continue, "I know you're already helping me out a ton, but I'd like to go to Mitch's game tomorrow. I was wondering if you might hang out with Noah for me?"

Ronda leans back in her chair and crosses her arms. She looks unamused. "You mean Mitch Anderson? The grumpy athlete who never smiles and who's...what were your words... *totally not your type*?"

I sigh heavily. "Okay, I lied. He totally *is* my type. And tomorrow's his first game back after his suspension."

She looks at me through narrowed eyes. "Fine. But only

because he's helped Noah so much. But mark my words, if he hurts you…"

"I know, I know. A slow, painful death."

She nods her head slowly… It's actually pretty creepy.

"Thank you!" I wrap my arms around her in a giant hug. "Mitch is a good guy, I swear."

She swats at me. "Okay, enough, get back to work."

Giving her a big kiss on the cheek, I pull back, grinning from ear to ear. She smiles back at me. "It *is* nice to see you so happy."

"The big man will grow on you, I just know it."

―――――

"But I want to go to the game!" Noah argues as I'm trying to leave. He's dressed in all of his finest Eagles gear, as if that'll cause me to give in to his whining.

"Noah, you're staying here with Ronda," I say, for what feels like the hundredth time.

He throws his hands up. "But you don't even know anything about hockey."

Ronda, who's leaning against the wall near the front door, quirks a brow like she's silently agreeing with him on that point.

"I'm not going to watch hockey, I'm going to watch Mitch."

"I knew you had a crush on him." Noah rolls his eyes.

"Yep, you were right. Now let me go swoon over your coach, you wouldn't want to see that anyway."

His face twists in disgust. "That's a good point."

"Come on, buddy. I brought brownies and we can watch the game on the T.V." Ronda sweeps an arm around his slim shoulders and he concedes with a heavy sigh.

"Okay, fine. But I get to come to the next game."

"Deal," I tell him, leaving through the front door before he changes his mind.

———

When I arrive at my seat with my huge bucket of popcorn, I see a pretty brown-haired woman in the seat beside my own. She has the biggest blue eyes I've ever seen and she's wearing an Eagles jersey just like mine, but the number on hers is different. She shoots me a friendly smile and stands up. "Hey! Are you Andie?"

"Yep, that's me," I answer.

She pulls me into a hug then introduces herself. "I'm Melanie, you can call me Mel. I'm West's fiancée."

"Oh! The blond guy?"

She laughs again. "Yep, that's him."

We sit down in our seats, which are in the stands this time and not the fancy box. I glance around us, noticing the girls right in front of us are all wearing Weston Kershaw jerseys. "Is it super annoying being with someone so popular with the ladies?" I whisper.

She side-eyes the girls in front of us. "A little. But they don't really *know* him. And he doesn't pay attention to them. Trust me, if they knew he spends half of his freetime playing NHL on the Xbox, or how he never puts his socks in the dirty laundry basket, they'd realize he's just another normal, some-times irritating, man."

"Good point."

"So, you and Mitch?" Her eyebrows raise in question.

"Me and Mitch." I feel a blush creeping onto my cheeks.

"What's he like? He's such an anomaly."

I bite my bottom lip, thinking of how to explain Mitch Anderson. "Mitch is like... eating crab."

Her brow scrunches together, clearly confused. I start laughing at myself for being so bad at explaining things.

"No, no. Hear me out. Crab looks all hard and difficult... and it's a ton of work to get the meat out of it. But then, once you get inside, it's tender and delicious." I wink and her brow smooths back out.

Mel huffs out a laugh. "Ahhhh, weird analogy... but it makes sense."

I lean my bucket of popcorn toward her and she grabs a small handful. "Thanks." She smiles. "It's so nice to have someone to sit with. I keep trying to get my friend, Noel, to come with me. But she refuses."

"Not a hockey fan?" I ask.

She quirks a brow. "You could say that. So, what do you do?"

"I'm a nurse. You?"

Her smile drops. "I was a political assistant to a congressman, but he didn't run for reelection. So, now I'm just taking time off to plan the wedding."

"You miss it?" I ask, noticing the disappointed look on her face.

"I really do."

The announcer comes over the speakers and we both look toward the ice as the voice announces the players. The entire first line is announced, but they save Mitch for last since it's his first game back in over a month. When the announcer welcomes *Mitch 'The Machine' Anderson*, my heart skips a beat. The crowd cheers, but there are still a few boos, I'm assuming from the opposing team. I cheer loudly and so does Mel. Mitch flies out onto the ice, skating in a large circle in the center of the ice and waving once before taking a seat on the bench with the others.

Mel leans over and asks in a hushed voice, "Have you ever seen him smile?"

I glance over at Mitch, who's frowning at the ice, and burst out laughing. "He does. And it's magnificent. Like seeing a rare animal in the wild."

The puck drops and we turn our attention to the ice. I enjoy watching Mitch in a similar way to watching Noah. I may not know anything about the game, but I enjoy watching someone I know. A feeling of pride washes over me as I watch the entire first period and Mitch stays calm and collected the entire time. I mean, sure, he body checked a few opponents, but from what I know, they were clean hits. Not a single penalty for the big man so far.

Mel and I go get some snacks during the intermission. Mine is a pretzel and soda, hers is a bottle of water and a banana. She catches me staring at her so-called *snack* and explains, "Eating healthy helps my anxiety. You do not want to see me hyped up on sugar." She widens her eyes to dramatize her statement.

We head back to our seats just in time for the second period to start. Mel points to the Jumbotron halfway through the second and I look up to see the two of us on the screen. We both wave and dance to the music they're playing. It's weird, I feel like I've known Melanie way longer than I have. I think I officially have a friend my own age here in D.C.

The second period, and half of the third, go by without any penalties from Mitch. The Eagles are ahead 3-1. One of those goals being from West, with Mitch getting the assist. I'm learning this hockey lingo quickly. I feel bad that I don't pay this much attention to Noah's games, but I'm going to start now that I'm a bonafide hockey expert.

"I can't believe Mitch hasn't racked up a single penalty!"

Mel yells over the crowd. "I've never been to a game where he hasn't been in the sin bin at least once!"

"Really?!" I yell over the crowd. I knew he tended to get penalties, but I didn't realize it was quite that extreme.

She nods and we turn our attention back to the game. One of the opposing players gets a breakaway and flies toward our net. Bruce hunches down, getting into position to block his shot, but the guy slips and slams right into him. They both tumble to the ice, the player on top of Bruce inside his own net. The guy on top of Bruce jumps up, as does Bruce. I can tell there's an exchange of words between the two and the guy charges Bruce and shoves him. Mitch is there quickly, yanking the guy off of Bruce. I can tell by his posture he's pissed. Colby skates up beside Mitch and tries to pull him away, but Mitch doesn't budge. He's clearly speaking his mind to the fool who messed with Bruce, but he doesn't throw any punches. Finally, he lets the guy go and the refs call a minor penalty on the opposing player for roughing.

"Goalie interference is a big no-no. The guys get pretty protective of their goalies," Mel explains, probably reading my worried expression.

I breathe out a sigh of relief. "Gotcha. I'm just glad Mitch didn't beat the crap out of that guy."

"Me too," Mel says. "He must be motivated with you being in the crowd."

I weigh her words before responding with, "Yeah, maybe. But I think he's working hard on keeping himself in control too. I've seen it when he's working with the kids at practice."

Her eyes brighten. "That's right! He coaches your little brother, right?"

"Yeah. He was a jerk at first. But I think he started to enjoy it. Noah, my brother, adores him. But he'd never admit it."

Melanie laughs. "Okay, that's pretty freaking cute."

"It really is," I agree. "I'm really going to miss ogling him at practice."

She smirks. "I bet. What's going on with you two anyway?"

I shrug. "Not sure, we had one date. Sort of. I'm not even sure it was a date, actually."

Mel gives me an empathetic pat on the shoulder. "He'd be crazy not to nail this down. Plus, I need another girl to hang out with. It's always just West, Remy, Bruce and me."

"Mitch doesn't hang out with you guys?"

She huffs a humorless laugh. "In the last year, I've only seen him at one party. They always invite him, but he's kind of a recluse."

I think about his instagram account where he follows zero people. "Yeah. That adds up. Well, if we ever define…" I gesture between myself and the ice where Mitch is playing. "Whatever this is. I'll make sure he comes to social events."

"Sounds like a plan to me!"

———

After the game, Mel takes me down to the same large hallway outside the locker room where Tom Parker took me and Noah last week. When the guys finally filter out one by one, my breath catches in my throat when I see Mitch. He's wearing a game day suit, this one is navy blue with grey stripes and a green tie. It doesn't sound like it would look good, but with his muscles and his whole bad-boy vibe, he's seriously pulling off the look.

He spots me and his whole demeanor changes. Lips titling up, eyes twinkling, posture more relaxed. If he keeps looking at me like that, I'll be a goner. Actually, I think I already am.

"Hey, Blondie," he says in that rumbly voice as he ambles toward me.

"Hey, Big Man."

I glance briefly at Mel and see her watching us. She winks at me. Just then, Remy and West walk into the hallway and she rushes toward her man.

Mitch stops directly in front of me and we stare at each other for a second. His eyes shift and I can tell he's unsure how to greet me. That's okay, I don't mind grabbing the proverbial reins. Placing my hands on his suit lapels, I stand on my tiptoes and place a kiss on his bearded cheek. His scent wafts around me and it's intoxicating. His hands grip my waist tightly and he turns his head so our lips meet.

*Smooth, Mitch Anderson, very smooth.*

He gives me a short kiss, nothing like the ones we shared at his penthouse. But it warms me nonetheless.

He leans back with a confident smirk firmly on his face. "Thanks for coming to the game."

"Not a single stint in the sin bin. I'm proud of you."

His face grows serious and he stares at me with a stunned expression, then blinks a few times. I swear I saw his eyes get hazy, but he blinked it away so fast, I wonder if I was imagining the emotion there.

"You guys coming out with us?" Bruce asks, appearing next to Mitch and resting his chin on the big man's shoulder just to annoy him.

Mitch shoves him away quickly. "Get off of me you leech."

Bruce just laughs. "Come on, Blondie. Come get drinks with us. You're the only one who can get this guy to join us."

Mitch looks at me with what I think is hope in his eyes. Which warms my heart since he, apparently, never joins in on the team fun. And I hate to shatter that hopeful look. But I have to. "I'm sorry, I have to work early in the morning."

Mitch's shoulders slump just enough for me to notice the movement. "I'll walk you to your car," he says, his voice not sounding quite as happy as it did a moment ago.

Offering him an apologetic smile, I turn to Bruce again. "Thanks for the invite, though. You guys have fun. But not too much fun." I wink.

Bruce shoots me a devilish grin, then struts off to find his other teammates.

Mitch steps toward me and laces his hand through mine. I look up at him and he looks hesitant again. "Is this okay?"

"More than okay." I give his hand a gentle squeeze, letting him know I'm totally okay with this hand holding situation.

Mitch got me a parking pass so I could park in a special lot saved for teammates and their families, which is a huge perk. D.C. traffic—and parking—is a nightmare. We walk outside in comfortable silence, I'm just soaking up the feeling of his hand enveloping mine. The night sky is dark, but it's difficult to make out the stars with the city lights surrounding us. But it's quiet and romantic all the same. The parking lot is peaceful now that the game is over, there aren't many cars near my own. As we come close to my car, I reach for my door handle, but Mitch grabs onto my waist and swivels me around to face him in one smooth move. His hands move up so they're resting on the hood of my car, one on each side of me, pinning me in. I've never felt so thrilled to be enclosed in a small space. He smells good too, back to his mountain waterfall scent. As much as I adore Captain Bubbles, I prefer the mountain scent when it comes to Mitch.

There's a desperation in his eyes as he looks at me, a look so mesmerizing, I don't miss the stars at all. Then he's bending down to bring our faces closer. I close my eyes and wait for him to kiss me, but he takes it slow, like he's savoring the moment... or maybe memorizing my face. Finally, his soft lips brush against mine, just barely. Just a tease. He kisses the corner of my mouth and I smile against the feel of it.

Keeping my eyes closed, I wait raptly in anticipation of what he'll do next. My skin tingles when I feel his nose running along the side of my neck, and then his lips. I think he must enjoy the scent of my skin just as much as I enjoy his. His mouth moves higher and he places a sweet kiss on my jawline, and then another one right behind my ear.

I could keep my eyes shut tight and let him do this forever. I feel his breath on my lips again right before he kisses them. Bringing my hands up under his open suit jacket, I allow them to rest on his waist, relishing in the way his muscles move beneath my fingers. I really, desperately need to see him with his shirt off.

Nearby smooching sounds pull our attention back to the present, both of our heads snapping up to see what's going on. Mitch growls when he sees Remy, Colby, Bruce, West and Melanie walking toward us.

Mel shrugs her shoulders and mouths the word *Sorry*, like she tried to get them to leave us alone and failed. I mouth back the words, *It's okay.*

Bruce blows out a low whistle. "Well if it isn't little miss *I have to work early in the morning*."

Colby fans his face dramatically. "Goodness. Is it hot in this parking lot, or is it just me?"

West grins and pumps his eyebrows up and down. "It's definitely not just you."

I laugh at their teasing, it's like being around a bunch of college guys. But Mitch is still growling as if he's about to pounce on them. I place and hand on his thick chest and pat him gently a few times, calming the tiger.

"I really do need to head home." I stand on my toes and give Mitch a kiss on the cheek and turn to open my car door.

Mitch's teammates and Mel say their goodbyes and walk toward their vehicles. Mitch leans inside my car, his voice low. "Thank you for being here. Just knowing you were out there tonight, somewhere in the crowd, made me want to play my best." He groans. "Wow, that sounded stupid."

I shake my head. "No, it didn't. Thanks for sharing tonight with me, I'm sure it was nerve-racking being back after a month."

He blows out a breath. "It really was. When can I see you again?"

"Well, you could come to Noah's game Saturday."

He smirks. "I can't kiss you in front of Noah."

"Well, you *could*. But he'd probably never speak to you again."

Mitch huffs out a laugh. "When can I take you on a real date?"

My heart speeds up at the thought of a real date... in public... with Mitch. Not just because it's Mitch, but it's also the realization that our relationship will be in the public eye, and that it will likely be picked apart by gossip blogs. But Mitch is worth it.

"Well, Noah's game is Saturday, but I'm off on Sunday too. Let me see if I can secure a sitter."

"Okay," he says evenly, looking into my eyes in a piercing gaze. "And if you can't, the three of us can hang out."

"Really?" I ask, but I can tell by the look in his eyes that he's serious. That he'd bring Noah along if that meant he got to spend time with me. The thought makes me feel warm on this cool night.

"Of course." He leans in and kisses my forehead, then pulls back. "Have a good day at work tomorrow."

# CHAPTER 26

# MITCH

THE DAY AFTER MY GAME, I'm waiting for Noah to arrive for our last session together. There's a large part of me that wants to continue working with him, and I wish my schedule would allow for it. But even squeezing one last practice in today was difficult, with Eagles practice this morning and working with my trainer this afternoon. But the kid has so much potential, I can't help but want to be a part of helping him hone it in.

Ronda strides inside the rink, Noah is probably in the locker room getting his skates on. Her stare isn't filled with mirth today; instead, she eyes me curiously like I'm a mystery to her. One she probably doesn't want to solve. I know she's important to Noah and Andie, so I force a smile and say hi.

She tilts her head dramatically, making her charcoal curls bob. It's clearly a gesture for me to come talk to her, and since she's terrifying, I quickly skate over. She peeks her head through the door in the glass and says in a low voice, "You make two of my favorite people happy… so I'm going to help you out."

My eyes widen, surprised by her words, and also a little

flattered. The fact that I could make someone happy? Especially people as amazing as Andie and Noah. The knowledge does something funny to my chest. "Okay, I'm all ears."

"Nurses, specifically ICU and ER, rarely get lunch breaks. Our girl packs a pb and j every single day, and usually, she has about ten minutes to eat it." Ronda shakes her head and huffs a laugh. "She has to be sick of them by now."

I nod, urging her to continue.

"You want to woo an ICU nurse? Take her a lunch, a *good* lunch. But something she can stick in the break room fridge and eat quickly when she has time. Don't send her flowers or any of that nonsense. The girl simply wants a well-made sub." She raises her eyebrows as if to say, *you get me?*

Nodding enthusiastically again, I thank her for the advice. "I owe you one."

She winks and steps back when Noah walks inside the rink. He's dressed for practice and has his skates on. He doesn't seem as happy to see me as usual. He's not angry, but maybe... melancholy? He skates onto the ice and levels me with a steely look. Perhaps I'm rubbing off on him too much.

"Are you dating my sister?" he asks, his tone serious.

I stare back at him in surprise. I should've known this was coming, but I guess I didn't think he'd put it together so fast. "If I wanted to... would I have your approval?"

He wrinkles his nose and looks up at the ceiling. The fact that he has to think about it so hard should probably offend me, but I find myself resisting a smile instead. If I had a sister, I'd like to think I'd be protective of her too.

Finally, he meets my gaze again. "Yeah, I guess so." He looks a little sad as he says it and I wonder if he feels left out, like after all our one-on-one time, I'm leaving him behind for his sister.

"Thanks, man." I skate toward him and bend down so

we're eye to eye. "But I need you to know…" I clear my throat, not used to sharing my thoughts and words so freely. But Noah has always been honest with me. "Just because I want to get to know Andie, doesn't mean I don't want to hang out with you too."

His chin dips down in a nod, and I swear he already looks happier and more relaxed. "Okay," he says, a content smile on his face. "Enough talking, let's get to work."

He skates off toward the net and I zoom after him.

We warm up by shooting pucks into the empty net, seeing how many we can get in within thirty seconds. His shot has really improved in just a month, I can't wait to see what he can do in a year. If I'm not in the stands at one of his NHL games in ten years cheering him on, I'll be shocked. If he keeps working this hard, he can make it. I just know he can.

We start working on stick handling and Noah stops abruptly and looks at me. "Are you coming to our game Saturday?"

"Yeah, I planned on it. Is that okay?"

Even though I won't be coaching anymore, I'd like to come to their games when I can, to see how they're doing. And… added bonus? I'd get to sit beside Andie. Maybe keep her warm since she always looks freezing.

He shrugs, feigning indifference. But then he gives up on the facade, allowing his shoulders to slump. "I'd like it if you came… It's gonna be kinda weird not to have you there anymore."

A smile plays at my lips. "You're not going to cry are you?"

He narrows his eyes. "Of course not, that's *your* job."

Friday, we have a light practice, basically just warming our muscles for the game tonight, but not so strenuous as to wear ourselves out before we play. I'm definitely feeling bummed that Andie works tonight and won't be at the game. Something about having her in the stands Wednesday made me want to play better… and just be a better person in general. Hence the zero penalties. My game has never been so good.

But I know she can't be at every game. And I can't count on another person to keep me from losing my temper, I can only count on myself for that. At least she said she'll turn the game on when she gets home from work, so I know she'll be watching.

I park in the hospital parking lot, the hospital where Andie works, with a sub sandwich in hand. Thank you, Ronda.

I have just enough time to drop this off to her before heading back to my penthouse and taking a pregame nap. Plus, I really want to see her. Maybe she can send some luck my way before the game even starts (I wouldn't say no to a pregame kiss either).

When I get inside the giant building, I stop at the large map on the wall and find the ICU. After an elevator ride, I come to a big door that's locked but has an intercom. Pressing the button, a female voice comes through the speaker, asking what I need.

"Yeah, I have lunch for Andie Downsby," I say into the speaker.

There's a pause and some muffled whispering before Andie's voice comes over the intercom. "I'll be right there, Big Man."

Just the sound of her voice makes my heart feel lighter than it did two seconds ago.

There's a beep and a click, then the double doors swing

open. Andie stands before me in all of her sexy scrub-wearing glory.

"Hey, Blondie."

She steps through the doors, several nurses at the desk a few yards away watching us and giggling. Andie has an intense blush coating her cheeks and I can't help but smile at her.

"I brought you lunch."

Her eyes soften, but her blush remains. "Oh my gosh, you did? That's so thoughtful. I planned on eating a—"

I hold one hand up, cutting her off. "Peanut butter and jelly sandwich?" With my other hand, I hold up the takeout bag.

Her eyes widen in surprise for a second before they narrow. "Ronda."

She snatches the bag from me and peeks inside, stepping out of the way of the double doors so they can close automatically behind her. Andie opens the bag and gasps. "Bacon, lettuce, tomato? That's my favorite. And barbecue chips? Are you trying to make me fall in love with you?"

This time *I* blush. I'd never allowed myself to imagine that anyone would fall in love with me, or that I was even capable of falling in love myself. But suddenly, it doesn't sound so bad.

"Sorry, I didn't mean that, I was just teas—" I cut her off mid-sentence again, but this time I do it by pressing my lips to hers.

Not a bad way to shut her up, actually. I could get used to this. She softens instantly and melts into me. I wrap my arms around her waist and she does the same to me. She ends our kiss, giving me a cute smile, before laying her head on my chest and squeezing me. We stand there holding each other, and I realize… she's hugging me. An affectionate, comfortable feeling envelops me. This is the hug I've waited for all my life. Right here, with this girl. A hug that makes up for a lifetime of not being held, not being loved, not being enough. This is the hug to end all hugs.

But I definitely want more hugs in the future, and only from this woman.

I'm not sure I'll *ever* get enough hugs after this.

I decide right in this moment, that if by some miracle I ever have children, I will hug them, and hug them often. What a simple, but life-changing gesture.

Kissing is great... epic... amazing. But hugs are severely underrated.

# CHAPTER 27
## ANDIE

I HAVE NEVER, in my twenty-six years of life, had a man bring me lunch at work. It was the most thoughtful gesture. And knowing he has a game tonight, it means even more that he made the time to do that for me.

They say food is the way to a man's heart, but I'm pretty sure they meant a *nurse's* heart.

After Mitch left, the other nurses—male *and* female—were in a tizzy about seeing a professional athlete. The girls want me to hook them up with his teammates, and the guys want to know if I can get them good seats at any of the games. I tell them no, on both fronts, and go on about my day. We don't have much time to chitchat in the ICU anyway.

At the end of my shift, I have to catch up on charting that I was too busy to do during the day, and don't make it home until eight thirty. When I walk inside, Noah is on the couch with the game already on. He's wearing his new jersey and baseball cap and munching on popcorn. He looks up when I enter the room and smiles. "Hey, you missed Mitch's goal."

"Dang it!" I plop down onto the couch beside him and grab a handful of popcorn. "So he's playing well?"

"Really good. And only one penalty, but it was a stupid call."

I breathe a sigh of relief that it wasn't a fight or anything crazy. All players get penalties once in a while. Peeking at the score in the top left corner of the television, I see that the Eagles are ahead 4-2 in the second period. A guy on the opposing team fakes out Colby and breaks away toward the Eagles' net. He shoots the puck right into the corner. Poor Bruce. Now the score is nearly tied and I find myself scooting to the edge of my seat on the couch, focusing on the plays. My eyes are pinging back and forth as I keep them firmly on the puck flying across the ice.

Noah snorts a laugh and I look over my shoulder to see him watching me. "Never thought I'd see you get so into a hockey game."

Forcing myself to relax and lean back, I respond, "You and me both."

There's a line change and Mitch skates onto the ice. A grin spreads across my face as I watch him. His movements on the ice are brutal and beautiful, and I can't take my eyes off of him.

Before I can stop it, a sappy sigh escapes my lips and Noah groans. "Oh, my gosh. You're ruining hockey for me."

I shove him and steal the popcorn bowl.

"Hey!" he yells, grabbing for the bowl. "Hockey is my thing. Don't make it gross with all your lovey-dovey crap."

Giving up the popcorn bowl, I gasp and bring a hand to my chest. "Noah Gregory Downsby! Sassy jar!"

"Crap is not a swear word."

"Oh, it definitely is," I tease.

He laughs at me, rolling his eyes, and snatches some popcorn. I notice Mitch has the puck and turn my attention back to the game. Mitch passes the puck to West, but he's blocked by the other players and there's no way he can get a good shot in. He passes it back to Mitch. Mitch catches it easily then slaps the puck right between the legs of the opposing team's goalie. Noah and I both jump up from the couch, me screaming and Noah whooping.

"Good shot, Big Man!" I say to the T.V. Then I feel stupid and pull out my phone to text him. He obviously won't read it for a while, but at least it will be waiting for him.

ANDIE

> Some smoking hot Eagles defenseman just scored his second goal.

Noah groans, I hadn't realized he was reading over my shoulder. "You guys are so weird."

I sit back down, a wide grin on my face. "Oh, little brother. Some day you'll meet a girl who makes your heart feel all funny and you'll act stupid too."

His face twists up, making me laugh. "Yeah, I doubt that. I'll be too busy playing hockey."

Laughing, I roll my eyes.

A few hours later, the game is done. The Eagles killed it, winning 6-3. Noah is in bed asleep, and I check my phone.

BIG MAN

> I see how it is, you change your tune after I bring you food.

ANDIE

> What can I say? A twelve-inch sub is the key to my heart... but I can settle for a six-inch too.

BIG MAN

> Oh, I can do better than a six-inch, Blondie.

I snicker and wish I could see his face right now. Is he smirking? Blushing? Or does he have that broody expression so no one around him knows he's actually in a good mood?

Also, is he in the locker room, and does he have his shirt off?

ANDIE

Are you still in your hockey gear?

BIG MAN

Why?

ANDIE

No reason.

BIG MAN

I'm cooling down with my shirt off.

ANDIE

*gif of a woman fanning herself and swooning*

BIG MAN

You're trouble.

———

The next morning, a friend of Noah's from school called and invited him to come over and play Roblox. He thought I was the best sister ever for saying yes and promptly driving him across town, but really, it was totally selfish of me.

I love my brother with all my heart, but I also want to spend time with Mitch. Which is going to be difficult between our schedules and Noah's. Noah is pretty much going to have a front-row seat to me and Mitch's courtship, or whatever you wanna call it.

I barely make it through the front door after dropping Noah off before I'm calling Mitch to see if he's free today. The other end of the line rings and rings. Remembering he had practice this morning, I leave a message.

"Hey Big Man. I'm surprisingly free today, sans brother. I thought you might like to squeeze in a sporadic date? Call me back when you can!"

On the off chance he's free after practice, I run upstairs to take a quick shower. I even do the long routine I never take the time to do these days. Shaving, exfoliating, polishing, deep conditioning the hair. All the things Mitch won't notice, but will make me feel like a goddess.

When I step out of the steamy shower, I wrap my body in one towel and my hair in another, then go to the closet. I find my favorite jeans quickly, but remember I put the rest of my clothes in the dryer this morning. They should be done by now. Making sure my towel is secure, I run down the stairs to the utility room where the washer and dryer are located. The dryer is still spinning round and round and I can hear a few hard items in there clunking around.

I roll my eyes. When you live with a boy under the age of thirteen, your dryer is essentially just a rock tumbler. The dryer comes to a stop and dings. I open it and grab the top I want to wear. It's a long-sleeved bodysuit in a caramel brown color, it makes my eyes stand out and I think Mitch will love it.

Running back up the stairs, I'm out of breath by the time I check my phone again. One missed call and a voicemail from Mitch. I press play while I dry my hair.

"Blondie," his deep voice oozes over the phone. My spine tingles just from his voice. I'll never delete this message. I will play it right before I fall asleep every night. "It's your lucky day. I'm free after practice. Call me back so I know what time to pick you up."

I walk back inside the bathroom, phone in hand, hang my towel up, and grab a comb for my hair. I call Mitch back and put the phone on speaker, then start combing through the tangles in my hair.

"Hey," his voice rumbles through the phone and under my skin. I shiver, and not because I'm cold. "We finally caught each other."

"Hey," I say back. This game of phone tag is a reminder of how opposite our schedules, and lives, are.

"Can I pick you up in twenty minutes?" he asks and I nearly gasp. I look in the mirror and see my wet hair that's only half combed out and my still towel-clad, dripping wet body.

"Have you ever known a woman to get ready in twenty minutes?"

A breathy laugh comes through the other line. "Okay, so how much time *do* you need?"

"Forty-five minutes?"

He sighs. "Alright, see you in forty-five."

"Okay, and Mitch?"

"Yeah?"

"This is our first date."

"The penthouse was our first date," he argues.

I shake my head and make a nu-uh sound. "That was to schedule something for my brother. Doesn't count."

"You and I both know that's not why I had you over."

"Sorry, no time to argue. Gotta get ready for our first date."

"Fine. See you in forty." I can practically hear the eye roll in his voice.

"Forty-five," I argue.

"Nope, you wasted five minutes arguing with me."

I groan. "Fine, okay bye!" I hang up so I don't lose any more time, and quickly finish combing and then blow drying my hair.

Forty minutes, exactly, later... my doorbell rings. Thankfully, I had a feeling Mitch Anderson would be punctual, and I'm ready to go. *And* I smell great.

Grabbing my coat off the peg in the entryway, I throw it over my shoulders and open the door. Mitch is standing there looking like a snack in dark-wash jeans, a green sweater, and a black leather jacket.

Yes, ladies... a black... leather... jacket. I manage to squeak out something that sounds like *hi*.

Mitch scans me slowly, starting at my hair and moving down to my feet. I feel his gaze like a caress and have to hold back the urge to turn away. When his eyes meet mine, his are molten and heated. His voice is low when he says, "I don't think I'll ever get used to how pretty you are."

I hold back a whimper. Before I've recovered from his sweet words, he leans in and kisses my cheek, allowing his talented lips to linger on my skin for a few seconds. He hums as he pulls back. "You smell really good. Not like bubble gum today. Although, I like the bubble gum scent too."

"Of course you do," I say, stepping out the front door then locking it behind me. "Because you love Captain Bubbles."

He snickers and takes my hand, leading me down the front steps and to his shiny black whatever-it-is parked on the street in front of my house. (I know anatomy, not cars.)

Mitch opens the door for me and I slide inside the fanciest car I've ever been in. The shiny, leather seat squeaks when I slide in, and the lights shift when Mitch closes the door. As he's walking around the car to the driver's side, I notice there's a small screen and it's displaying a crackling fireplace. When

Mitch gets in on the driver's side and closes his door, my mouth is still gaping.

"Why do you look like that?"

My eyes that are already wide open, grow even wider as I gawk at him. "*Why* does your futuristic car have a fireplace?"

"You've never seen a Tesla?" He asks, his eyebrows drawing together.

"No, Mitch. I'm not a quadrillionaire like you!"

He chuckles and starts to pull out of the parking spot, actually, the car might be doing it for him. He's just sitting there for looks.

"Teslas are actually pretty affordable."

I scoff. "Yeah, okay." Looking around and into the backseat, I notice how clean it is and how nice it smells. "Wow, no hockey gear and random shoes scattered about. I'm impressed."

"Oh, trust me, when I was Noah's age, my granddad's car was a mess of hockey gear and dirty socks." He shakes his head with a smile, as if remembering something. "And the smells that came from that old Buick... worse than a locker room, no doubt."

I smile, watching him intently. "Tell me more about your granddad, he sounds special."

"He was." He sighs, gripping the steering wheel a little tighter. "He had a temper, I came by it honestly. But the eight years I lived with him were the best years I can remember." Mitch pauses, looking over at me and then back toward the busy road in front of him. I note that he's a safe and cautious driver, something I've come to look for and appreciate about people. "He taught me to work hard, and to own up to my mistakes. But more than anything, he gave me an education about all things John Wayne related." His mouth pulls up in a smile.

"John Wayne... like the cowboy actor guy?"

He reaches one giant hand over and squeezes my thigh gently. "Oh, Blondie. I'm so relieved you know who that is. I can forgive you for Wayne Gretzky, but not knowing John Wayne might've been a deal breaker."

Laughing, I place my hand over the top of his. He stares at the road, his demeanor calm. "I want to tell you everything, about my past, my family. But it's not easy, it'll take time. It'll be in bits and pieces, when I can get it out."

"That's okay. Whenever you feel like sharing, I'm here." I rub the back of his hand with my thumb, but keep my gaze on the side of his face. On his sharp profile, a profile not even his soft beard can disguise.

"So, have you ever seen a John Wayne movie?"

He looks over at me as he comes to stop at a red light and I give him a hesitant smile. "I haven't."

He tsks. "Then I know what we're doing today."

Thirty minutes later, Mitch parallel parks outside a small, old-looking theater. One of those that plays movies that have already been out for years. The kind of place a couple goes just to make out and not actually watch a movie. The large sign above the ticket box at the front of the brick building reads: *Stage Coach 11:00 & 2:00, Funny Face 4:00 & 7:00.*

"Are we gonna sit in the back and kiss the whole time?" I tease.

He shakes his head. "Your mind is always in the gutter."

Mitch gets out of the car and comes around to open my door. We walk to the ticket box hand in hand. A giddiness builds inside of me at how date-y this feels. Like a normal boyfriend and girlfriend. No little brothers around to make fun of me, and no fans around to berate Mitch. Just the two of us at a practically empty theater.

We walk up to the ticket booth where a teenage boy with

blond hair draped over his left eye ignores us. He's reading a book and doesn't seem to care that there are customers needing assistance. Mitch clears his throat and the boy looks up slowly. He heaves an annoyed sigh, places a bookmark in his book and mutters, "How can I help you."

"Two tickets to Stagecoach, please." Mitch says, extending cash for said tickets.

They make their exchange and as we walk away the boy mumbles something about John Wayne and toxic masculinity under his breath. Mitch stays calm, taking my hand again, and heading inside to the concession stand. We wait there, looking around for someone to help us, when the front door opens and the teenage boy steps inside and around behind the register of the concession stand.

"On your own today?" I ask.

He just rolls his eyes and asks what we want. Wow, what customer service. I take a moment to appreciate that Noah isn't like this, and also steel myself for the angsty teenage years. Yikes.

We get snacks and sodas. Mitch goes for the beef jerky, and I get the sour straws. Of course, he ordered the most protein-packed snack option available. Sweet and salty... both wonderful in their own way, but don't really go together at first glance. Kind of like us.

Mitch leads me inside the one and only theater room. Not multiple like the modern ones. The place is kind of run down, and looks like no one has vacuumed all week. Little bits of popcorn litter the floor. Not too surprising, considering the only employee I've met so far.

"I know it's not fancy," Mitch says as he kicks at an empty soda cup. "But the privacy here is top notch."

I laugh. "That's okay. I'm happy just to hang out with you. Also, I'm now terrified for Noah to become a teen."

He huffs out a laugh. "Hormones are the worst."

We sit down in the very center of the back row and I hum to myself. Mitch's head whips in my direction at the sound, a question on his scrunched up face. "What?"

"Back row."

His face eases into a cocky smirk and he does something I never thought he'd ever do… he winks.

Giggling, I take my seat next to him. His mountain man scent making the stale popcorn smell fade away. I lean my head on his big shoulder and the previews start playing on the big screen. Being an old theater, the arm rest between us isn't one of those that can be pushed up for better snuggling. Dang it. Apparently, we're actually watching this movie then.

Mitch notices me wiggling the arm rest and smirks. "You can just sit on my lap if you're that desperate to get close to me."

"I'm not desperate. Just checking this thing in case there's an emergency." I pound on the armrest a few times to get my point across.

"Right."

We sit silently, watching previews for movies that were released years ago. The title for Stagecoach finally pops up and the long credits start scrolling across the screen. I forgot they used to play before the movie. Mitch leans over and whispers, "Tell me about your parents?"

Taking a deep breath, I whisper back, "Let's make a deal. I'll tell you one thing about my parents, then you tell me one thing about yours."

He rolls his lips together while he thinks it over. "Okay, that's fair."

"My mom was the exact opposite of me in every way," I begin. "Except for our physical appearance."

"I noticed," he says with a smile. "From the photo in your house."

I smile back at him. "She was calm where I'm wild, wise where I'm scattered, and I never heard her complain once… while I'm dramatic about, well, most things. She was just the best. And I'm not just saying that because she's gone and I'm only remembering the good things. She was really the greatest person ever, I always wanted to be just like her."

He chuckles, but takes my hand and rests them both on the arm rest. "I didn't know your mom, but I happen to think you're pretty great, even if you aren't just like her."

I squeeze his hand. "Thank you." Leveling him with a serious stare, I say, "Okay, your turn."

He looks away from me, body tensing. He clears his throat and speaks in a low voice. "I don't have a lot of memories of my mom, but I do remember she had hazel eyes like mine, and her hair was long and dark." He huffs a laugh. "When I was really little, I used to wrap my finger around the ends of it when she put me to bed. The times she was there to say good-night to me stand out, because she was gone a lot even before she left. Probably running around with different men. When she did officially leave, I was sad, of course, but I mostly remember my dad's reaction. I remember him completely changing."

"I'm sorry, Mitch," I say, not knowing what words to describe how sorry I am for that little boy who grew up without love and hugs from his own mother. I place my free hand on his arm, hoping the touch lets him know I'm here, and that he can talk to me.

"Your turn," he says, his voice thick with emotion.

The movie starts playing, but it's just background noise to our conversation. I'm assuming he's seen this movie before, because he doesn't seem to care that he's missing it.

"My dad worked a lot, and he was quiet. A lot like Noah. I wasn't as close with him as I was with my mom. He was a good man, just a man of few words. But he loved hockey, especially the Eagles." I grin at Mitch, then look down at our clasped hands. "He would've loved you."

Mitch stares ahead at the screen for a while, his face looks concentrated and intense. Not like he's watching the movie, but like he's deep in thought. Finally, he looks at me. "I wish I could tell you something good about my parents. Something nice. That they'd love you, or how much fun we had. But I just… can't."

"Mitch, I'm here because I like you. Because I want to get to know you. I'd like to hear whatever you feel comfortable telling me about your family. Good or bad, I just want to know what makes you… you."

He nods. "Well, I already told you my good memory. The one about the tiger at the circus." He sighs. "But after my mom left, Dad started drinking. I imagine he wanted to numb the loss. But then he got into drugs too… At first he just purchased them. But the real trouble started when he couldn't afford to buy them anymore, and started dealing."

He bends over and rests his elbows on his knees.

Taking my hand off of his arm, I move it to his broad, muscled back, moving it back and forth over the expanse of his shoulders. I hate that his parents were so awful.

"Is that why you don't drink?" I ask.

He nods. "I don't want to be anything like either of them."

"You're not," I tell him honestly. Because he's a genuinely good person. And I want him to believe that as much as I do.

I continue to rub his back, hoping to comfort him, but he starts shaking silently. I think he's crying at first, then realize he's laughing. It's a humorless laugh, but definitely a laugh.

"You're telling me how wonderful your parents are, meanwhile my Dad is literally a drug dealer." He shakes his head, looking over at me. "You have to admit, it's almost funny how mismatched we are."

"I like you for you, and it has nothing to do with your parents. But I am sorry they suck so bad."

He huffs out another laugh.

"My parents weren't perfect, maybe they weren't pimps or drug dealers, but they were far from perfect."

"Did you just say *pimps*?"

"Uh, yeah."

He snorts a laugh. "You know, my therapist would be jealous of you."

"Why?"

"You've gotten me to talk about my parents more in one week than he has in over a month." He turns his expression back to the screen again.

"I'm more than happy to listen." I squeeze his hand. "But you should talk to him about your family. It would help. After losing my parents, I didn't stay in therapy as long as Noah, but in the few months I talked to a counselor, it helped a lot."

"Is that how you're able to stay so positive? Because of therapy?" he asks.

"Maybe, although I'm definitely not always positive. I do this weird thing, actually…"

"Yeah? What?"

I bite my bottom lip, feeling self-conscious. "Well, I think of three things I'm grateful for every day. And I try to focus on those three things."

"Really? He asks, not judging me, but clearly surprised. "And it works?"

I sit up in my chair, angling myself to look at him. "Try it!"

"Nooooo…."

I nudge him with my hand. "Come on. Just three things. That's it."

He begrudgingly agrees, squinting as he thinks. "Andie's lips. Andie's legs…" He thinks some more. "And Andie's belly button."

I burst out laughing, thank goodness we're alone in this theater. "You're ridiculous."

He opens his eyes, grinning wolfishly, then leans in and gives me a slow, tender kiss. When he settles back in his seat, I'm still fuzzy from the kiss.

"I think I want to stay in therapy. Technically, my month of counseling is done. But I'm going to talk to him about continuing," he whispers.

His words instantly clear the fog of the kiss and I look over at him. "I think that's great."

"So, you're okay with dating an emotional basket case with daddy *and* mommy issues?" he asks, looking over at me with a smirk.

"Well, I guess so. But only because your abs make up for it."

He quirks a brow. "You've never seen my abs."

Tapping my index finger on my temple, I say, "Oh, but I have a very over-active imagination."

Mitch's head drops back and he laughs. I soak up the sound, relish in it, saving it in my internal 'Mitch's laugh' bank.

We watch the rest of the movie in comfortable silence, holding hands and enjoying the nearness… even though the armrest won't budge. I tried three more times.

———

Mitch dropped me back off at my place just in time so I could go get Noah from his friend's house. Our date was much too short for my liking, but at least I get to see him again tonight at Noah's game.

Wow, I think I'm officially a Mitch addict.

Noah rests in his room for his game tonight while I catch up on chores around the house. We make it to the rink and he heads straight to the locker room to suit up.

When I walk inside the arena, I'm greeted instantly by a sour-faced Steph.

"Really, Andie?" She asks me abruptly, getting way too close to my face.

"Really what?" I ask, completely confused.

She huffs and points to the bleachers. My heart nearly leaps out of my chest when I see not only Mitch, but Remy, Colby, Bruce, West and Mel. Mel waves at me with a big, friendly smile that warms my heart and I wave back enthusiastically. I completely forget Steph is in front of me until she clears her throat indignantly.

"I'm sorry, what's the problem?"

She purses her lips so tightly, it almost looks like she's sucking on an imaginary pacifier. I kind of wish she was, because that would keep her mouth shut. When I first met Steph, I thought she was a little annoying, but I never imagined she was a mean girl.

"It's really petty of you to not only sleep with the coach, but also befriend the team, just to get back at Declan for 'teasing' Noah." She uses air quotes with her gloved hands when she says *teasing*.

"My relationship with Mitch isn't anybody's business, Steph. And honestly, I have way bigger things to worry about than getting revenge on a ten-year-old boy." I work hard to keep my face neutral and be the bigger person here.

Because the idea of me plotting all of this is absolutely laughable.

"He's twelve!" She defends. "And I think you're jealous that he's more talented than your brother. So you're trying to keep Noah in the limelight."

My facade breaks and I release a breathy laugh. "Steph, do you realize how ridiculous that sounds?"

"All I know, is you're acting like a hussy." She spits the last word in a venomous tone.

I gasp, horrified by how awful she is. Mitch is beside me, towering over both of us so quickly, I didn't even see him coming. He places his big body between both of us like a wall of protection.

I can't see his face, but he very slowly, and very sternly says, "Do *not* speak to Andie that way."

Tori walks through the doors to the rink and notices the altercation. She rushes over toward us. "Guys, what's going on?"

"Your *friend* called my girlfriend a hussy," Mitch says, crossing his arms.

I step out from behind him so I can see what's happening. Tori's eyes widen and she whips her head to stare at Steph. "What? Steph…"

She pouts. "I said what I said. And I was standing up for Declan!"

Tori puts an arm around Steph's shoulders, and drags her away silently.

"Girlfriend?" I ask, my heart pounding in my ears. That's pretty much the only word I heard during this super weird altercation.

Mitch's head turns in my direction, his gaze meeting mine. He looks serious, contemplative. I can't read his expression or what he's thinking. His eyes shift down to the floor, his hand coming up to scratch the back of his head. "Uh, yeah. Sorry about that. It just came out."

"That's okay." I try not to let my face fall and place my hand in his. I want to ask what he means by *it just came out.* Did it just come out because he was defending me and it didn't mean anything, or did it just come out because he really thinks of me as *his*?

Because I think I'd really like to be his.

Silently, we walk to the bleachers. I take a seat beside Melanie, and Mitch sits next to me. West is on Mel's other side, and Remy, Colby, and Bruce are in the row behind us. I can barely contain my smile when I notice they're all wearing Wombats gear. I feel a little bad that I don't have a single Wombats item. Bad sister move.

"I can't wait to see your brother play, I've been told he's basically a prodigy." Mel oozes warm friendliness that is rare to find. Her smile is so genuine as she talks about Noah that it brings tears to my eyes. I quickly blink them away and swallow.

"Thanks, he works really hard."

"He's infinitely better than Freckles," Mitch mutters the words so quietly, I barely hear him. I turn and give him a mulish glance, but he doesn't even look a little abashed. He just stares right back at me.

He's obviously still perturbed by Steph calling me out like that in public. I'm annoyed, and even a little embarrassed by it, but those feelings are overshadowed by the satisfaction of Mitch defending me. It's been a long time since I had someone to defend me, to stand up for me. And it feels pretty freaking good.

Turning my attention back to Mel, I note that West has an arm around her waist and the smile of a man completely in love. Watching them makes me want to breathe out a happy sigh.

Mel leans into West, but keeps her eyes on me. "So, you had a date this morning?"

"Yeah, Mitch took me to see a movie."

Colby and Bruce snicker behind me, I look over my shoulder just in time to see Remy elbow Bruce in the ribs and shush him.

"What's so funny?" I ask.

He uses air quotes when he says, "To see a movie."

Remy rolls his eyes like he's babysitting two small, hyper children and needs a break. "Some guys can take a woman to a movie and actually watch the movie, you know."

"We didn't watch the movie," I say with a suggestive smirk. "I couldn't begin to tell you what it was about."

Remy blushes so hard that he looks ten years younger and so boyish. I laugh. Mitch's rumbly, low voice comes from beside me, "We didn't watch the movie because we were talking." He pins them with a steely glare. "Get your minds out of the gutter."

The kids get in place on the ice for the start of the game and everyone on the bleachers quiets down. I wish youth hockey had announcers like the NHL, maybe then I'd actually have a clue what was happening during these games. Instead, I just copy the people around me. If the crowd is cheering… then I cheer too.

Noah's on the first line as usual, but not Declan this time. I'm sure Steph somehow thinks that's my fault. The kids start playing and the guys chat the entire time about what's happening and comment on the kids' abilities. It's like having my very own announcers to sit with.

"Dang, Noah really is good," West says, looking over at me and Mitch. "Reminds me of myself when I was that age."

Melanie pats his cheek. "Yeah, you wish."

Noah scores a goal and we all jump up and scream, cheering for him enthusiastically. The guys' antics, along with the sheer size of them, are probably shaking the bleachers. Noah looks over at the stands and shakes his head slowly, like we're so embarrassing. It's such a Mitch thing to do; it makes me laugh.

"Oh, my gosh. You're rubbing off on him," I say to Mitch.

His eyebrows raise slightly. "You mean because his game is on point?"

"No," Bruce answers for me. "Because he's got the *Mitch 'The Machine'* glare down pat."

We all laugh, except Mitch.

Shifting in my seat on the cold, uncomfortable bench, I realize that I was so high from my date with Mitch that I forgot to grab my bag that contains my mittens and hat before leaving the house. Thankfully, I'm wearing a sweater over my bodysuit, but my hands and face are freezing. I release a little shiver and Mitch looks at me with those adorably furrowed brows.

He shrugs off his sexy leather jacket and gently places it over my shoulders. It's so big, it's practically a blanket. And the scent of the big man himself envelopes me... it's like entering a bakery and being overwhelmed by the smell of freshly baked bread... but the Mitch Anderson mountain-scented version.

"Where's your hat?" he asks quietly as he takes both of my hands and presses them between his own to keep them warm.

"You noticed my hat?" I'm a little surprised he was paying enough attention to note that I typically wear a knit-beanie to hockey games and practices.

He leans in close to my ear, his soft lips and beard brushing against my earlobe. I shiver at the feel of him being so close. "I notice everything about you," he whispers in that deep, manly tone.

In my opposite ear, Bruce's voice whispers, "Hey, can you guys talk a little louder? It's really hard to eavesdrop when you're whispering."

Colby nudges his head in between me and Mitch's. "Yeah, I'm with Bruce on this," he says in the loudest whisper I've ever heard. A whisper so loud and dramatic I burst out laughing and shoo them both away with my hands.

Mitch sends them both a *we'll be talking about this later* look. I realize then that he and Remy are the dads of the group. The stern ones. A thought enters my head that Mitch would be a great dad. I push the thought away, because *wow…* way too fast, Andie.

Just then, a tall woman with short, blonde hair walks through the doors of the arena. Her eyes brighten when she spots our group and starts walking toward us. Her smile is natural and pretty and she reminds me of a 1920's swinger-goddess… with her long limbs and lean figure. Her curly hair coils gracefully around her face. But despite her reed-like figure and her short hair, she oozes femininity and beauty.

Mel stands and rushes toward her, they hug each other and chat enthusiastically.

Bruce giggles behind me. Yes, the man giggled like a school boy. I hear Colby tell him to shut up. Turning around, I pin them both with a curious stare. "What am I missing?"

Remy, being the only mature adult in the row behind us, answers, "That's Noel, Mel's best friend, and Colby's unrequited love."

"Oooooooooh." I pump my eyebrows up and down to a now very red, Colby.

Mel and Noel amble toward us, arm in arm. "Andie! Meet my friend Noel," Mel says, gesturing toward her gorgeous friend. I stand up to shake Noel's hand, but she releases Melanie and pulls me into a big hug.

"Great to meet you!"

"You too," I say, pulling back from the hug. Noel is a good six inches taller than me, but her hug is warm and she smells really good. I can see why Colby is enamored with her.

Colby, who's recovered now from Noel's unexpected appearance, is back to his charming self. "Noel, baby," he drawls. "Where's *my* hug?"

Noel shoots him an annoyed look. Mel chuckles at their encounter and gestures for West to scoot down and make room for her friend. Noel takes a seat between me and Mel, then Colby leans down, still trying to win Noel's attention. I have a feeling he's used to being the center of attention, and doesn't often fail at getting the attention he desires… especially from women.

"So, you'll come to Noah's games but not mine?" he says.

She sighs heavily. "I'm here to hang out with my friends, Knight. I couldn't care less about hockey."

He jabs his fist into his chest like it's a knife and then groans dramatically. Noel ignores him.

"So, you don't know who Wayne Gretzky is, then?" I ask.

She glances at me, a question in her eyes. Probably wondering why the heck I'd ask about Gretzky. "Of course I know who The Great One is. Everyone knows that," she huffs out a laugh as she says it.

Mitch starts snickering beside me and the rest of the guys laugh so loud, I swear they rattle the bleachers again. We're going to get kicked out at this rate.

But I also can't help but laugh right along with everyone else. A happiness filters through me that I haven't felt in a long time. That feeling of belonging, of having friends. Of having a tribe. I always sit alone at these games, and I never realized how lonely that was until now. Until I had these people here, making me laugh. I scoot a little closer to Mitch and relish in the feeling of being surrounded by him and his teammates. He may not consider them close friends... but deep down, I think he's a lot more fond of them than he even admits to himself. I feel his chin rest on the top of my head and close my eyes.

*Three things I'm grateful for: Mitch, his goofy friends, and not sitting alone during Noah's game.*

# CHAPTER 28
# MITCH

SUNDAY, WE PILE ONTO THE EAGLES' private plane and head to Canada for a series of away games. Bruce is thrilled, he'll get to see his family in Quebec. Normally, I'd be happy too. Five days away means not having to watch the guys with their families. No Daddy jerseys, no wives, no girlfriends. But Andie disintegrated that damn lockbox in my chest, and now I just want to be near her. Five days now seems agonizing.

I'm utterly and completely whipped… and I like it. Yeah, I don't even know who I am anymore. But I like this new version of myself, and Dr. Curtis probably would too.

I take a seat by the window on the plane and pull my phone out to text Andie that we're about to take off when West slumps down in the seat next to me. I get it, we've been tolerating each other. And if I'm honest, my chest doesn't tighten whenever he's around anymore. But sitting next to each other on the plane? That might be taking things a little too far.

My thoughts must be reflected by my facial expression because West takes one look at me and huffs a laugh. "Come on, man. Us *taken* guys have to stick together." He winks.

I sigh in resignation and make myself comfortable. The seats on the Eagles' plane are large enough for us to relax. The smell of clean leather fills the space around us, and the seats even swivel so we can face each other and play games when we want to. I had planned on texting Andie this entire flight, but West has other plans. Apparently, he's in a chatty mood.

"So, Andie's great," he says with a wide grin.

"Yep."

"I think she's good for you. You've changed."

I pin him with a serious stare. "I can still beat the shit out of people when I want to."

He smirks. "Not sure I believe you. I think we should change it from Mitch 'The Machine' to Mitch 'The Lover.'"

I flip him the bird and he laughs.

"Anyway, I just wanted you to know I like you guys together. Don't mess this up, man."

I tilt my chin in a nod and finally send Andie a text that we're on the runway. Then, I lean my seat back and take a nice long nap.

————

I wake up to West blowing on my face. My eyes fly open and he pulls away from me just in time to avoid my fist connecting with his jaw. "Time to wake up, sleeping beauty. We've landed."

Blinking a few times, I look at my watch. I can't believe I passed out for the entire four-hour flight. Must've stayed up too late texting Andie last night. Great, now I'm never going to fall asleep tonight... which means I'll probably stay up too late again... and will probably be texting Andie the entire time... again.

I stand and stretch my arms and legs, then reach up for my

carry-on in the overhead compartment. We get off the plane and the team grabs their luggage and heads toward the line of SUVs sent from the hotel to taxi us. Remy, Colby, Bruce, West, and myself pile inside one of the vehicles. Once I'm settled, I pull my phone out to check it. My eyes widen in alarm when I see ten missed calls from Max, and another eight from Andie.

"What the..." I tap on Andie's name and it rings a few times before she answers.

"Mitch. Oh my gosh," her voice is breathless, she sounds shaken up.

I lean forward in my seat, feeling annoyed that I'm not there to help her with whatever is going on. "Hey, what's wrong?"

"You haven't seen the article?" Her voice sounds strangled, like she's holding back tears.

"Article?"

"I'm texting it to you right now. Mitch, this looks so bad. I'm so sorry." She chokes out the apology and I know she's really crying now.

"Hey, it's okay," I tell her, having no clue what's happening.

I pull the phone back and tap on the link to the article she sent me. The link takes me to the D.C. Tribune. The article is titled: *Mom Takes Advantage of Hockey Bad Boy to Get Her Son to the Top.*

I groan, then put the phone back to my ear. "You've gotta be kidding me. This is ridiculous, and completely untrue." The guys are leaning in, whispering and trying to figure out what's going on.

I place a hand over the lower part of my phone and whisper, "There's a gossip article about me and Andie."

Remy, who's beside me, pulls his phone out and googles the article. He scrolls through, reading it and showing me all the pictures. It really does look bad. There's a photo of me with Andie over my shoulder on that first day of practice. Another one of us standing very close to each other in a heated argument. Then, there's another one of us at the Eagles' game on Noah's birthday. This one includes Noah in it too, which pisses me off. They could at least leave minors out of this.

"How the hell did they get these photos? And who took them?" I ask through gritted teeth.

"It was Steph," she says. "There's a video of their interview with her toward the bottom of the article." Her voice sounds choked and I wish I was there to hold her.

I close my eyes, fighting back anger and frustration. I remember last night at the game, how mad she was and the accusations she made. Throwing a fit because she wasn't getting enough attention. Like mother, like son, apparently.

"I can't believe her—" I'm cut off when my phone begins to vibrate in my hand, I pull it back to see my manager trying to call me again. "Andie, can I call you back? My manager's been trying to get ahold of me."

"Yeah," she sniffs. "I'll talk to you later."

I pause for a second, thinking of something to say to console her, but I come up short. "Okay, bye."

She whispers goodbye and I feel like a tool for not saying something sweet to her. All I feel is anger, though not at her, but at everything else. And it's so difficult to think when I'm angry. I let my phone go to voicemail while I breathe in for seven and out for eleven.

Max, of course, calls right back. This time I answer. "Hey."

"I'm assuming you've seen the disaster?" he huffs.

I drag a hand through my hair. "Yep."

"I told you this would happen." It sounds like he's gritting his teeth while talking.

"Yeah, I get it. So why don't you tell me how to fix it? That's your job right? Making this all go away?"

"Oh, there's a really simple way to make this all go away. End things with the hockey mom. It's a no brainer. Then, accept the sponsorship from the Franklin Distilleries, and this will all fizzle out within a week. *And* you and I will be even richer than we already are."

My heart stops, the familiar sense of overwhelming dread coiling in my gut. I can't imagine ending things with Andie. I'm pretty sure I'm already in love with her, and I didn't even think my heart knew how to work like that. But Andie made it beat again, made the blood pump again, made me see everything in a new light. And being with me includes stupid drama like this. Us being photographed, being gossiped about.

And Noah, he's an adolescent boy, now in the spotlight for less-than-positive reasons.

I should've known I couldn't make their lives better. I should've known I'd drag them into my wasteland. Into this pit.

Faintly, I can hear Max yelling at me over the phone, asking if I'm still there. I hang up and let the phone drop to the floor, leaning forward and cupping my face in my hands. I just need the world to fade away for a minute while I think. I need silence for my brain to work.

A firm hand grips my shoulder, I know it's Remy. In a low voice, I hear him say, "How can we help?"

# CHAPTER 29
# ANDIE

"IT'S GONNA BE OKAY, ANDIE." Noah consoles me. I should be the mature person here. The one telling him it's going to be okay. But it's Monday morning and I still haven't heard back from Mitch. I've tried calling and texting. Nothing.

"I know. You're right," I tell my brother with the best smile I can muster. He arches an eyebrow, obviously unconvinced. I continue packing his lunch for school and he heads toward the front stoop where he waits for me in the mornings when it's not too cold. He and Dad used to sit there together in the mornings while Dad drank his coffee.

I manage to drop Noah off at school and make it back home, my brain is in such a thick fog, I barely remember the drive there and back. Thank goodness for muscle memory. I head straight toward the home gym, knowing I'll feel more clear-headed after a good workout.

Starting with pull-ups, I add my band for assistance. My arm strength isn't as good as my leg strength, but my goal is to do pull-ups unassisted soon. I wonder how many Mitch can do with those big arms? I groan. *Stop thinking about Mitch!*

When I'm done with a set of pull-ups, I move on to Arnold

presses. Halfway through my set, I hear my doorbell ring. I throw my weights down and rush to the door, hoping Mitch will be there. Even though I know he's in Canada and has a game tonight.

I swing open the door and find Melanie there. I blink in surprise but she steps inside and pulls me into a hug. "Hey, I saw the article and got your address from the guys."

I melt into her arms and return the embrace. It's nice to be comforted by a friend. "I'm glad you came. Honestly, I'm going crazy."

We pull back and I lead her into the kitchen. "You want coffee?"

"I'm okay," she says, taking a seat on a bar stool. I sit beside her and she looks at me, her eyes full of concern. "The guys said Mitch is a mess."

My eyes blur with tears. "He won't talk to me."

"Oh, Andie. I'm sorry." She pauses. "Maybe he's just over-whelmed and needs to clear his head?"

"I hope you're right."

"I know this isn't my business, but he's working on his temper, right?"

I nod.

"So, it makes sense that he'd allow himself time to think instead of lashing out at someone he loves."

My heart does something funny when she says *loves*. It feels like it's pumping extra fast and twisting at the same time. "Maybe. I just want to talk this out. It's neither of our faults."

"It's not. The media can be brutal." Her eyebrows go up when she says it. "West's reputation before we got together was less than stellar."

"Really?" I ask, feeling surprised. They just seem so perfect, it's hard to picture either of them before they were engaged.

"Oh yeah." She releases a small laugh, but there's no

humor in it. "When we started dating, an article came out about how I was his newest bed warmer… well, that's putting it nicely. It was humiliating."

"I bet. That sucks." I grimace. "I know what that blog said about me and Mitch is bogus, but it surprised me. Like, I just wasn't expecting to be in the public eye so soon, and in such a negative way."

Melanie pats my arm gently and I continue. "But I'm already falling for Mitch. Hard. I know we can get through this stupid gossip. But he has to talk to me! He has to communicate for this to work."

"Definitely," she agrees. "In a way, it's good you got initiated into this life early on. To see if you can handle the gossip and the mean comments. And it sounds like you can." She smiles warmly, then her expressions grows more serious. "But you're right, he has to talk things out with you. This is probably overstepping, and just tell me to shut up if it is, but I think you're going to have to be patient with him on this while he figures out how to be a good partner while also controlling that temper of his."

I take a deep breath. "You're right, I do need to be patient with him. He's never had anyone show him what a healthy relationship looks like."

"Love conquers all, right?"

"Let's hope so."

———

Monday evening, we walk inside the ice rink for hockey practice. I've been dreading this all day, as has Noah, I'm sure. I feel so bad for him, he must be so humiliated. And the idea that Mitch only worked with him for my sake, when in reality,

Noah got Mitch's attention with his own hard work and talent. I hate this for him.

Noah heads straight to the locker room to change and I reluctantly walk inside the rink to find a seat on the bleachers. I bundled up even more today, like if I cover myself I'll somehow be invisible. I have a scarf, my beanie, knit gloves, a big coat, and furry boots. The realization hits me that I look ridiculous and am actually drawing more attention to myself and not less.

As anticipated, everyone looks up and stares at me when I walk in. Steph is literally standing there by the doors with her arms crossed like she's been waiting for me. She looks pretty pleased with herself.

Knowing she loves drama and is probably hoping that I'll confront her, I ignore her instead. *Be the bigger person, Andie.* That's what Mom would've told me.

I keep my chin up, but don't make eye contact with her. But she can't leave well enough alone.

Her teasing voice grinds in my ears. "What, no Mitch Anderson here to protect you today? I wonder why."

I turn to face her. "You know what, Steph? Attack me all you want. If your life's so pitiful that you have to tear me down to feel better about yourself, then so be it. But don't drag Noah into this. He didn't do anything... other than being really stinking good at hockey."

Her jaw drops as she stares at me. I don't wait for whatever sneering retort she has, I turn and head toward the bleachers, sitting as far away from the other parents as I can. When the kids file onto the ice and practice starts, I feel a tap on my shoulder. I look over to see Tori, her dark eyes filled with sympathy. She wraps her arms around my shoulders. "Andie, I'm so sorry." She sniffs and I hug her back.

She releases me but stays by my side. "I didn't realize

Steph was so conniving, I should've stood up for you right away. Right when she made those first comments about Noah overdramatizing Declan's bullying. I've seen it happen right before my eyes, and to my own son too. But I didn't want to cause drama, so I stayed quiet, and tried to keep the peace."

"It's okay, Tori. Really. It's not your fault."

She puts her hand up to stop me. "It's not okay. You're my friend, you're a good person, a great sister to Noah. For months, I've watched you hustle, taking care of him, grieving, *and* working. No one, not one person, should have to take on that load alone. But *you* did, and you've done amazing. And when you needed a friend, someone to look out for you? I failed. But I won't fail again. I'm here for you, okay?"

Tears are streaming down my face now. I couldn't get them to stop even if I wanted to. I had no idea how much I needed someone to acknowledge how hard these past nine months have been, how exhausting… until now. Until someone *did* acknowledge it. And now, all of the pent-up emotion and sadness is pouring out. Tori pulls me into another long, motherly hug.

"Thank you, Tori," I whisper into her shoulder.

At that moment, the doors to the rink burst open and Ronda waltzes in, still in her scrubs from working today. She locates me quickly, eyes blazing angrily, and walks toward me and Tori with long, urgent strides. Ronda sits beside me and wraps her arms around me. Well, crap. Now there's no way I can hold my tears back anymore.

My shoulders shake with silent sobs and I sniffle into her winter coat. "Oh, sweetie," she says, stroking my hair. "I came straight here after hearing about the article. I'm so sorry."

"It's okay." My words are muffled by her coat.

"It's not, but it will be." she whispers.

I pull back, nodding my head. She keeps one arm around

me and I lean my head on her shoulder. On my other side, Tori pats my hand that rests on the bleachers and I give her a sad smile.

Tori and Ronda sit beside me the rest of practice… and suddenly, I don't feel so alone.

# CHAPTER 30
# MITCH

AFTER MORNING PRACTICE, we arrive back at the hotel. It's only been a day since the article about me and Andie came out, so when my phone rings, my chest tightens. I squeeze my eyes shut, knowing it's probably Max.

I answer it, knowing I won't be able to fall asleep for a pregame nap anyway. I'm so wound up from that stupid article, and worrying about Andie. Wondering how long it'll take before she breaks up with me.

"Yes?" I ground out.

"Good day to you too, Anderson," Max says in that fake-nice voice of his. "So, did you give Franklin Distilleries any more thought?"

He's pushing so hard for me to accept this contract with the distillery, and it's just another red flag with this guy.

"I've already told you, I don't drink. I don't want to start drinking. And I don't want my name on a bourbon bottle."

An exaggerated groan comes through his end. "You don't even have to drink it! They just want to slap your name on the label and to have you hold the bottle in commercials." He sighs. "We can even fill your glass with maple syrup for advertisements, Canadians love maple syrup!"

I squint my eyes. "Max, I'm not Canadian. I'm from Wisconsin."

"Whatever." I can practically hear the shrug in his voice. "Can't you pretend to love bourbon for millions of dollars?"

Slowly, I inhale and exhale a calming breath. "You know what, Max? This conversation has given me some much-needed clarity."

"Good!" He sounds genuinely happy. "I can send the contract to your hotel for your signature."

"No."

A stifled, confused-sounding laugh comes from Max. "Excuse me?"

"You're fired, Max. I'm getting a new agent, someone who understands my boundaries, my life, anything. You're only worried about your own paycheck. I want to make money and have security after retirement as much as anyone, but I won't sell my soul in the process."

"Mitch, come on, man!"

I hang up before I have to listen to his annoying voice any longer. This is one decision that I'm entirely confident in, and one that's been a long time coming. Slumping down into an uncomfortable modern chair in the hotel lobby, I yawn loudly. I barely slept last night.

I'm sharing a room with Bruce, and he finally threw a pillow at me at three in the morning and yelled at me to quit tossing and turning.

Light sleeper much?

Bruce is in our room napping, and I'm not about to ruin it for him since I apparently kept him up last night. My phone is still in my hand; I tap the screen and find Andie's contact info, then allow my finger to hover over it. I know I need to call her, but the feeling of not knowing what to say, and the fear that she's going to end things, is overwhelming.

Everyone leaves, and she will too. She'll figure out that I'm not worth the drama, that her life will be better off without me. She'll find a nice guy and settle down in the suburbs where they'll raise Noah and drink pina coladas and have a labradoodle.

And I freaking hate that guy. I hate him with every fiber of my being, whoever he is. As much as I love punching people, there's no one I've ever wanted to punch more than this imaginary man who's going to marry the love of my life.

I lock my phone and slide it into my back pocket. I can't do it, can't call her. Can't listen to her voice as she shatters my heart. Leaning over, I grip my head in my hands, tugging at my hair. I probably rip out half of my hair in the process, but I can't bring myself to care. Unsure what to do to distract myself, I head to the hotel's gym. Exhausting myself before a game when I'm already running on very little sleep is probably a terrible idea. But better than going out and finding someone to beat the crap out of.

———

"Dude, are you going to be okay?" Colby whispers from his seat beside me in the locker room before the game.

Coach Young already gave us a pregame talk, and now Remy is pumping us up. I haven't heard a word of what they're saying. When I got dressed earlier in my burgundy suit, I made the mistake of looking in the mirror. Pretty sure I've never looked worse, despite the expensive, tailored material. Dark circles under my eyes, my beard longer and scruffier than I usually keep it, and my hair messy and unkempt from running my anxious hands through it. It looks like they found a homeless man on the side of the road and threw him into a suit, thinking it would fix everything.

I grunt at Colby, but he nudges me with an elbow, obviously not content with just a grunt. "I'm fine," I spit the words. But in my defense, he's annoying.

His head rears back. "Yeah, you seem totally fine."

Bruce makes a *pst* sound from my other side. Unfortunately, even though we're in the Quebec Wolverines' guest dressing rooms, our seating arrangements are the same. I'm really wishing they'd have seated me between two rookies who are still too terrified of me to strike up a conversation.

Groaning, I grit out the word, "What?"

"It's just a gossip article. Don't get into trouble tonight and add fuel to the fire." Bruce is abnormally serious as he says it. But his words just make me even more annoyed.

"*Just* a gossip article?"

"I didn't mean it like that," he whispers, trying not to disrupt Remy's speech. "I just meant that there's always going to be stupid gossip and then a week later everyone forgets about it."

A growl ripples through me, shocking Bruce and Colby. They stare at me like I'm a bomb about to explode. "Most gossip doesn't include kids, Bruce."

He nods. "I know, man. I'm sorry. I'm just trying to help."

"Don't."

The guys in the room clap after whatever the hell Remy just said and we file out onto the ice. As soon as my skates hit the ice, I feel a little more controlled. The familiar air of the cool arena hits my face. I relish in the feel of the crisp, icy air, closing my eyes and breathing it in. Willing it to freeze my heart so I don't have to *feel* anymore.

After a few laps around the ice, we take the bench while the Wolverines are announced. Couch Young squeezes between me and Colby and pins me with a look so serious, it's almost a glare.

Tilting my head to the side, I crack my neck. I'm sure that muscle in my jaw is clenched too. I'm really freaking sick of everyone fawning all over me. I'm *fine*.

"You seem tense. Are you good?"

"Yep. Good to go."

He studies me. "Okay. No stupid penalties."

I nod and he goes back to standing behind us.

# CHAPTER 31
## ANDIE

NOAH TURNED ON THE EAGLES' game the moment it started. I told myself I wouldn't watch, that I couldn't bear to sit there and see Mitch on the screen when he hasn't spoken to me in nearly twenty-four hours. But with how much Noah was yelling at the T.V., I finally caved and started watching five minutes into the second period.

And now we're both yelling at the T.V.

The Wolverines aren't even having a good season like the Eagles are, but you wouldn't know it from this game. The Wolverines are ahead 5-2. It's getting more and more unlikely that they'll make a comeback. It would be a miracle at this point… with only nine minutes left.

Even as someone who knows nothing about this sport, I can tell they're playing like amatuers. Namely, Mitch 'The Machine' Anderson. He's been in the penalty box three times already, and there's still half of the third period to go.

Is there an eensy-weensy part of me that's happy to see Mitch struggling so much? That he's as miserable as I am by everything going on? Yes, okay!? At the end of the day, I'm only human.

Noah groans as we watch Mitch get into it with yet another Wolverines player. The guy got a little too close to Bruce, and that's all it took for the gloves to come off.

"What's gotten into him?" I mutter to myself.

Noah gives me a judgmental side eye. As if to say, *you and I both know this is about you and that gossip article.*

And he's not wrong. But is Mitch mad about the article? Or mad at me? Does he think I caused this? Does he think I wanted to become famous or something?

Ugh. I hate second guessing everything. I'm trying to be patient with him and let him work things out in his own mind. But this isn't how a relationship works. You take a few hours to think and cool down, not a few days!

I remember Mel's words about being patient with him. But where do I draw the line between being understanding and feeling like I'm his mother? Because I can't be raising a boy *and* a giant man-child.

Burying my face in my hands, I block my view from the T.V. where Mitch and #97 from the Wolverines are going round and round in their petty fight. The refs are standing around with their arms crossed and their faces say, *Here we go again.*

"This is painful to watch," Noah says. I feel the weight on the couch shift, telling me he stood up. Then I hear the T.V. click off. "I'm going to bed. Are you going to be alright?"

Popping my head back up, I give him a small smile. "I'll be fine. Goodnight."

He surprises me by stepping toward me and wrapping his slim arms around me. I bring my arms up to hug him back and nearly cry at the sweetness of his gesture. He hasn't hugged me since Mom and Dad died. The simple token of affection is so sweet, and makes me feel like no matter what, everything is going to be alright.

He stands and starts toward the stairs while I'm left on the sofa, feeling a little weepy.

# CHAPTER 32
# MITCH

WE MAKE our way back to the locker room once the game is over. My fist meets the metal of the door as I pass by it. Bruce, Remy, West and Colby stare at me. None of them dare to be the first one to poke the bear.

The air in the room is thick, laced with simmering tempers and regret. Or is that just me?

Everyone is quietly removing their gear, no one wanting to break the silence. Even Coach Young seems at a loss for words. I was off tonight, I get it. But so was everyone else. I wasn't even the only one in the penalty box, although I spent more time there than anyone else.

Finally, West takes a step toward me. "You should've sat out, Mitch, taken a mental health day. We get there's a lot going on, but you've gotta be real with us."

I lunge for him, grabbing onto his jersey and causing both of us to topple to the ground. He's really going to blame this entire game on me? I don't think so.

I've wanted to mess up West's angelic face for over a year now, and this is finally my chance. The only issue? I'm worn out, running on barely any sleep, and even my rage isn't giving me any added strength. I'm spent.

And the thought of kicking West's butt doesn't give me the same thrill it did a year ago, anyway.

West easily shifts our weight to where I'm on the floor and he's holding my arms down. "What the hell, Mitch? Do you really think beating the crap out of your own teammate is going to solve anything? Or make you feel better?" He starts to move himself off of me and I swing at him while he's distracted.

West's forgiving mood is gone now, he punches me back, right in the eye. I deserve it. Remy and Coach Young separate us. Coach lets go of West as soon as he's on his feet again, but Remy keeps his hold on me.

West looks at me, he's mad, but there's another emotion there too. Like he's hurt… not physically, but emotionally. "That article sucked, man. But we've all been there. That's the shitty thing about constantly being in the public eye. We're here for the world's entertainment… even outside of the game. And sometimes fans can be cruel. But *we're* here… look all around you." He pauses, looking around the room. I do the same, my eyes catching on Bruce and Colby behind West, looking at me without any anger or judgment. "*We* are your family. We're here to support each other. But we can't do that if you won't talk to us."

Remy's grip on me loosens. He gives me a friendly shake, like the Remy version of a hug. Before I can move away, Bruce and Colby are rushing toward me and wrap me in a giant hug.

I groan. "No, please no hugging."

But I don't fight to get away. It's not an Andie hug, but I guess I'll take it. After a minute, I brush them off, pretending to be annoyed. I have a reputation to keep up, after all.

"I-I'm sorry guys. Tonight was a disaster." I scratch the back of my neck and look down at my skates.

"We were *all* off tonight," Bruce says.

Coach Young scoffs. "You can say that again."

———

We made it back to the hotel last night way too late for me to call Andie, and then this morning we got on our jet too early for me to call her. We have another game tonight in Thunder Bay, then a late flight back to D.C.

I can't stand not being there with her to make this right. To tell her I'm sorry, to beg her forgiveness. There's never in my life been something that would bring me to my knees, that would make me grovel and beg… but Andie? Yeah, I'd do that for her. I'd do anything.

I'm still miserable, but my anger has dissipated a little since West knocked some sense into me last night. And he's right, the whole team has always been there for me, has always been my family in a roundabout way, but I was too stupid to see it. Or maybe I just didn't want to. Maybe I wanted to wallow a while longer. But I'm done wallowing now. I want to live, want to love, want to do more than just survive. And I want to do it all with Andie by my side.

When we land in Ontario and get settled in our hotel before tonight's game, I try to call Andie. It goes straight to voicemail. I can't remember if she's working today, or if she's ignoring me. I deserve her silence.

I type out a text instead.

> Andie, I know I'm sorry isn't good enough. My head has been such a mess, I couldn't even think straight. Call me when you can. Please.

Settling in a comfortable armchair in the hotel's lobby, I call Dr. Curtis. I desperately want to fix this, and to show Andie I'm here for her. But I don't know how, and I feel like I'm going to mess everything up even more than I already have.

He picks up after two rings. "Well, good morning, Mitch." His voice is calm like it always is. And I find myself wishing I was in his peaceful office.

"Hey." I sit back in an armchair the hotel has in their lobby. It's a Monday right before noon, so it's completely empty except for me. "I need some help."

"I'm glad you called. What's going on?"

I explain to him the issue with the article, and how my manager is down my throat, and how I stupidly ghosted Andie for a day and a half. He hums every ten seconds or so, letting me know he's still there and still listening.

"Well," he says in his steady voice. I hear wrestling like he's shifting in his seat. "It sounds like you know you reacted poorly, and that you need to make things right. The only way you can do that is to talk to her. Tell her how you've been feeling, how the anger took over, how you're afraid it's too much and she'll abandon your relationship. Lay your heart out there, even if it's hard. You have to be vulnerable."

I swallow slowly. "And if she leaves me?"

He waits a few seconds before responding, "Focus on what you *can* do in the situation. Not what you *can't* control. Love is risky, Mitch. You *can't* make someone stay. But you *can* put in the work, and you *can* communicate with her."

I nod my head even though he can't see me. "Yeah, okay. You're right."

"Are you still listening to your audiobooks?"

"Yeah," I tell him with a sigh. Not feeling better after this conversation... but also not feeling worse, I guess.

"Prepare your mind for the conversation with Andie, take a long walk, listen to your book, calm your mind."

"Okay, I can do that."

"Good," he says, and I can hear the smile in his voice. "I have faith in you. And I can tell you really care about this girl. Whatever happens, remember you're worthy of love, worthy of happiness."

"Thanks. Hey, Doc?"

"Yes, Mitch?"

I roll my lips together, trying to get the words out. The words I need to say, but am not sure I really want to. "I know my mandatory anger management is done, but can I continue seeing you?"

"Of course." If he's surprised, he hides it well. "Should I save your Tuesday morning slot?"

"Yeah, sounds good."

Fifteen minutes later, I'm changed into joggers, a long sleeved tee, and a puffer vest to keep my core warm. I turn on my noise-canceling headphones, then check my phone, seeing nothing from Andie. My heart sinks but I force myself outside for a long walk. It's cold here in Canada, but at least it's not snowing. My new audiobook is a self-help book about building healthy relationships and improving your emotional intelligence.

You know, just a little light reading to calm my stress.

Maybe I'll go back to the smutty hockey one instead. I cringe at the thought.

Thirty minutes into my walk, my phone rings. My heart

nearly leaps out of my chest when I see it's Andie. I fumble around with my headphones, trying to figure out how to answer the phone while wearing them. Thankfully, I must tap the correct button because I hear her sweet, perfect voice filling my ears. I swear my heart rate calms just at the sound of her, and the stress of the last few days eases just a little.

"Mitch?"

"Andie, thanks for calling me back."

She's quiet, waiting for me to speak.

"I'm so sorry. I have a lot to say, I'm trying to find the words—"

"I'm at work. We're swamped today. Can we talk later tonight?"

I release a heavy sigh. I wish I could go to her right now. But my contract with the NHL and all that. "It's okay, don't apologize. As soon as our game's over tonight, we're getting on our flight back to D.C. Can we talk tomorrow?"

"Okay, I'm off tomorrow." She sighs. "I hate that we haven't talked."

"I know." I shake my head. "I'm so sorry. I just—"

A voice comes over the intercom at the hospital. "I've gotta go, talk to you later."

She hangs up before I can say goodbye.

———

Our game went better tonight. We won 3-2 in overtime. I feel like our defense, namely myself, sucked. So Bruce held us together by blocking forty-one shots from the Thunder Bay Thunderbolts.

How the guys stay focused when they have families back home is a new mystery to me. I always thought they might enjoy having a break, some time away. But no. It sucks. It really freaking sucks.

Being away from someone and trying to sort things out is excruciating. It's so much simpler to talk things out in person, to see their face, their reactions. To hear their tone clearly.

We get on the team's private jet exhausted and ready for a few days off. I'm not just physically exhausted, but mentally too. Probably because instead of sleeping at night, my mind has raced. West takes a seat next to me again. Rather than glare at him, I nod my head. A silent *We're good.*

His words after our fight are still stuck with me. *Look around, we're your family.*

This whole time, I chose to be blind to the family right in front of me. Brothers. A whole freaking slough of them. Half of them annoy the hell out of me, but still.

I don't sleep during our flight. And I don't go home afterward. No, I race to my vehicle and then drive straight to Jimmy John's for some sandwiches.

# CHAPTER 33
# ANDIE

IT'S four in the morning when my phone startles me awake. With a quick, bleary glance at the screen, I see it's Mitch calling me. I answer because I'm too sleepy to make rational decisions.

"Mitch. It's the middle of the night."

"I know, Blondie. And I'm sorry. But I've wasted enough time. Please come talk to me."

"What?" I ask, feeling confused. Isn't he in Canada, or on an airplane… or, something?

Then I hear the doorbell ring. I jump out of bed and rush downstairs before the doorbell wakes Noah up.

When I yank the front door open, Mitch is standing there with a huge tray in his arms. A huge tray of… I squint, trying to make out what exactly he's holding. It's a tray full of sub sandwiches. Like the kind you'd get to cater a huge party. No clue where he got those at this time of night…

"I couldn't wait any longer to see you."

I rub my eyes, thinking I might still be dreaming. When I look again, I still see Mitch Anderson, in all of his sexy, muscular glory, standing on my front porch, holding a tray of sandwiches. I tug him inside, close the door behind us, and lead him into the kitchen.

He places the tray on the counter and looks at me with the most heartbreaking expression. His face is half joy and half misery. I can tell there's a war going on in his mind, that he's fighting someone. Probably himself.

Unable to keep myself from touching him, even though I'm still pissed at him, I cup his bearded cheek with my palm. "Where'd you go, Big Man? What's happening in there?"

He closes his eyes and leans into my hand. I see his throat work as he swallows. "I sort of convinced myself I had ruined yours' and Noah's lives... that I added more challenges instead of happiness. Then I avoided talking to you, thinking you'd figure that out, and then... you'd leave me behind."

A tear streams down my cheek at his honest and brutal confession. And his very real fear of abandonment. And that he'd think something so small—a stupid gossip blogger—could make me leave him. "Mitch, you add nothing but joy to our lives. Monday night, Noah hugged me. I can't remember the last time he hugged me. You know why? Because you've been good for him. You've helped him come alive again. You're a good man, Mitch Anderson. And that's why I love you... even when you're an idiot."

His eyes open and one slow tear drips down his cheek, across the faded scar below his eye. The eye that's now purple. That's a story I'm going to want later.

He lifts his hand to his face, covering mine. "Andie, I need you to know that I'm a broken man. I have a lot of work to do. But I *am* doing the work, I'm trying to be better." He pauses, looking into my eyes. "And I promise," he squeezes his eyes closed for a second. "I promise that I'll never stop working to heal. I'll never stop working to become the man you deserve, because I love you too. And I'm sorry, so sorry that I hurt you."

More tears stream down his face, and my own. I wrap my arms around his neck and allow myself to cry against his thick chest. I never want to let go.

This is more than him messing up, more than an apology. This is the admission of a broken and abandoned boy. A boy who's still inside there somewhere, learning not only to love, but to receive love... unconditionally.

We stand like that for a minute before he lifts me up so I can wrap my legs around his waist. He holds me to him with those big, strong arms that I love.

And I feel safe.

I feel hope.

Because we're all a little broken... and we're all healing.

———

I wake up on the couch having no clue what time it is. I'm so warm and still wrapped in Mitch's arms. Waking up in his arms is definitely something I'd like to repeat. I nuzzle into the broad expanse of his chest and enjoy his warmth. Mitch is still sound asleep, poor guy must be exhausted.

I'm just about to close my eyes again when I hear someone clearing their throat. I look up and find Noah hovering above us, his arms crossed like a father who just found a boy bringing his daughter home past curfew.

"Is this going to become a usual thing? Because it's really gross."

My eyes shift to the side to look at Mitch, whose eyes are open now. "Sorry, Noah," he says in a groggy, just-woke-up voice.

Noah rolls his eyes and runs up the stairs, probably to get ready for school.

"School!" I squeak and lift myself into a sitting position, then jump up from the sofa. Mitch follows suit, looking confused and like he's barely awake. I rush into the kitchen to see it's already 7:30 and grab Noah's lunch box to start packing it.

"What can I do?"

I look up at him and see his messy hair, rumpled clothes, and black eye and can't help but smile at him. "For starters, why don't you tell me how you got that black eye?"

He gives me a sheepish smile. "West gave me this."

I gasp and he puts a hand up, a silent plea for me to not freak out.

"I deserved it, believe me."

"Hmm. If you say so." I peek inside the fridge, smiling when I spot the tray of probably one hundred sub sandwiches. I grab two of them and stick them inside Noah's lunchbox. Thankfully, we still have ten minutes before we need to leave.

"Want me to take Noah to school?" Mitch asks.

I'm about to tell him he doesn't have to do that when Noah comes down the steps and answers for me, "Yes, please. That's so much cooler than my sister taking me." He stands next to Mitch and the big man reaches down and ruffles his hair. Noah shoves him away, making Mitch chuckle.

Noah turns and starts walking toward the front door, toward his spot on the front porch, and Mitch follows him.

When I've packed his lunch and thrown on some sweats, I go in search of the boys. The boys... I like the sound of that.

I open the front door slowly and find them both sitting on the steps. It's a cold February morning, but with the sunshine filtering onto the small stoop, it seems warmer than it is. The sun shines on Mitch, bringing out the flecks of gold throughout Mitch's hair. I take a moment to watch them. Mitch's large shoulders fill the impossibly small space, and it does something to my heart. It's a reminder of the space in our lives that was empty after losing our parents. But this giant man with his fragile heart came in and filled it when we least expected it.

Clearing my throat, I say, "Hey, here's your lunch."

They both turn and look over their shoulders at me. They both stand. Noah takes the lunch and thanks me. "See you after school, Andie." He waves and walks toward Mitch's Tesla that's parked nearby.

Mitch takes a step toward me, and slips one of those big hands around my waist, tugging me close until I collide into his chest.

"Good morning, Blondie." He kisses me again. This time longer.

I hum into the kiss, then pull back slightly. "Careful, I'm going to get used to waking up to your kisses."

"That's alright with me." He closes his eyes and kisses my forehead. "I love you so much it hurts a little."

"Are you sure that's not the black eye?"

He huffs a laugh. "Definitely not."

I sigh happily. "I love you too, Big Man."

"Oh my gosh, I'm going to be late for school!" Noah yells from the sidewalk next to Mitch's car.

We snicker and I mouth the word *Sorry* to my brother. Noah groans when Mitch gives me one more kiss before letting me go and walking toward his car.

I lean against the doorframe, watching as they interact with each other. Noah says something that makes Mitch laugh. They open the car doors and both have smiles on their faces. They look so happy. A sob catches in my throat and I choke it back.

Mitch Anderson, with his tender soul and his commanding presence, was everything we didn't know we needed.

And now, this feels like a family. A whole, complete unit.

*Three things I'm grateful for: My little brother, Mitch Anderson, and family.*

Because family looks different for everyone. Sometimes it's not the family you're born into, but the one you build. The one you work for. And this is mine.

# MITCH

TEN MONTHS LATER

WATCHING Andie walk toward me in a wedding gown leaves me overwhelmed and breathless.

My heart squeezes as I take her in… the silky fabric of her dress that hugs her hips perfectly, then flares out just a little at the bottom. Her hair pinned back to show off that beautiful face that I adore. Her smile pulled up, showing off her dimple. The flowers she's holding, an assortment of bright red roses, greenery, and little white buds of something I can't name.

I'm a little surprised it's not a bouquet of Jimmy John's subs.

The venue in downtown D.C. is lit with Christmas lights and decked out with pine trees. It feels like we're in a forest instead of a ballroom. The rich reds and greens lining the room and the elegant table settings make the space feel cozy and romantic.

I can honestly say this was the first time ever that I've looked forward to our holiday NHL break. Because today, this gorgeous woman walking toward me becomes *my wife*.

I finally understand that giddy feeling people get around

the holidays, the one where they're about to open a present they've dreamt of for months. And that's how I feel.

I've never been so excited to unwrap a gift.

Feeling a nudge at my elbow, I turn slightly to see my best man, Noah, smiling at me. I glance up to find my groomsmen: Bruce, Colby, Remy, and... you guessed it, Weston Kershaw.... waggling their eyebrows like fools.

With a sigh, I turned back to my bride. She's halfway down the aisle now, escorted by Ronda. I think Ronda likes me now. A little. Ronda looks distinguished in a silver dress that hits the floor and has long sleeves.

After Ronda kisses her cheek, then releases her, Andie finally arrives at my side. Right where she belongs. I have a difficult time not grabbing her and kissing her right away. But during the rehearsal, I got yelled at for that. Oh well, plenty of time for that later tonight.

Andie smiles up at me with tears in her eyes as we clasp hands and stand before our wedding officiant, Dr. Curtis. She turns and hands off her bouquet to her maid of honor, Melanie. Her other bridesmaids, Tori and Noel are all smiles. Their dresses look similar to Ronda's, but in a forest green color.

When Andie focuses those brown eyes back on me, I nearly melt on the spot. Her eyes are shiny from the tears she's holding back. I know they're happy tears because of her genuine smile and the way she clutches my hands like she never wants to let go. Well, Blondie, you never have to. Because I'm not going anywhere.

Dr. Curtis says some wise words before having us repeat our wedding vows and exchange rings. They're both simple gold bands because tomorrow we're going to get tattoo rings together. Andie can't wear large rings at work, and neither can I. Plus, permanently marking myself with our wedding date just feels right. Not that I could ever forget today. But her name, and the day we became one, will be permanently part of me... mind, soul, and body.

When we're announced as Mr. and Mrs. Anderson, I don't waste any time pulling her body against mine. The silky material of her figure-hugging dress feels like butter against my calloused fingers. I clutch the fabric at the sides of her waist and kiss her. She must've been just as antsy for this kiss and leans into me with a soft sigh. Her hands cup my face as she kisses me back, her head leaning to the side to get a better, deeper angle. Her lips feel soft and she tastes so sweet.

And then there's that lingering bubble gum scent on her skin, making me wonder if she took a hot bubble bath this morning before getting ready. I allow myself to think of her in the bath, covered in nothing but translucent bubbles. We're married now, I can picture her naked all I want.

A current shoots through me, thinking of having her all to myself tonight. Just the two of us, skin to skin, tangled up in the sheets in that giant four-poster bed in our suite upstairs.

I hear Noah mutter the word, *Gross*, behind me and I reluctantly pull away from my bride. I'll kiss her more later. *Much* more.

The crowd claps as the D.J. starts to play *Paradise* by George Ezra. Andie grins at me as we turn to exit down the aisle together. She reaches her hand out to hold mine, but I surprise her by bending down, grabbing her behind her thighs, and hoisting her over my shoulder. It just seems fitting to start off our married life with this woman lugged over my shoulder. The same way we met. She squeals and doesn't resist me as I carry her down the aisle like that. The small crowd eats it up, clapping and laughing.

We exit the ballroom doors and I set her down, knowing

we have about one minute to ourselves out here before the wedding party joins us.

Andie pulls my head down for a kiss, then pulls away laughing. "You're not just *a* big brute… you're *my* big brute."

"Forever," I say, kissing her back.

———

### Andie

After hours of greeting guests and dancing with friends, I'm ready to get to our suite. Not only am I exhausted, but I'm anxious to get the Big Man alone. Just us. After ten months of being chaperoned by my brother, I'm about to rip this man's clothes off like a savage.

Mitch uses a key card to unlock the door to the suite, then instead of carrying me over the threshold, he hauls me over his shoulder again. Such a romantic.

He walks through the sitting room and straight into the bedroom before throwing me onto the big bed. I giggle as he crawls on top of me, tugging at my dress and kissing my neck.

"Finally," I breathe, closing my eyes and enjoying the feel of his beard against my sensitive skin.

He growls against my skin. "You can say that again. I love Noah, but your brother isn't a very good wingman."

"Not the best time to talk about my little brother."

He pulls back, looking at me with that handsome smirk. "True. Sorry."

Mitch meets my eyes, his expression growing serious. His eyes are dark, so dark I can barely detect any of the usual blue and green in them. He studies me, his heady gaze making me squirm.

"You're so damn beautiful," he whispers.

My eyes fill with tears at how earnest his words are, how sincere. I can't believe he's my husband, *mine* for life. He gently rolls off of me and I instantly miss the weight of him. Before I can pout, he unbuttons his suit jacket and lets it slide to the floor.

He starts to loosen his tie, but I jump up and walk toward him. "No, allow me." I shoo his hands away and remove his tie, then work on the buttons of his shirt.

He grins wolfishly, bringing his hands to my waist, then around my back to the clasps on my dress. Mitch feels around, trying to figure out how to get the dress off. By the time I slide his shirt off of his sexy, tattooed arms, he's groaning in frustration at the dress.

I lean in and kiss his chest, whispering, "There's a tie at the nape."

He spins me around quickly and I gasp. Mitch finds the tie quickly and the entire dress unravels, falling to the floor. His sharp inhale makes me feel so sexy, so desired. He turns me around to face him, but instead of devouring me with his eyes, he pulls me against him. My warm skin against his. He holds me, hugging me close. I feel damp heat on my shoulder and realize he's softly crying.

"Mitch, what's wrong?"

He angles his head to look at me, his eyes still wet. His chin quivers slightly as he looks at me. "What's wrong? Nothing, Andie." He huffs a laugh. "Absolutely nothing. I'm so completely happy, so content. I can't even express how amazed I am that you're mine. That you chose *me*."

Mitch leans in and rubs the tip of his nose along the edge of mine. I never knew nuzzling could be so sensual, but geez, someone get me a fan.

"I'm so proud to call you my husband," I say through tears. He uses his thumbs to gently wipe the tears from my face.

"I can't believe I made you cry on our wedding night," he teases.

"You can make it up to me." I flutter my lashes.

Mitch slowly moves forward, causing me to walk backward. My knees hit the edge of our mattress and I fall back onto the fluffy bedding with an *oomph*. He hovers over me, now allowing his eyes to rake over my body. I'm hot all over, just from having his eyes on me. Finally, he crawls onto the bed beside me and pulls me against him. "Are you hungry for some protein, Blondie?"

I burst out laughing, and then I kiss my husband.

# ALSO BY LEAH BRUNNER

**Under Kansas Skies Series**

Running Mate

House Mate

Check Mate

Cabin Mate

**D.C. Eagles Hockey Series**

Passion or Penalty (prequel novella)

Desire or Defense

Flirtation or Faceoff (preorder)

# LEAH'S LIT LOVERS

Come join the fun in Leah's Lit Lovers Facebook group! It's like a party… but you don't have to leave your house!

# ACKNOWLEDGMENTS

Thank you so much to my amazing, lovely, talented BETA readers! Madi, Katie, Amanda and Meredith. You guys rock! Your input helped me refine Mitch and Andie's story and make it even more beautiful… and, of course, adding *more* kissing! LOL.

To my ARC readers, thank you for being so excited about this book! I love how y'all hyped Desire or Defense up! You guys are the best. Every post, every share, every TikTok… it all makes a huge difference and I appreciate it so much!

To my husband and children, thank you for being my biggest fans and supporters. Thank you for becoming hockey fans with me, going to hockey games with me, and just overall making hockey our new personalities. I love you guys.

# ABOUT THE AUTHOR

Leah is a Kansas native, but currently resides in Ohio with her family. She's a proud military spouse and has moved all over the country, (and hopes to move a few more times)!

When she was a child, she dreamt of writing children's books about cats. Even though she ended up writing romance, she's pretty sure her childhood self would still be proud.

instagram.com/leah.brunner.writes
bookbub.com/profile/leah-brunner
tiktok.com/romcomsaremyjam

Made in United States
North Haven, CT
06 December 2024

61869446R00169